Born Again Hustler

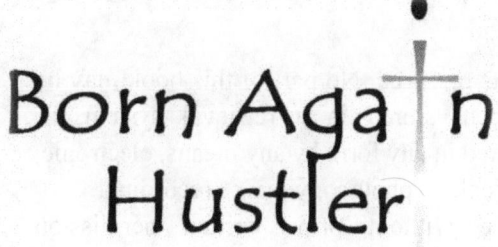

From Pimping to the Pulpit

Diane Martin

http://dianemartin.weebly.com

10 09 08 6 5 4 3 2 1

First Edition

Edited by Dr. William A. Martin & Diane Martin

Interior Design by Diane Martin

Cover Design by Diane Martin

Printed by Createspace

Printed in the United States

ISBN 10: 0-9975761-2-x

ISBN-13: 978-0-9975761-2-2

Disclaimer: This is a book of fiction and not based on actual events. Any similarities to current events, characters, names and locations are purely coincidental and based solely on the imagination of the author.

My writing legacy would be my true depiction of life; exploring the entire colorful spectrum of people, both good and bad, capturing it in words and exposing it to all cultures in a respectful manner - In a way that would stand the test of time. - Diane Martin

Acknowledgements

A special "thank you" goes out to everyone who has supported me. It is because of all of you that I continue to do what I do, so from the bottom of my heart, I appreciate you.

A special "thank you" to the men in my life...they helped me to keep this book authentic. ☺

"Beware of false prophets, which come to you in sheep's clothing, but inwardly they are ravening wolves."

Matthew 7:15 KJV

(King James Version)

Translation:

"Beware of preachers, who come to you cloaked in God's word, but inwardly they are nothing but pimps."

— Diane Martin, IWBBNIS

("I was blind, but now I see...")

Prologue

So you're probably looking at this book and thinking to yourself, "Not another fucking pimp narrative..." Sorry, but I have to be honest, it is. I know that you think that you've heard it all. The story of some low-life who decides to prey on the weakness of some woman - who also convinces her to fuck every lowlife that rolls up on her to prove her love and loyalty to him. Yes, it is the same old story, different characters, but always the same old tired ass story. And sadly, that's the world of pimping. I wish that I could tell you that it's different – that instead of hoes, johns, tricks, and pimps, there's a sleeping princess who falls in love with a toad who's actually a prince that sweeps her off of her feet and they live happily ever after, but I would be lying. It's an ugly world and no matter how many people try to ignore it, wish that it didn't exist, it does. It ain't going nowhere and like life, it almost always, has an "unhappy" ending.

And I live in that world. My name is Trey Miller, the youngest male of ten kids, and I profit off of the women who sell their bodies for a living. The money that they make on their backs and knees, is my money. I cash-in on their low self-esteem, ignorance, and their desperation. I make them think that their survival depends on me - not knowing that their value rests in their ability to continue to please the "Johns" and me; and not in that order. Once they outlive their usefulness, I will toss them out like a used paper-towel and move on to the next broken-soul that I can find. I know that this sounds horrible – that I make my money this way, but why shouldn't I?

Human beings make it easy for people like me to exist and I come in all forms. My parents like to call me, son. Some like to call me a criminal. While others call me evil. People have even accused me of stealing the souls of the weak, but I don't have to steal what's being given away. I've been called the Devil, and like the devil, I am able to "shape-shift" and become whatever it takes to get your money. I can be whatever I need to be.

I like to call myself an equal-opportunity "opportunist." I feed off of your misery, hopelessness, and anguish. It's like the Food Chain. Those on the bottom either get the scraps or they get eaten. I decided at an early age, that I didn't want to be eaten and people like me who are starving prefer a meal over scraps. I wanted to eat and I wanted to eat the finest the world had to give, but why should it be at my expense when so many people are willing to give it to me?

And I was hungry and didn't want to wait until after I'd spent twelve years sitting in a classroom to graduate only to spend another eight years in a classroom just to end-up flipping burgers for minimum wage. That bullshit was for folks who were paying their way through college and still living with their parents or for folks who planned on living below the poverty line for the rest of their lives. I just couldn't see myself being given the gift of life only to squander it away in some drive-thru window asking folks if they want to "Super-size" their fries. I needed to find another way out and in the hood, there's only so many ways to do so.

I also thought about becoming a drug dealer, but drugs fuck people up. Now, that's not to say that I'm above it, but I wanted to look into other options first. Dealing requires upfront money. While pimping only requires a hoe that needs protection from the johns that she has sex with.

And contrary to popular belief, pimping is actually pretty easy. All you need is some sheep who are in need of a Shepard.

That's it. You would be amazed at how many women want to get paid to fuck. At one time, I was just like you. I believed that pimps had to force women into the trade, but they don't. Have you ever heard of the phrase, "Build it and they will come?" It's true. Now, don't get me wrong, there are a lot of animals out there who snatch little girls and force them into prostitution, but a real pimp doesn't have to do that. Pimping is pimping. Pimping ain't kidnapping and rape. A real pimp knows how to get a woman to do what she would normally do for free and get paid for it.

When a woman knows her value, the only way that you are getting that ass for free, is because she loves you and she knows for a fact that you love her, but even those women expect you to buy them dinner, take them to the movies, buy them flowers, or buy them a gift every once in a while. Those who don't know their value will give it up for a bag of potato chips and a Mood Ring - without the promise of love in hopes of one day obtaining it. The game is full of those people, from the hoes to the johns and that's where I come in.

The only time that pimping gets hard is when you have to deal with the police. Unless you want to spend the rest of your life getting "three hots and a cot" and trying to keep rapists out of your butthole, you have to be smart. You don't want to come into this game as a man and end-up institutionalized or as somebody's bitch.

I know…it takes a "special" kind of person and when I say "special", I mean "morally depraved individual" to decide to get into the game. To wake up one day and decide that you're going to profit off of the pain of another individual means that you don't give a shit – you don't give a shit about them, you don't give a shit about their families, and you don't give a shit about their community. You don't care about nobody, but yourself and the money and if you're lucky enough, you will stay out of jail while accumulating it.

I bet you hate me already and that's okay. Sure, it's easy to blame me for the fucked-up shit that grown people are willing to do to each other, voluntarily. I'm cool with that as long as this motherfucker gets paid…y'all can keep on hating.

But eventually, all good things must come to an end…After a while, the hoes get old, the pimps get old, and the game gets old and what's a pimp to do then? Go into the retirement home for pimps and live off of all of the tax-free money that he saved over the years? No, he turns to one of the other oldest professions in the world. He becomes a preacher.

Chapter 1

Another glorious Sunday Morning...

"**A**men?" he asked.

"Amen," we responded.

"Let the church say 'Amen' again."

"Amen," we all said, again.

"Can we give the choir an 'Amen'?" he asked. "They sang so beautifully."

We said, "Amen."

"And can we give the Praise Dancers an 'Amen'?" he asked. "They danced so gracefully...don't you agree?"

"Amen," we all said, again.

"And can we give the musicians an Amen?" he continued.

I noticed that everyone was saying "Amen", but my father. I looked at him and noticed that he was pouting. He was still pissed, because my mama made him go to church on Super Bowl Sunday, and he was not a "happy camper."

Finally, he looked at me and said, "If that motherfucker asks for one more 'Amen…'"

I started laughing. My mother looked at us and said, "Shhhhhhhhh…."

"I'm just saying…" He folded his arms across his chest.

Our pastor continued. "Today is a good day."

"Amen," the congregation said.

"And why is today a good day…you may ask?" he said.

My father looked at me and said, "I didn't ask his ass shit."

I started laughing, loudly. My mother threw us the "look."

Our pastor continued. "Today is a good day because this is the day that the Lord has made…let us rejoice and be glad in it, Amen?"

My father looked at me and said, "Just one more time…I swear…one more time."

My mother looked at him and said, "Stop."

My father frowned. "Why don't you tell him to 'stop'? That's at least twenty 'Amens' in the past five minutes…I mean, really…how many do he need?"

She looked at him and frowned.

"Frown all you want…I'm not giving his ass not one mo' Amen," he said, folding his arms and pouting.

The pastor continued. "Today is a good day because you and I are here today…Amen?"

"Amen," the congregation said.

"A lot of folks went to the mall last week, purchased a fancy outfit to wear to service, today…got up last night and ironed that outfit, spent all of last night dreaming about how good they were going to look in that outfit, and guess what? Some of those same folks didn't get to wear that outfit. Why? Because, in the middle of that dream, they were called home to be with Lord."

The congregation nodded in agreement.

He paused for a second and looked around the room. "The Bible tells us that tomorrow is not promised," he said. "Amen? Not promised."

"Amen," they all said.

"Let's pull out your Bibles," he requested. Suddenly, they turned on two big flat-screen TVs that sat off to the right and left side of the altar. The scripture flashed across the screen. He continued, "Matthew 6:25 says, *Therefore I tell you, do not worry about your life, what you will eat or drink; or about your body, what you will wear. Is not life more than food, and the body more than clothes?* He paused for a second and said, "Do you see what's happening here? Let's read further."

I looked at him. I began to position myself for a long awaited nap when I heard him make a hacking sound. I looked up because I thought that he was choking, but he continued on without missing a beat.

"Now, let's skip to Matthew 6:27-28. It says, *'Can any one of you by worrying add a single hour to your life? 28* says *And why do you worry about clothes? See how the flowers of the field grow. They do not labor or spin.'* He stopped and made that hacking sound again.

I began to look around to see if anyone else was waiting to see what he was trying to cough up, but no one else look concerned or seemed to care that he was preaching and trying to cough up phlegm at the same time.

He continued. "Now, skip to verse 31. *So do not worry, saying, 'What shall we eat?' or 'What shall we drink?' or 'What shall we wear?'* (Hack)

Suddenly one of the ushers walked up and handed him a glass of water, but that didn't seem to help. He kept "hacking." Some of the members of the congregation began to stand. "Preach!!!" one woman shouted. I began to notice that his "hacking" was stirring up the crowd. It was a part of his performance.

"Let's continue…33 says, (Hack) '*But seek first his kingdom and his righteousness, and all these things will be given to you as well. 34 Therefore do not worry about tomorrow, for tomorrow will worry about itself. Each day has enough trouble of its own.* (Hack) Why are you worried about what you look like (Hack) when you have more than enough to worry about? But If you BELIEVE (Hack)…"

"Preach!!!"

"I said, 'If you BELIEVE (Hack)'…that God will provide (Hack) then focus on living your life TODAY (Hack) because tomorrow is not promised. (Hack)"

"YES!!!"

"Oooooooooo Lord…y'all ain't ready today…God has been so good…turn to the person on your right and say, 'You don't need no new clothes. (Hack)"

"Ain't that some shit…" My father looked at my mother and frowned. "Says the man who got on a new suit…." He shook his head. "I ain't never seen that suit before…have you?" he asked my mother, but she ignored him. Then, he turned and asked me. "Don't that suit look new?"

If I was thinking about answering him that was quickly shot-down by the look on my mother's face.

Then everyone turned to the person on their right and began to chant "You don't need no new clothes!!!!" I thought that this was odd because when everyone turned to their right, they ended-up looking at the back of somebody's head, but they did it anyway. Then, I began to get caught-up in the excitement too. I got so wound-up, I began to join them, but when I said it, I ended it with a big loud HACK!!!!!! The whole congregation turned and looked at me. When I noticed that all eyes were on me, I pretended that I had something caught in my throat and slid down into the pew. My mother looked at me and shook her head.

My father looked at his brand new shoes and then looked over at us. We were all wearing brand new clothes. My father said, "I wish we would have read those scriptures before we spent all of that damn money. Even God wants us to stay out of the damn stores."

My mother looked at him and then said, "Shhhhhhhhh…"

"I'm just saying that we could have worn what we already had and saved some money," he continued.

She shushed him again. "Shhhhhhh…"

"Shush, yourself…I work too hard for my money…"

She frowned and he stopped talking. He folded his arms and slumped back down into the seat.

"TODAY is a good day, because we are here today…here…another day to serve the Lord. Amen?" the preacher continued.

"Amen," the congregation said.

"Another reason why today is a good day is because TODAY is my birthday." he said.

My father and I sighed loudly.

"When I woke up this morning, I had to use the bathroom really bad…it must have had something to do with those prunes that I'd eaten the night before…you know you gotta get your fiber…Amen?" he said.

"The Lord don't want his servants to be constipated," a woman said. The people on the side of her, nodded in agreement.

"Well, I was sitting on the toilet and I was pushing and I was pushing and then all of a sudden, the Lord said, 'Son, you don't need to strain…relax…BELIEVE and watch what happens.' And you know what? I relaxed, I believed, and then it happened. PRAISE THE LORD…I was set free, Amen?"

"Amen," the congregation said.

"And while I was sitting there…the Lord asked, 'Son…isn't today your birthday?' And I said, "Why, yes, Lord…how did you know? And He responded by saying, 'Boy, I know everything. Am I not the Lord?'"

The congregation erupted in laughter and he continued. "I'm not kidding…He said, 'You need to tell your congregation that today is your birthday.' And I said, 'Why

Lord? Why should I tell them about my birthday? And the Lord said, 'Because what they sow into you, they sow into Me.' And I said, 'Are you sure Lord?' And He said, 'Yes, ask and it shall be given...' Then, I wiped myself, flushed the toilet, and as I washed my hands, I thought about what He said. Then I asked myself, 'What would I ask of my congregation?' And I thought long and hard about it as I drove here in the Bentley that you all bought me for Christmas and it came to me."

The congregation grew quiet. They were all sitting on the edge of their seats.

"Now, to keep down confusion and to make it easy for you...I'm asking that each one of you give $100. Now, understand...I'm not asking you because I want to, but because GOD told me to and remember, when you give, you get. Your blessings are determined by how much you sow. If you only plant one seed, then you'll only get one blessing...but if you sow abundantly, then your cup will runneth over....and remember, that today is a special day."

A few people began to pull out their wallets and purses.

He continued. "Yes, I could have asked for a card, but God doesn't want you to sow a card...I can't go on vacation with a card...I can't buy new suits with a card, but if you put a hundred dollars in that card, I can get a suit and still go on vacation. Amen?"

More people started to open their wallets.

"Now, for those who are hesitating, we must remember that we have to be obedient. I could have said, 'No, Lord...I can't ask my congregation to give me MORE money, but I have to be obedient too, because what is disobedience? It's a sin and the wages of sin is what?" he asked.

The congregation answered, "Death."

"Say that again," the pastor requested.

"DEATH!!!!" they shouted as more people opened their wallets and purses.

"Yes, 'The wages of sin is death'…Now, for those of you who have their money in their hands…I want you to flip that money over to the back and look across the middle…what does it say?" he asked.

In unison, the congregation said, "In God we trust…"

"In God we trust," he confirmed. "You have to trust God and trust me to know God's will…now, hold that money in the air and say, 'In God we Trust,'" he said.

"In God we trust!!!" they repeated after him.

"Now, put all of that 'trust' in the collection plate and then let's bow our heads." he said.

I looked at my father. It looked like his head was going to explode.

Slowly, the collection plates came down each aisle. Each parishioner placed their "seed" into the plate. I watched my father reach into his wallet and next to his lottery tickets was a $5 bill, $10 bill, and a $20 bill. My father reached for the $5 bill, but my mother gave him the "look" and he pulled out the $10 bill. She gave him another "look" and said, "You better stop playing with God."

Hesitantly, my father pulled out the $20 bill. He mumbled, "I better win the lottery or I'm going to be pissed."

Chapter 2

After service, my dad took us to a local "all-you-can-eat" buffet restaurant where most of the congregation went after church. We were all in line, getting our plates, napkins, and silverware when, Sister Baker and her husband arrived. She walked up to us.

"Well, hey Sister Miller," she said to my mother. My father, brother, and I stopped to look at her.

My mother put her plate down to hug Sister Baker. "Hey Sweetie, how are you? Didn't you just love the Pastor's sermon?" she asked.

"Girl, yes…he spoke to my spirit…yes, he did," she said, placing her hand on my mother's shoulder. "Well, look, I will talk to you in a second…enjoy your meal." She stopped and looked at us. "Hi kids…" She waved at us.

We all waved back and politely said, "Hi."

She smiled and walked away. We watched her as she walked to her seat. As soon as she was gone, my mother looked at my father and said, "Talking about he spoke to her spirit…" she paused to shake her head. "More like he spoke to her breasts…did you see how her chest was sticking out of that dress?"

"No…no…we didn't see…I mean, I didn't see…I mean…can you hand me a spoon?"

My mother narrowed her eyes and said, "She should be ashamed of herself. If she had of sneezed, I would have been saying 'Hi' to her nipples…talking about he spoke to her spirit…I wonder if her husband knows that he's speaking to her spirit." She grabbed her plate and started filling it with food.

My father laughed and said, "Didn't you just get out of church?"

My mother turned up her nose and said, "It ain't a sin if you're speaking the truth."

My father smiled and shook his head as we smiled back.

After filling our plates, we all sat down to eat. Everyone had already started eating when I felt something burning the side of my face. I looked up to find my mother staring at us.

"Ummmmmm...didn't you all forget something?" she asked.

My father looked around and said, "Did I forget the ham? Did they have ham up there?"

My mother frowned. "Ain't nobody talking about ham. Did y'all say Grace?"

"Man, really? I'm hungry," one of my sisters complained.

"Yes, really..." she confirmed.

"And y'all better get full...I better not see none of y'all in that refrigerator," my father said.

My mother was still staring at us. "Y'all better not embarrass me...now, bow your heads and say 'Grace."

We all sighed and then bowed our heads. Two seconds later, our faces were back into our plates. After we ate the first time, we decided to sit and talk to give the food enough time to settle before eating again. Suddenly, my father walked back up to the buffet and then returned with a plate full of chicken and a hand full of napkins. He sat down and said, "Hand me your purse."

"What? Wait...no...no...no...please do not embarrass me," my mother said.

"Look...I'm not worried about embarrassing you...I know how these damn kids are. They are going to wait until we leave and then holla' hungry and I ain't buying nothing. I gave my last to that church. Now, keep an eye out while I put this chicken in your purse."

My mother's face turned red. "I can't believe you."

My father said, "If you can see it...then believe it...I paid for this damn chicken."

As they argued about the chicken, I stood to go fill my pockets with dessert.

Chapter 3

My father is an interesting character. He and my mother are polar-opposites. My father says whatever is on his mind; whenever and wherever he feels like saying it. And if you don't like it, you have the unique pleasure of kissing his Black-ass. If you didn't want to kiss his ass, you had another option and that was getting the fuck out. It was one or the other and whatever you decided to choose made him happy, because either way, he wins, and winning is what he likes to do.

He was a hustler. He was once a low-level dealer and gangbanger on the Chicago's Westside. He was eleven years old when he was recruited into a gang. As a young soldier, he hustled other little kids into becoming gang members. Although, he never talked about it, we knew what it took to get in, we knew what it took to stay in, and we knew how hard it was to get out. While pointing out the scar on his face that was once a tear-drop tattoo, he told us scary stories about that "life." He was slowly moving up the ranks – doing whatever he had to do to get there, until the day he met my mother.

He was cool and smart as hell – not book smart, but street smart. He couldn't tell you the Process of Photosynthesis, but he could look at a bag of weed, weigh it with his eyes, smell it and tell you what kind it was, tell you where and when it was grown, and give you a price for it. He was true to the game, but eventually, the game dealt him a hand that would ultimately change his life. He told the story so many times that I can recite it better than I can recite the Lord's Prayer.

He began, "Son...did I tell you how I met yo' mama?"

"Only a million times, but could you tell me again? I think it'll be better if you tell it a million and one times," I said, sarcastically.

Frowning, he said, "With your smart ass...for that, I will tell it again."

"I thought that you would," I said. "Should I use the bathroom...grab a pillow and a blanket...maybe apply for Social Security first?" I asked.

"Sit your butt down," he said, smiling. "Well," he began. "I was "pushing" one day and had to drop some stuff off at this house. The house was a shack – one of those buildings that was supposed to be torn down, but the city hadn't gotten around to it yet. Anyway, when the door opened...the smell nearly knocked me off my feet...it smelled so bad. It smelled like a damn zoo in there. The furniture looked like the kids were using it for a toilet. It was nasty. Both the mother and father were 'hypes.' They barely had ten teeth between the two of them. They were "tweeking" and needed a fix quick." He paused for a moment and continued, "We made the deal and we were getting ready to leave when I asked them did they have a bathroom. Now, you know that I must have really needed to piss to even ask them. They were too busy shooting-up to even hear me, so I decided to find it for myself. I looked all over the place for it. I would have been able to find it if the whole house didn't smell like shit. Anyway, I didn't find it, but while I was lost, I heard this voice. It was so sweet. She sounded like an angel. She was singing, 'Oh Mary, don't you weep...'" He paused, again, to make a nauseating face, one that most men who are in love make and said, "I took her out of that pile of shit and married her. Ten kids and a hundred pounds later, we are still together."

"Zzzzzzzzzzz..." I said, pretending to be asleep.

"Boy, you know that's some good stuff. If I hadn't met your mama, you would probably be a stain on a piece of toilet paper," he said.

Now, this is the only part of the story that seems to change every-time he tells it. "I thought that you said that I could have been a stain on a sheet."

"Sheet, napkin, toilet paper, sock…" He laughed. "Still would have been a stain if I hadn't met her…"

"Tell me about the good stuff…"

"What good stuff?" he asked.

"…About all of the money that you made."

"Boy, the thing about fast money is that you lose it as fast as you get it. Sure, you gain a lot, but you end-up losing more."

"But you gain a lot…"

"But you lose a lot…it's not worth it in the end…believe me. People who do that shit end-up in one of two places; prison or

41

a grave and I wouldn't recommend either one of them to nobody. I was lucky to find your mama...she probably saved my life."

As I listened to him, I couldn't help but feel like my father is a little "pussy-whipped." I understand why he loves my mother, but I have to admit, she's a little crazy. He really respects and loves her – so much so, that he turns a blind's-eye to her closet-craziness. Why? Because he didn't want her to cut off his supply. When she shook her butt, all of a sudden it was time for us to go to bed – no matter what time of the day it was. We were probably the only kids on the block who took naps two or three times a day. Everything stops when the "booty" calls. We would lie awake in bed with our pillows covering our heads until the screaming and banging stopped. Then, they would walk out of their bedroom looking like they'd just run a marathon.

She was always complaining about something. He once joked that if we weren't around, she probably would argue with herself. There are some mothers who can beat the "black" off of you. My mother was one who could accomplish the same feat by arguing with you. I mean it…she could argue with you so long that your "blackness" would pack its shit and leave. Then, you're left walking around, looking stupid, cause your "blackness" is gone.

"Women…you can't live with them and you can't get them to shut the hell up," he joked, but never in front of my mother because he knew what would happen to him.

Chapter 4

I was raised by a woman who devoted her life to her family and to God. Normally, this wouldn't be a bad thing but my mother ate, slept, and drank Jesus. She was a religious junkie who had to have her daily fix of the "Word". If she didn't get it, her withdrawal came in the form of screams and complaining about how life had dealt her a bad hand.

She would point at her stretchmarks and say, "Y'all did this to me." She would point at her gray hair and say, "Y'all did this to me." If she could, she would point at her hemorrhoids and blame that on us too. Day in and day out, she was whining about something. I'm sure that if she could, she would have blamed us for her having so many damn kids, but she couldn't. She had to blame that on a husband that humped everything that moved, blame it on R&B, and blame it on that bottle of wine that she calls, "The Blood of Jesus" that she kept in her nightstand.

I always wondered why she had so many kids if she didn't want them, but she wouldn't dare say that out loud, because then she would have to admit that she made a mistake and Mrs. Holier than Thou never made a mistake. She was always right. Even when she was wrong, she was right, and we believed everything she said.

Now, don't get me wrong, I don't doubt that she loved us. Any woman who has ten kids and don't beat the shit out of them every day has to love them. Cause you see, we were bad as hell. We used to do things just to see if we could get away with it and many times, we did. She tried to keep up with us, but while she was talking to one of us, the other one would be knee-deep into something that they didn't have any business being into. She used to look at us and say, "God is watching you" and I used to look at her and wonder why God was stalking us.

The poor thing really had her hands full. I remember one time, she'd sat us all down for lunch. She looked at the table and noticed that one of us was missing. She looked at me and said, "Where's your brother?"

I looked at her and shrugged my shoulders. "I don't know."

"Get down and go find him," she demanded.

"Ahhhhhh man, why me?" I complained.

"Because I told you to…now, go and find him," she said.

I jumped out of my chair and stomped all through the house until I found him sitting on the bathroom floor. I turned and walked back to the kitchen.

"Where's your brother?" she asked.

"He's in the bathroom eating chocolate," I said, snickering.

Confused, she asked, "Chocolate? What chocolate? We don't have any…" With her eyes bulging out of her head and veins popping out of the side of her neck, she said, "Oh my God, nooooooooo…"

My brothers and sisters began to laugh hysterically.

Before she ran out of the kitchen and down the hall, she said, "You better not move. I swear…if one of y'all move all Hell is going to break loose."

I shrugged my shoulders, and climbed back into my seat – joining the rest of them in laughter.

Suddenly, we heard a scream. "What are you doing? Boy!!!!! What are you doing??!!! This is not chocolate, boy!!! THIS IS NOT CHOCOLATE!!!"

Suddenly, we heard the shower come on and she yelled at him until he was clean. By the time, she returned to the kitchen, it was full of smoke because she'd burned everything. She turned the stove off.

"Why didn't one of you come and get me?" she asked, opening the window to let the smoke out.

We all looked around the table. My sister broke the silence. "You told us not to move."

Breathing heavily, she asked, "The house could have caught fire...what were you thinking? You're smarter than this...you can't expect me to do everything..."

"But you said..." my other sister said.

"So you gon' sit there and burn to death? God-damn-it kids...use your God-damn heads..."

Yes, my mother cursed, but she only used one word, "God-damn-it." She felt that it if she used it, God would hear her, stop everything that He was doing, just to help her with her bad-ass kids. She had Him on speed-dial. She would call on Him all of the time and always for the same reason – her bad ass kids. Too bad He never picked-up his phone. Maybe it was because He was too busy dealing with real issues like sickness, poverty, war, and natural disasters. But she felt like they had a special connection like the one that most Fathers have with their daughters. It didn't matter that He has a lot of other daughters who probably has some bad-ass kids too. Also, she felt that anything with the word "God" in front of it had to be okay. It didn't bother her that it had the word "damn-it" on the end of it.

We all looked around the table and waited to see who would respond to her first. I guess my brothers and sisters thought that it was my turn to get yelled at, so they all turned and looked at me. I smiled and said, "Mama, God is watching you."

If looks could kill, I would have fell out of my chair, hit the floor, and died on the scene. She didn't appreciate the comment and she responded to me by making us all go to bed without eating, but I didn't care. It was worth it.

I love her, but she can be annoying. My mother used to have these things that she called her "Private Summers." I used to think that my mother was really special because God had given her her own Private Summers. Until one day, we caught her in "Mid-Season." She was going-off about something. I wish that I could tell you what she was going off about, but it starts to all sound the same when you hear it a thousand times a day. Anyway, she was yelling and screaming when all of a sudden, beads of sweat formed on her forehead, then those beads turned to streams of water that poured down the sides of her face, next she started peeling off her clothes like she was getting ready to take a shower, until finally, she was standing in front of us wearing nothing, but a bra, a slip and a pair of panties. I'm only assuming that she was wearing panties. At least, I pray that she was. Then, she would dismiss us to fan herself while drinking a glass full of water, and rubbing herself with ice cubes.

God must have blessed her with her own "Private Winters" too because if she wasn't hot, she was cold. On those days, she dressed in layers, and turned on the heat – no matter how warm it was outside. Then she had this "friend" who visited her every month who used to really piss her off. When this "friend" came to visit, my father would load-up on chocolate, painkillers, and tell us to stay out of our mother's way, because when her "friend" came to visit she could kill any one of us and get away with it. I never had a friend that caused me as much pain as hers did. I used to wonder why she never dumped her "friend", because with friends like that, she didn't need any enemies.

As I got a little older, my granny explained to me what was happening to my mom and why. What I couldn't understand was why, would a merciful God, put women through such a terrible thing.

"We are all created in God's image…" My granny explained. "And, you will find, after you read the Bible, that God's a little Bi-polar, jealous, indecisive…and He has multiple-personalities too…got that whole "Us" and "Our" thing going on…He is one and many at the same time…just madness…I can go on and on, but what more can you say about a guy who writes, directs, produces, and plays lead in His own movie?"

Finally, I asked her, "Well, what do men go through?"

She looked at me and said, "Well, men go through the same thing, but just a different version of it…now, add some balding, nose hair, ear hair, back hair, ass hair, the ability to fart at all the wrong times and places…"

The look on my face made her pause. "I could tell you more, but then you will never want to grow up."

"Thanks, grandma…that's depressing…"

"And it only gets better or worse depending on your view of things…just keep living, son…just keep living…"

Chapter 5

Grand-mama is the matriarch of the family. My grand-mama loved the Lord, but she took great pride in being a sinner too. She straddled the fence of good and evil and you could never tell, on any given day, what side she was on. She used to drink, fight, curse, and chew tobacco like a man and dared you to say something about it. She felt that she could do anything that she wanted to do because God knew her heart. My grand-mama was another person who claimed to have a special connection with the Lord. Didn't matter that she could curse you out so bad that it left you in tears, or that she drank whiskey from sun-up to sun-down, and it didn't matter that she could spit tobacco 50 feet into a can that sat across the room – she and God had an understanding.

I love my grand-mama. Like my father, she said exactly what was on her mind. My father had to be provoked where my grand-mama was just waiting for the opportunity. And you talk about fighting. She was always ready to throw-down – anytime or anyplace. It was weird thinking that a woman her age would be willing to jump on somebody, but she felt like you were never too old for an ass-whooping. My grand-mama didn't care if you were a man or a woman – if you had a weapon or if you wanted to go "toe-to-toe." Once she got a hold of you, it was over. If you walked up on her, you better have your "affairs" in order because you were going home in a body bag.

I remember one time, we took my granny grocery shopping. My mother was still in the store shopping when this all took place. Everything was going along just fine until a child pushed a shopping cart up against the heel of my granny's foot. She jumped and screamed when it happened, but when she saw that it was a child, she didn't say anything. She just rubbed the back of her foot and mumbled curse words under her breath. Then she looked up and saw that the child's mother saw the whole thing, but didn't say anything. As I saw the look on my granny's face change from pain to anger, I began to count backwards in my head because I could tell that it was about to go down. *10,9,8,7,6,5*...by the time I got to number four, she said, "You need to keep an eye on that child...he just rolled that cart on the back of my foot."

Now, a normal person with any kind of home-training would have just apologized. My grand-mother was an elder and everyone is raised to respect their elders, but instead the woman said, "OR if you wasn't rubber-necking those damn candy bars, you would have seen us coming."

My eyes widened and I stepped aside to make room for the ass-whopping that this woman was about to receive. My granny turned and said, "Whether I was looking at candy bars or not...you should be keeping an eye on that kid."

"Well, from the view back here, YOU DON'T NEED TO BE LOOKING AT NO DAMN CANDY BARS..." the woman said.

My grandmother's eyebrows were now touching each other. "Hold my purse." She turned to the cashier and said, "You might want to go on break because I'm about to shut this lane down...oh, and call housekeeping because you gon' need a clean-up in aisle 9."

The cashier didn't call housekeeping. Instead, she called the store manager.

I walked over and grabbed her purse. She walked around the woman's shopping cart and said, "You might want to call your next of kin..." as she removed her earrings and rolled up her sleeves.

Realizing that my granny wasn't playing, the woman said, "Look…he didn't mean to do it…" she looked at the boy and said, "Tell the woman that you didn't mean to do it."

The boy didn't respond.

My granny said, "With your bad butt and your messed-up ass mama…that's what's wrong with you damn kids today."

Suddenly, the store manager walked up. "Is there a problem, Mam?"

Frowning and taking her purse from me, she said, "Naw…ain't no problem."

Then, the boy's mama said, "She threatened me and said that she was gon' kill my son."

My grand-mama couldn't believe her ears. "Bitch…after I was gon' let you slide…you lie on me?" She looked at me. "I'm 'bout to whoop this lying bitch's ass."

The manager grabbed her by the arm. "Mam, you need to leave."

My grandmother gave him a look that said, "You don't want none of this," and then he quickly released her. "I ain't going no-where."

Suddenly, security arrived. As they were escorting my grand-mama out of the store, my mother arrived just in time to hear her say, "Fuck this store...you hear me?...fuck this store...and bitch, if I catch you on the street, your ass is mine...fuck you and that little bad-ass child of yours...and all of y'all can suck my dick. You hear me? SUCK...MY...DICK!!!!"

My mother looked on in complete horror. She didn't come to my grandmother's aid. Instead, she acted like she didn't know her. As I carried her purse to the car, I couldn't help but wonder if my grandmother really had a dick. It was scary enough to hear her say it, but to think that under that polka-dotted housecoat was a penis, made me want to lie down in the middle of the parking lot and wait for someone to run me over.

Chapter 6

If the Miller family were a vehicle, religion was the fuel that kept us going. Seven days a week, 24 hours a day, it was always time to praise the Lord, but it was a struggle for me, because I've always known that something wasn't right. Now, I know that we are not perfect and 'all fall short of the glory of God,' but some fall farther than others. They may have a good reason for why they do so, but it is the unwillingness to admit their imperfections that has always left a bad taste in my mouth.

Again, there were ten of us. My dad is now a Postal Worker. Although, he made a decent wage, we were still struggling. It takes a lot to feed ten kids and they needed help. They couldn't go to the church, because the church wouldn't help them. Sure they would throw us some powdered milk and some of that cheese that block-up your bowels every once in a while, but that's every once in a while. We needed to eat every day, so they turned to the government for help and they said, "No." Even though, we were at the poverty line, they still refused to give us assistance. While the government isn't responsible for them making all of those babies, they couldn't change what they thought was God's will, so my mother felt that she needed to figure out a way to feed all of us. But the government will not help a family if the father is still in the household. They would prefer that the children who were on welfare had no fathers, so my mother had to lie to keep food on the table. It didn't matter that they barely had enough money to pay the rent or the bills – the system favors a "broken" home over a family who was trying to make it – together.

So she spent most of her life looking over her shoulder. She was afraid that the Welfare police were going to come and snatch her away from her children because she wanted to feed them - and was willing to commit a crime to do so. So while we were taught that lying and stealing was a sin, what we were learning is that it applied to everyone, but my mama. It was okay to lie and steal as long as you had a good reason for doing so, but it's that type of "education" that messes up a child. As a result, we learned to hate a government that would rather see us starve to death rather than having a father in the home and we learned not to trust parents whose actions spoke louder than their words.

And that's what kids do – we watch you. From Monday through Sunday morning, we watch you - lying and sinning. Then on Sunday morning, we watch you waving your hands in the air, crying, running up and down the aisles like folks who are possessed - banging on a tambourine until you break every last one of those "press-on" fingernails just so you can turn around and start the sinning all over again on Sunday night. Sure, we could call you on your hypocrisy, but if we like chewing our food instead of drinking it through a straw, we better keep our mouths shut.

I actually found it quite entertaining. You see when you don't drink the "Kool-Aid" and you know the truth, you can view it all for what it is – bullshit, but you better not say anything. Young or old, people don't like you questioning their religion or their relationship with God. Even if you can see that something's not right, you better keep it to yourself or you could find yourself on the wrong end of an argument.

≈

There was one woman who used to come to church who made every grown man in the church smile – even the married ones. Her name was Sister Adams. If Sister Adams didn't show up, there would be no reason to come to church. Sister Adams was fine as hell. She used to come to church looking like she'd just slid right off of a stripper's pole. She used to wear blouses that were so tight that you could hear the buttons that were trying to hold her cleavage in, screaming. Her skirts barely covered her ass and she wore those glass slippers that those women in the Nudie magazines wore. Everyone in the church couldn't wait for her to get the "Spirit." The men couldn't wait because it turned them on and the women couldn't wait because it gave them something to gossip about later.

When the pianist started banging on the piano's keys and the drummer started banging on those cymbals, we knew that it was just a matter of time before she stood up and gave us what we all came to see – that pink spot between her legs. Oh,

I forgot to mention that she never wore any underwear either, NEVER, and when her legs flew open, there was not one man still sitting in his seat unless he was married and didn't want to get stabbed in the church. I'm sure that if the church hadn't taken all of their money, they would have thrown "singles" at her.

The congregation complained about her attire, but the Pastor reminded them that they had no right to judge her, but we knew the truth. You see, the "First Lady" was a troll. I'm sorry. I know that it isn't "Christian-like" to say such things, but it was the truth. She was not a beautiful lady. I know that beauty is skin-deep, but hers was so deep that it was nonexistent. I wouldn't want to get caught in a dark-alley with her unless I was using her face for protection. She was a "beast" with make-up on, so I could only imagine what she looked like without it. You talk about being in the right place at the right time. I don't know what the pastor was thinking, but the First Lady must have had some "skills" or a whole lotta money.

The Pastor didn't say anything to Sister Adams because, and I'm just assuming, that was all of the "action" that he was getting. The "First Lady" could not stand Sister Adams. I would say that you could tell by the look on her face, but she always looked like that. If the Commandments didn't say anything about murdering folks, Sister Adams would be dead along with every other cute woman in the church.

And her moves were classic. She would stand, adjust her clothing, start with the "Nay-Nay" until she was in front of the whole congregation, do a little "Running Man", break into the "Hustle", "Drop it like it's hot", add a little twerking, and then finish with a cartwheel back to her seat. *Whew.* I'm getting hard just telling you about it. It was funny watching all of the men lean-in, making sure that they didn't miss a thing. I was right there with them – beads of sweat on my forehead, mouth wide-open, tongue hanging out of my mouth, and eyes bucking out of my head. When she was done, I sat down to adjust myself and my growing erection. Watching her bounce all over the place was nothing short of Heaven. For a little boy, it was the next best thing to staring at the old lady who lived next door - her pink rollers in her hair and flannel nightgowns weren't sexy, but beggars can't be choosey.

My mother looked at my father to see if he was staring. As soon as she caught his gaze, she nudged him in the ribs, but as soon as she turned back around, he looked at us and smiled.

Chapter 7

One Sunday, after hours of sitting, half of the "church" was now asleep, and my butt was numb. Now, it was time to start handing them more money. I found it amazing how many times they asked for money. They had the Building Fund, the Sick and Shut-in Fund, the Pastor's Anniversary Fund, the Choir's Anniversary Fund, we had to pay the musicians and the visiting preachers, there was a special fund for whatever the pastor needed on that day, and then after all of that, they required that people pay their "Tithes" – these funds were collected twice a day, during the morning and afternoon services. Not to mention the money that they collected for the First Fruit Offering, Choir Rehearsal, Bible Study, Usher Board Meeting and any other auxiliary meeting going on at the church. They also got paid for weddings and for funerals and in the Black community, sadly, funerals can add up.

I asked my father why the church needed so much money. You could tell that this was a touchy subject for him. You see, my father didn't "believe" like my mother did. He walked on egg-shells when it came to the subject because he didn't want to argue with her, but if he had a choice, he would keep every dime of his hard-earned money in his pocket. I used to think that it would be easier and would probably save a lot of time if people just walked in and deposited all of their money and valuables at the altar or maybe the church could install a drive-thru window like they had at the bank, but then they would miss-out on all of the entertainment.

I was curious about all of this, so I asked my father about it.

He looked at me with the most serious face I've ever seen and said, "Son...look around you...what do you see?"

This sounded like a trick question. "Ummmmm...people?"

"What you see are a bunch of kind and loving people...a bunch of delusional, kind, and loving people...who want to do the right thing for the right reasons...only to give their money to the wrong man who's going to do a lot of wrong shit with it."

"Huh? What?"

"Ask yourself this...we all pay tithes, right?"

"Yes..."

"Does the pastor pay tithes?"

"Ummmmm...yes...I guess..."

"Who is he paying them to?"

"Ummmmm…the church? God?"

"God never sees a dime of that money…use your head…does God have a bank account that churches make deposits into?"

Confused, I said, "I don't know…"

"NO…that money goes right back to the pastor, the musicians, the bill collectors, and the bank…the bank is the landlord…the real 'lord' of the 'land'…they're supposed to take care of the poor, but they don't…if they did, we wouldn't still see them on the street."

"Wow…"

He patted my hand. "Son, let me tell you something…"

"Okay…" I said, eager to hear what he had to say.

"This is all bullshit…"

My eyes widened. "Huh?" I asked.

"Yep, bullshit...I'm only here because I don't want to hear your mama's mouth..."

Confused, I looked at him.

"Look son...church is not for men...this shit is for women..."

"Really?"

"Yes, really..."

"Why do you say that?"

"Think about it...men are not emotional, while women are...religion is all about the 'warm and cuddly shit'...love, giving love, being loved..." He paused and then continued. "Churches give women the shit that they are not getting at home..."

"Like what?" I asked.

"Easy access to a hundred women on any given day...this is like one big-ass country club...and Jesus is the kind and loving man that most women don't have in their lives...they can talk to Him all day long and He never gets tired of listening to them...He and God will love them unconditionally. They will be there when no one else will."

"Interesting..."

"No man wants or cares about another man loving them...unless, it's his father or unless it's something that he's into..." He paused and continued, "Listen to that song that they are singing...have you ever sung a love song to another man? Especially, one that you can't see?"

I couldn't answer his question because my brain was numb.

"Men read the Bible because we love the action, the gore, the scandal, and the scary shit...other than that, we wouldn't read it...unless we're using it to control people and men love control...that's why every version of it has been written by men...kinda makes you understand why there's so much sick shit in there."

I looked at him in complete shock.

"As soon as we walk in the door, we feel like we're being emotionally castrated…like they cut our balls off at the door and then hand them back to us when service is over. We would rather be getting a root canal with a rusty drill then to be sitting here, but we do it. If I took a poll right now, you will find that most of the men who are here, are here because they don't want to argue, they don't want their 'supply' cut off, or they are trying to get them some…OR they are trying to make sure that their wives don't put all of the bill money into the collection plate…" He paused and pointed at the pulpit. "Or like him…The men are trying to get paid…and that's where tithes come in…"

"Wow…" I said.

"That money that your mother put in that collection plate is the price that I pay for peace…If I know that coming to church is going to get me some ass at the end of the day or some peace and quiet…I'm going to hurry up and put this suit on and shut the hell up…"

"Wow…" I said, again, trying to process all of this.

"Churches wouldn't exist without women…cults wouldn't exist without women…all of this shit exists because of women…and women spend money. Look around you…women buy clothes for other women…women buy clothes for their kids for other women…" He looked at himself. "If it was up to me, I would die in this suit, but your mama ain't gon' let that happen."

"Man…that's ummmm…"

"Boy, look…I'm just keeping it real…that's why churches appeal to women…to keep them hooked and they will pay any price to keep their men…Jesus and God…happy…and their men know it."

"That's kind of messed-up…"

"Hey…a man don't mind his woman loving an invisible man…until that relationship disrupts the real one. Then there's a problem."

76

I looked around the church at all of the men's faces...wondering what they were thinking about.

He continued. "And women are drawn to preachers...they're like celebrities and the women are like groupies...while that man is up there, not one woman is thinking about the man that is sitting next to them or the one that she has at home...believe me...not even your mama."

"Wow...well, thank God for Sister Adams, huh?" I said.

He smiled and mumbled, "Amen."

Chapter 8

Because of the "disconnect" between my mother and father over their religious beliefs, we challenged and disobeyed them. Everything that they said and did required an explanation. This frustrated my mother because she just expected us to go with the flow. Her answer, to every question, was always the same. "Do it because I told you to." Even if it made absolutely no sense, we still had to do it and God-forbid if we asked questions about things that she felt was "grown-folks" business. When that happened, and after the smoke cleared from all hell breaking loose, we would be forced to listen to the Adam and Eve and the Tree of Knowledge of Good and Evil story. If you don't know the story, you will find it in the Book of Genesis. I would tell you what it's about, but if I have to hear it again, my head is going to explode. Spoiler alert: Contrary to what you've heard, it wasn't Eve's fault.

Anyway, she used to get so mad and frustrated at us when we asked her questions, that she would dismiss us and make us get out of her face. She wasn't like my father who tried to talk us through it, even though he didn't know the answer. No, by getting us out of her face, she could avoid us, the answer, and the truth.

If they only had one child, the disagreements and disobedience wouldn't be so bad, but when there are ten kids working on your nerves, day in and day out, you find yourself praying to that invisible being in the sky for the strength to keep you from choking the shit out of your kids.

Now, out of all of us, usually there would be one or two of us who got into trouble all of the time, but in the end, we were all punished. Why? Due to something called, "association." That's when a person is blamed for something because they know the person, are related to the person, they look like the person, or simply because they are the same color as you. It's terrible, but it's true. It happens all of the time to Black people - all of the time.

There's no difference growing-up in a Black household. You are guilty until proven innocent. So when things went down in my house, my mama would round us all up, interrogate us, and then use what she knew best to beat the hell out of us? She would use the Bible. Scripture after agonizing scripture, she made us listen to her. She would start early in the morning and wouldn't stop until you couldn't think about nothing else, but the "word of God."

"Honor your father and your mother, so that you may live long in the land the

LORD your God is giving you," she began.

I looked over at my sister who was picking her nose and rubbing boogers on her clothes.

"Cursed is anyone who dishonors their father or mother..." she continued.

I looked at my other sister who was falling asleep and trying to play it off. One time her head fell back so hard, it hit the wall behind her. She woke up just long enough to wipe the drool off of the side of her mouth before falling back to sleep. While watching her, I noticed that both of my legs had fallen asleep. This torture needed to end and soon or I wouldn't be able to walk again.

Then, she said, "Whoever spares the rod, spoils the child..."

Now, one thing that I've learned, in all of these sessions of torture, is the Bible. It wasn't because I wanted to, but after having it stuffed down your throat day in and day out, you learn a few things. I raised my hand.

She tried to ignore me, but I began to wave frantically like a person who had to pee really bad. She finally acknowledged me. "Yes, Trey."

I lowered my arm. "That ain't in the Bible."

She frowned and said, "Yes, it is…how you gon' tell me that it isn't?"

I frowned, folded my arms and said, "What scripture says that?"

She laughed and then began to flip through the pages, but she couldn't find it.

I said, "Proverbs 13:24 says 'Whoever spares the rod hates their children, but the one who loves their children is careful to discipline them'….it don't say nothing about spoiling them."

My mother continued to look in the Bible for the scripture, but was still unable to find it. Slowly, she looked up from its pages. "Everyone go to bed, but Trey." As they all stood to leave the room, they stretched their legs as they said "good-bye" to me. Not a "good-bye" that indicated that they would see me later, but the type of "good-bye" that you give a man who was on his way to the electric chair.

She slammed the "book" onto the table. "Who are you to question me?" she asked, with a scowl on her face.

"Mama, I wasn't trying to question you, but what you said is wrong," I said.

"God's word ain't never wrong," she said, waving her hands in the air.

I reached for her Bible and she handed it to me. I flipped through the pages and found 1 Peter 3 and like most preachers, I only read the parts that I found important in getting my point across. '*Wives, in the same way submit yourselves to your own husbands so that, if any of them do not believe the word, they may be won over without words by the behavior of their wives, Your beauty should not come from outward adornment, such as elaborate hairstyles and the wearing of gold jewelry or fine clothes. Rather, it should be that of your inner self, the unfading beauty of a gentle and QUIET spirit, which is of great worth in God's sight. Like Sarah, who obeyed Abraham and called him her lord.'"*

Suddenly, she fell quiet.

I waited for a second and said, "The 'Lord' and 'Master' of the house hates going to church and so does his kids...can we stop going?"

She looked at me for a long time. Then, she looked herself up and down – done-up in her fine clothes and jewelry; hair done-up in an 'elaborate hairstyle.' For the first time, in a long time, she was speechless. She looked at me and then said, "Take your butt to bed."

≈

The next morning, she barely looked at me. As she placed each bowl of oatmeal on the table, the child who received it dropped their head and began to pray. This happened nine times until she walked over to where I was sitting. She held the bowl as she stared at me. Finally, the silence was broken when she said, "You keep playing with God…your days are going to be long and hard, son…long and hard." She slammed the bowl down in front of me. I wiped oatmeal off of my face as I watched her walk away.

Chapter 9

I was getting older and wanted to break free from the rules of our household and from the restrictions placed upon us by the "Word." I love my mama, but she didn't understand me. She tried to convince me that the only way was God's way, but by the time I was a teenager, I started to believe that maybe God didn't exist.

They kept telling me to believe because the consequences of not believing were great, but they were talking to a child. We gravitate towards the forbidden and automatically do the opposite. It's how our brains are wired. If you say, "Don't go to the left", we automatically begin to wonder "What's on the left and what's so good about it?" Then, we start to say to ourselves, "Damn, it must be some really good shit on the 'left' if you are trying to keep us from it." Then we go to the left, and some really messed-up shit happens, and we blame it all on you. It's what kids do.

It was when my Grand-mama got sick that things really started to unravel for me. She'd lived with us until I started middle-school. She was so beautiful. She was a mix of African and Cherokee Indian. She had the most beautiful long white hair. I used to sit and watch her and wonder what a woman like her thought about. She was "weathered" – her skin damaged from all of the days in the sun from picking cotton. She used to tell me that even though she worked on a plantation, she wasn't no slave. She said that although they enslaved her physically, she remained free in her mind.

She used to tell me incredible stories about her life and about the lives of those who were forced to work in the fields. She also told me about all of her family members who were lost to disease and to the brutality of slavery. She is an incredible person, so the thought of her being sick is hard for me. I spent my whole life watching her, learning from her, and loving her. She taught me everything. Why the sun rises. Why a kiss can heal a scraped knee. Why brothers and sisters are so gross and why it was okay to cry.

One of my favorite memories of her was when I got into a fight in middle school with three girls. I came home broken and bruised. When my granny saw me, she asked, "Did you win?"

Handing me a bag of ice, my mother said, "Does he look like he won?"

Holding the ice to my face, I said, "No granny."

She didn't say another word about the incident until the next morning. My granny went to the school with me and told me to point out the girls who beat me up. I pointed to them. She said, "I'll be back."

I didn't know what that meant, but I was hoping that she was going to go over there and beat the crap out of them, but that didn't happen. She walked back over to me and said, "You go in that class and you get your learning. I will see you later."

I didn't know what that meant either, but I did as I was told. When the school bell rang, she was waiting outside for me. She saw the three girls and stopped them. "So you jumped on my grandson?"

Confused, they looked at her. They were frightened to have an adult in their faces.

"Did you jump on my baby?" she asked again.

One of them began to stutter, "Ye…yes."

She grabbed me by the arm, pushed me towards them, and said, "Well, he wants to fight you again."

I was in shock. My eye would have popped out of my head, if it wasn't still swollen from the first fight. "Huh? Wait...what?" I asked.

"Yeah, he wants to fight a bunch of cowards who couldn't fight him one-on-one..." She looked at me and said, "You will fight them again and whoop their asses or I'm going to whoop yours."

I looked at them and then I looked at her and the choice was simple. Where my mother didn't believe in whooping her kids, my granny did not spare the rod, the broom, the brush, the comb, the shoe, the belt, the cord, a "switch" off of the tree, or the kitchen sink – she didn't spare anything. Whatever they had in store for me was going to be ten times better than what she would do if I lost again. So without thinking, I ran up on them and started swinging. When the smoke cleared there were a lot of folks hurting.

We were all beaten and bloodied, but it was over.

She looked at me and said, "You did good…"

"Granny…you just made me beat up girls. I thought that you said that men shouldn't hit a woman?" I said, holding my swollen lip.

"And, in most cases, you shouldn't, but when one of them turns into three, that's a different story. It wasn't a fair fight, so you have to cater your ass-whoopings to fit the situation. Now, if I'd heard that you let one girl beat you up, I would have thought that was cute for about five seconds…then I would have still told you to kick her butt…" she said.

"Really? You would have made me fight a girl?"

"Yes, I would have, because people who don't want to get hit, don't hit other people. For every action, there's an equal reaction…should you hug a person who just slapped the mess out of you? No…a hug feels good and a slap does not. It has to be equal…it has to be fair…give them what they gave you. They slap you and you slap their asses back. That's how you teach people to keep their hands to themselves. It's physics…science…you don't plant apples and expect pears…"

"Okay…we just went from girls to fruit…"

"That's cause your granny's hungry…"

"But wouldn't it be better to just walk away?"

"Sometimes you should, but what kind of message is that? You can hit me and get away with it? Now, every fight isn't worth fighting, but if you gon' walk away, they better know that it's because you're being generous and not because you're some kind of bitch and the next time around, they won't be so lucky."

"Okay…" I said, rubbing the side of my face.

"Your granny won't be here forever to protect you. You don't let nobody jump on you and get away with it. I ain't taking an ass-whooping from nobody and neither will my grandson. Do you understand? An eye for an eye…"

I looked at her with my 'good-eye' and nodded, "Yes" and from that day forward, no one messed with me. They were afraid of me and my crazy grandma.

Chapter 10

By the time, I started Junior high, things had gotten worse. After a while, we started to notice things about grand-mama that wasn't normal. At first, it was gradual. She started misplacing things. Which wasn't a big deal at first, but then she started accusing people of stealing things from her. After a thorough search of the house, we found the things that she'd misplaced, but that didn't stop her from accusing us.

One Thanksgiving, my granny decided to help make dinner. It was a tradition that she cooked, but once her health started to decline, my parents thought that it would be better that she stopped for fear of her hurting herself or burning the house down. But, on this day, she insisted and everything was going smoothly until we all sat down to eat. After my dad said a prayer, we all dug in. Suddenly, I looked up to find my granny looking for something.

"What's wrong, granny?" I asked.

She continued to look around.

"Granny? What's wrong?" I asked, again.

She looked around the table and said, "Has anyone seen my teeth?"

Suddenly, everyone dropped their spoons and forks. There was a look of horror on every face in the room.

She continued to look around. "I had them in my mouth...now, they are gone."

"No, I have not seen your teeth," my mother said, spitting into her napkin.

She pointed and said, "Which one of y'all got my teeth? I know you got them?"

"Ain't nobody got your teeth," my father said.

Suddenly, you could hear people heaving, gagging, jumping up from the kitchen table, and running towards the bathroom.

There was no one left but me and her. She looked so sad as she continued to look for her teeth. I reached over and touched her hand. "It's okay, granny…we will find them," I said as tears filled my eyes.

Now, tears filled her eyes, as she tried to make lite of the situation. "If your sweet potatoes are a little crunchy then you've found my teeth."

We both fell-out laughing. "Granny, you are too funny."

She smiled and said, "Funnier by the minute…huh?"

I said, "Yep," and we continued to laugh as we finished dinner – together.

≈

She started to forget things like dates and her grandbabies' names. We sort of ignored that because she had so many grandkids that it would be easy to forget or mix up one or two of them. But then she started calling me Sam. My name ain't Sam. Matter of fact, none of her grandkids were named Sam, but when she said it, out of respect, I just said, "Yes mam…"

Then one day we were in the grocery store shopping and I noticed that the side of my granny's face was drooping. I looked at her and asked her if she was okay. She said that she was fine, but she could barely talk. My mother looked at her, left a cart full of groceries in the middle of the aisle, and immediately took her to the hospital.

From there, her health really began to deteriorate. She was no longer able to care for herself. Her children took turns taking care of her. It was so hard watching the woman who was once so strong, who was once able to take care of everyone else, and who was now dependent on others. There were days when you could tell that when she couldn't remember everyone's name that she felt 'broken' and 'beaten' by what was going on with her, but at the end of every day, she went to bed knowing how much we loved her. We reminded her on the days she couldn't remember, how much of a wonderful and incredible woman she was.

Not so long after that, we were having a picnic. I took her outside to sit in her favorite lawn chair. She really enjoyed those moments. She would sit there silently for hours just listening to the birds singing and the children playing. On this particular day, it became cold out, so I went inside to get her a sweater. I left her with her other grandbabies in the backyard. Suddenly, one of them came running inside and said, "Mama, grandma's sleeping."

When my cousin first said it, I didn't respond because I just thought that she was taking a nap, so I remained inside -

even after I watched everyone drop what they were doing and ran outside, even as they placed her body in the ambulance, I still thought that she was just sleeping. Then when they lowered her body into the ground, I knew that something wasn't right. I stood over the hole in the ground waiting for her to climb out, but she never did.

Chapter 11

For days, I waited for her, but she never came back home. Then one day, I overheard my parents talking about her. They were in her bedroom packing-up her things when I walked into the bedroom.

"What are you doing?"

"We're putting your granny's things away," my mother said, wiping tears from her eyes.

"Why?" I asked.

"Because she won't be needing them and we could use this room," my dad said.

"Use it for what? Why won't she need it?" I asked.

They both stopped and looked at me. My father broke the silence and said, "Because she's dead," he blurted out.

"Dead?" I asked. "Dead 'as in never coming back' dead?"

My father frowned and said, "That's about right..."

"I thought that you said that only sinners die."

"Everybody dies," he said.

"It's God's will son..." my mother said.

My father frowned and shook his head. "Your ass is crazy..."

"What are you talking about?" she asked, confused.

"So...it's God's will for good, decent, kind, hard-working, and loving people to get murdered...raped...to get sick...to struggle...to suffer and die...and the assholes, who are behind that shit, is given 'life' for taking a life...this world is messed-up? If that's God's will, then God hates good people."

"Son, your grandmother is preparing to go to Heaven..." my mother said, interrupting and ignoring him.

My father became angry. "Stop lying to that boy..."

"And where do you think you're going after you die?"

"Shit, it don't matter cause I'mma be dead."

Frantically, she said, "Don't listen to him...the Bible says..."

He interrupted her. "Look boy...people die...then we put them in the ground and that's it. All of that bullshit about a resurrection...and souls going to Heaven...all bullshit."

My mother's eyes widened. "Don't say that. She's going to a better place."

My father frowned. "The ground is a better place? 'Cause that's where she's at."

"It's only until He comes back again…"

"He who? The grave-robber? Because that's the only way she's coming out of that ground."

"She has to go to the ground, first…because that's where we come from…the dirt…and then when He comes back, her soul will rise…"

"Are you a plant…a fruit…or a vegetable? 'Cause you're starting to sound like one…Humans don't come out of the ground. I didn't see my own birth, but I saw that boy being born and he didn't come out of no ground…he came out of your…"

My mama interrupted him…"STOP!!!!"

"I'm just saying…he came out of a hole, but it wasn't a hole in the ground."

"Honey…"

104

He shook his head and continued, "We go in the ground, but we don't turn into dust...bodies decompose...the flesh liquefies and the bones remain intact...and that's without being embalmed...matter of fact, bones stick around for years. Where do you think that shit from the museum comes from? Ever heard of dinosaurs? And the 'Mother of all Mankind'...what's her name?"

"Eve?" I said.

"No, Lucy?" he said. "...over three million years old...found in the ground...bones still intact...they didn't find dust..." He paused for a second and then said, "The only way a human turns to dust is if they are cremated...and if it is God's will that we turn to dust, first, then they are going to have to get those folks out of those boxes..."

"So you don't believe in Heaven and Hell?" I asked.

He frowned. "I'm sorry, but do you hear yourself...There is not one LIVING person who has died and gone to either one of those places and then turned around and came back to tell us about it…it ain't even possible and who the hell would leave Heaven and come back to this bullshit? Especially, if it's as wonderful as they say it is."

"Sweetie…" my mother said, grabbing my father's arm.

He snatched away from her. "Stop feeding that boy fairy-tales."

"But it's true…"

He shook his head. "I never understood how preachers could promise a trip to Heaven, if folks do God's will, when it clearly says that the 'Meek shall inherit the earth'…that alone says that we ain't going nowhere…it don't get no clearer than that.'"

"But…it talks about 144,000 who will go to Heaven…the virgin sons of Israel…" she began.

"Your ass ain't neither a virgin, a son, or from Israel..." He huffed and then continued, "God sounds a little sexist and racist...if you ask me."

"Not my God..."

He continued. "Please...my mama used to read the Bible to us to scare the shit out of us...especially with Revelations...talk about some scary shit...it's one thing for kids to believe that crap, but grown folks? Crazy...fear is the greatest motivator..."

"But..." she said, again.

"But nothing...it makes no sense...when you carefully read it, God starts to sound like a scorned lover...He gives you the gift of life...waves a Heavenly reward in your face...and whether you act right or not...He takes His gift back, but not before making you suffer first...then instead of letting you in the house, after you've proven your love for Him, He sticks you in the dog house...throw you a pillow and a blanket...make it all comfy for you while someone else gets to play in the clouds." He sighed and then shook his head. "Like I said...bullshit..."

"Then, what do you believe, dad?" I asked.

"I believe that we live and die...and we better make the most of the time that we have between the two of them...'cause you'll hate to be that motherfucker, who dies, wishing that he did or said some shit...you don't want no regrets..."

I thought about what he said. I will learn later that no truer words could have ever been spoken.

Chapter 12

I began to rebel. I didn't want to do shit or hear anything that they had to say to me. As a result, I stayed in trouble, failed every class, and then decided to drop out of school. My mama was mad as hell. When I came home, she was sitting in the middle of the living room with her Bible in her hand. "Where have you been?" she asked.

I walked into the kitchen. She followed me and then said, "Boy, do you hear me talking to you?"

I didn't respond. I wasn't ignoring her on purpose, but I was so hungry, the only "voice" that I heard was my stomach talking to me.

With her hands on her hips and her Bible still in her hand, she said, "Your school called. They said that you ain't been there in a week so where have you been?"

I grabbed some lunchmeat, some bread, and proceeded to make a sandwich. "Ma, school ain't gone do nothing for me." I was so hungry, I stuffed the whole sandwich into my mouth.

"Boy, who are you talking to?" she asked.

I didn't respond to her because I had too much food in my mouth.

She followed behind me. "I didn't bring you into this world to be a failure. You gon' take your butt to school. Do you hear me?"

I could tell that she was becoming agitated because I wasn't responding to her, so I turned to speak to her and accidentally spit some of my sandwich in her face. She wiped the food off of her forehead. I was still chewing when she said, "You did that on purpose." My mouth was still full when I tried to speak. It happened again. She wiped the food from her nose. She began to breathe heavily. Her eyes narrowed.

This time, I kept my mouth closed. I just stood there with both cheeks puffed out like a squirrel with a mouth full of nuts. I looked at her, and then I looked at the door to measure how much distance it was between me and freedom. I knew that I had to be smart because if I fell, she would be all over me like flies on shit. I counted to ten, ran, and jumped over the furniture like it was a minefield. I hit the door so fast and I didn't look back.

In the end, running didn't matter because I ended-up having to go back to the house that I ran away from. As soon as I walked in, she confronted me. She yelled at me until I fell asleep. When I woke up, she was still sitting there – going off. The whole time, I wished that she would just beat my ass like I owed her some money and get it over with, so that I didn't have to listen to her mouth all day.

"So...you want to drop out of school? What's your plan? Sleeping all day, scratching your butt, running up the electric bill, and eating up all of the dog-gone food?" she asked.

I didn't respond.

"Boy... do you hear me talking to you?"

I took a deep breath and said, "If I say 'yes' will that end this?"

Her eyes narrowed as she leaned into my face. "If I snatch your tongue out of your mouth and knock your teeth out, will you be able to say 'yes' or anything else for that matter?"

I rolled my eyes, because I knew that she wasn't going to do anything.

She snatched my face and then said, "Roll them again and you won't have them."

I sighed.

She shook her head. "Boy, you are testing me…I'm trying my best not to hurt you, but if it's God's will…"

I frowned.

"Boy, I'm not raising no bums. What do plan to do with no education?" she asked.

"Without an education…" I said, correcting her.

"That's what I said…with no education," she said.

"The proper way to say that is to say, 'Without an education,'" I said.

She laughed and shook her head. "You are really smelling yourself."

"Huh?"

"Your ass ain't done shitting yellow shit…" she said.

"What?"

"A hard-head makes a soft-behind…"

My head was spinning. "What are you talking about?"

113

"What I'm saying is...one day, you're going to wish that you'd listened to me."

"Why couldn't you just say that from the beginning? Instead of telling me that I'm sniffing myself, that my doo-doo is yellow, and that I have a soft booty? And how do you know that my booty is soft? I mean...I do moisturize..."

"Boy, ain't nobody thinking about your soft butt...it's a figure of speech..."

"Confusing is what it is..."

"Because you don't listen..."

"Mama, I hear ya..." *But you're right, I'm not listening.* I thought to myself. "It'll be fine, mama."

"Okay...what are your plans?"

"I'll get a job," I said.

My mother began to laugh – so hard that she grabbed her stomach and fell on the floor. When she was done, she sat-up and began to wipe the tears from her eyes.

"And what type of job are you going to get WITHOUT an education?"

I shrugged my shoulders. "I don't know, but I'll find something."

She shook her head and said, "Boy, you don't give up one plan without having another. Now, tomorrow, you're going to get your butt up and go to school. And before you open your mouth…think about this…the only reason why my foot ain't knee-deep into your butt is because God is watching me…and you."

Chapter 13

Going to school is for suckers, but I had to play the "game" until I was able to get out of my parents' house. Even if that meant getting up and going through the motions until I was old enough to tell them to kiss my Black ass. Well, I don't think that I'll ever be able to tell them that, no matter how old I am or how far away I am, but a guy can dream, can't he?

I was looking for a way to prove her wrong, but I needed to figure out how to do it without going to jail. I thought about cutting grass, but it was too hot for that. I thought about washing cars, but I didn't want to mess-up my clothes. I was still too young to get a job at Mickey Ds, so I didn't know what to do. I was quickly learning that things were 'easier said than done.'

The thought of becoming a gang-banger crossed my mind, but there was only so much shit I was willing to do. I never understood people who were willing to kill another person over territory that they didn't own themselves or killing someone over respect. I was always taught that respect had to be earned and a dead man can't give you anything that he takes in the ground with him.

While I was trying to figure out what I was good at, what I was going to do with my life, and how I could make money doing it, I noticed something about myself. The girls really liked me. It wasn't that I was particularly good looking, because I wasn't, but something about me drew them to me.

I found out something, really interesting, early in life. You don't have to be good looking to get what you want. You see...I was confident. When I was younger, I could sweet talk a girl out of her chocolate milk. Then, I got better and I was able to talk them out of their lunch money and by the time, I was a teenager, I could sweet-talk them into letting me touch their breasts. I'd gotten so good at it, they used to take turns letting me feel them up during recess. You see, all you need is game. Now, you may be asking yourself, "What is game?" First, let me tell you about the moment when I realized that I had "game" and then I will tell you what it is.

Let me preface this story, by again admitting that by no means do I think I'm fine. I have been told by a lot of girls that I have a nice personality and everyone knows that that is code for ugly. I had this girl in my class and I'm not trying to be mean, but, and I'm not exaggerating when I say this, this girl was ugly and I don't mean ugly in the normal sense. This girl, and let me apologize to all of the butts in the world before I say this, but she was butt-ugly. Okay, I'm going to describe her, so that you can get an idea of what I mean by "butt-ugly." Imagine your butt, throw some teeth in the crack of it, place an afro on top of it, and you had her. Matter of fact, if you told her to wipe her ass, she would probably blow her nose. That's butt-ugly. Her breath smelled so bad that every time she spoke, you found yourself checking the bottom of your shoes to make sure that you hadn't stepped in dog-shit. I wasn't sure if I should offer her some gum or some toilet paper.

Anyway, one day, I'd forgotten my lunch. My stomach was growling so loud, I couldn't hear myself think. When we entered the lunchroom, I saw her sitting by herself. Her parents used to make her the best lunches and I decided that I wanted some of it. Now, I had to be careful because if other kids saw me eating with her, they would talk about me, but if I had to choose between them and my growling stomach, my stomach was going to win. So, I saw her, sitting by herself, eating a sandwich, and I walked up to her.

"Is this seat taken," I said.

She looked around, then pointed at the spot next to her, and said through a mouth full of food, "This one?"

Praying that that piece of lettuce that was lodged in her teeth didn't fly out of her mouth, I said, "Yes, that one."

"Nope." She kept chewing.

I slid in next to her. "You know...I don't think I know your name."

She frowned and asked, "Why you wanna know my name?"

"Cause, I do," I said, as my stomach growled louder.

She looked at my stomach and asked, "You don't have any lunch...do you?"

This question threw me off because I planned to compliment a sandwich out of her and run, but she wanted to have a real conversation. "No, I forgot it."

She took her sandwich and ripped it into two pieces. I looked at her hands. They looked like they hadn't been washed in years, but I was too hungry to care. I took it from her. "So, you didn't really tell me your name," I said, examining the sandwich.

"Do you really wanna know my name or do you want to eat the sandwich?"

I didn't want to be rude, but she was right, I didn't give a shit about her or her name. I wanted to eat, so we sat quietly as she shared her lunch with me.

The next day, I was hanging out with my boys and she walked up to me. "Here," she said, handing me a bag and then walking away.

I opened it to find two sandwiches, an apple, a can of soda, some cookies, and a candy bar. My boys looked into the bag and teased, "Miller got him a new girlfriend."

I looked in her direction and stared at her until she was gone. When the lunch bell rang, we all gathered in the cafeteria. All of my friends sat in their normal spot. I was about to join them until I saw her sitting by herself. I walked over to where she was and asked, "Is this seat taken?"

She looked at me, sucked the food out of her teeth, and then said, "Look, let's not pretend. You don't want to be my friend and I don't know if I want you to be mine. My mom made me an extra lunch and I thought that instead of throwing it into the garbage, I could give it to you."

I smiled and then sat across from her. "If you don't mind…"

Picking her teeth with her fingers, she said, "Look…let's not pretend. I didn't give you that lunch so you can have lunch with me…"

"No, I want to…" I looked over my shoulder before continuing, "I want to have lunch with you."

"Okay…cause there's nothing that I hate more than fake-ass Negroes…"

I laughed at this comment because she was right. I was being fake, but she will never know that.

Curiously, she looked at me. We remained quiet for the remainder of the lunch period.

First, it was food, but then she started bringing me other things. She brought me a watch, a necklace, and she gave me some money. I think over the year, she gave me close to three hundred dollars in food and gifts. I didn't even have to ask her. She just did it. Mind you, as I share this story with you, I still can't tell you her name and knowing her name did not matter to her. You see, I did something that no one else was willing to do, I befriended her. Yes, in the beginning, I have to admit that I was using her, but by the end of the school year, I didn't mind sitting with her during lunch – it was the least that I could do. Now, you may be saying, "Miller, that's terrible," but it would only be terrible if things were one-sided. I gave her something too. She didn't want to be alone and for the rest of the school year, she wasn't – at least, not during lunch period.

And that's game – find out what a person needs and then give it to them. If there's a hole in their lives then you be the one that fills it and you fill it better than anyone else can. Once you do that, you can use it to your advantage. Now, this might sound like what normal people do in relationships and they do, but this is a little different. I'm not trying to get into any relationship, but I want them to think that I do. Now, that may be what they need and what they want, but I really don't care. They need something and I need something too. I can't be responsible for how they interpret my actions. As long as I leave them feeling good about themselves, and in turn, they reward me for it. Everyone's happy.

Chapter 14

While girls were learning about love, boys were being trained to be players. Girls wanted love so bad, and were willing to do almost anything to have it. But, sadly, most boys are only thinking of two things, and love ain't one of them. Unless, love can lead us to the "booty", we're not thinking about it. When you're young, your brain don't work that way. If we can get "it" without the headache of some girl sweating us that would be perfect, but girls don't work that way. They want you to call them, be nice to them, be their boyfriend, and who's trying to do that?

At age 15, I took great pride in breaking the hearts of the neighborhood girls. My eyes were always on getting the "prize." It was easy to convince them that I was going to be their boyfriend, be with them forever, and for some odd reason, they believed that crap. While forever meant a lifetime to them, to me, forever meant until the next piece of ass walked by.

You have to understand, boys start getting an erection from the moment they are conceived. Once we recognize what it's for, we are always trying to put it to good use. We will hump almost anything, and it doesn't have to have a heartbeat. We would like to rub-up against something nice and warm, but when you're a kid, you will take what you can get. Once we graduate from our "hands" to little girls, we are in a race to see how much "booty" we can get before we die.

Now, most boys like to "practice" on the nasty girls, but I avoided them, because they would have your "shit" all messed-up – burning, itching, and oozing all over the place. There are some boys who like the lonely girls or the nerds. They are easy-pickings for horny teenage boys. I didn't want that either, because once you give them some attention, they will follow your ass around in broad daylight with a flashlight. You'll almost have to get a restraining order or fake your death to get rid of their ass.

No...what I wanted was one of those stuck-up girls who thought that the sun rose and set because of them. They don't just let anybody touch their "stuff." They understand how valuable their pussy is, and they keep it under lock and key, until the right brotha comes along. See, what girls don't understand, guys will never, I MEAN NEVER respect a girl who is willing to show their stuff to every Tom, Dick, and Harry. It always amazes me how a girl, with her tits and ass hanging out of her clothes, wants a man to respect her. If you're walking around looking like you ready to get fucked – you gon' get fucked. And we will tell you everything that you need to hear to get it, but once you get "got", we are gone. We might keep you around for the "jump-off", but we are always looking for the good-one. The one that we can take home to mama. Only a lazy motherfucker wants pussy that's thrown at him. A real man wants a woman that he has to put some work into.

This also applies to the fake-ass girls who want a real brotha or a real relationship. I mean let's keep it real...literally. You can't have a head-full of weave, fake eye-lashes, fake nails, a push-up bra, a face full of make-up, a fake ass, and expect a brother to be "real" with you. If you walk around looking like a "blow-up" doll, expect to be treated like one. We may not say anything about it, because we have an agenda, but until we reach our "goal", we are always wondering what's underneath that shit.

I remember this one girl. We were leaving the movie theater when we saw her. She had on her "camel-toe" outfit – tits hanging out of her shirt while her pants left nothing for the imagination. Me and my boys were staring at her. She thought that we liked what we were looking at. We did, but not in the way that she thought. She looked like she was looking for something, so we decided to give it to her. I was bored, so I started to play with her head. I walked up to her, told her that she was sexy, said some other corny shit, and before I knew it, she was on her knees "blowing" every last one of us in the parking lot. It was six of us, and she moved from one guy to another – only stopping long enough to lick her lips before moving on to the next one. When she was done, she stood up, and asked me to call her. I looked at her ass like she'd just escaped from the looney-bin. *Bitch, please.* I was going to tell the "chicken-head" to kiss my ass, but she had some skills and might come in handy on a slow night, so I took her number and walked away, but I never called her.

Now, there was this other girl. Her name was Yvonne. Yvonne was beautiful. She had short curly hair, big beautiful brown eyes, big full lips, long legs, and a small waist. She was so smart. Everyone wanted to be her friend, but she didn't want to be bothered. She was on a mission. She wanted to get the hell out of Chicago and wasn't letting anyone get in the way of that. Now, because Yvonne was "hands-off" that made the boys want to put their hands on her. She was the forbidden fruit and we all wanted to take a bite out of her, but it wouldn't be easy and there lied the challenge.

I pursued her like a man who was dying of thirst and she was the last drop of water on earth. I paid her compliments, bought her gifts, everything. I was sweating that chick like the sun, but she wasn't interested. I was putting in a lot of "work" too, but instead of being rewarded for my efforts, she let a brotha down, hard.

One day, I was with my boys and I walked up to her and said, "Hello."

She looked at me and frowned. "Do I know you?"

Damn. I felt like I'd been kicked in the chest. I felt my heart break into two pieces. That shit hurt so bad. Immediately, that shit went from pain to anger – from love to hate. That mess pissed me off so bad. I'd been sweating that chick and giving her "mad-play" and she treated me like a brotha with a huge booger hanging out of his nose, but I played it off. I didn't even show how much she'd hurt me. I laughed and said, "Ahhhhh...it's like that, huh?"

She frowned and walked away. I felt like a fool and it didn't help that my boys went in on me.

"Damn man, she looked at you like your breath smells like balls-sweat."

Trying to keep my manhood intact, I said, "Naw man...she's just doing that in front of y'all...she don't want her business in the streets."

Another one of my friends said, "I hope that she's warmer behind closed doors…'cause the look that she just gave you almost made me put on my jacket."

"She's better than warm…she's hot as hell…" We all laughed and gave each other "dap." After that we went our separate ways, but I was still pissed.

I thought about it all the way home. Then, I sat down and decided that she would be mine. Not because I wanted her, because that ship had already sailed. No, I wanted to humble her ass. She played me like a chump and now, she was gon' get played.

All night, I wondered. *What does a girl like her need?* I stayed up all night thinking about it. Before I knew it, the sun was peeking through my bedroom window. I jumped in the shower, threw on some clothes, grabbed my books, and a slice of toast and darted out of the house. I was in such a hurry that I'd forgotten my shoes – had to run all the way back to get them, because now, I was on a mission.

When I got to school, I saw her talking to the girl who used to bring me lunch every day. I asked one of my boys what was going on and I found out that her and Yvonne were sisters. So I knew what I needed to do. I had to get to her through the "back-door." So I played "nicey-nice" with her sister, but I made sure that Yvonne saw me do it. After a while, she started to warm-up to me. She thanked me for the time that I spent with her sister and even thanked me for the stuff that I'd bought her that I knew that she'd thrown away. Things were getting really good between us. It's a shame that it didn't mean anything to me.

Then one day, I was walking her and her sister home. When her sister walked in, Yvonne turned, walked up to me, and she kissed me. I'd dreamed about that moment for months, but when it happened, there was nothing – no fireworks, no butterflies, no sweaty palms, no erection, no nothing. As her lips touched mine, all I could think about was all of the shit that I had to do to get that kiss. My mother was the one that told me that you have to work hard for the things that you want, but it felt messed-up when I finally got it and realized that I didn't want it. "My eyes were just bigger than my gut." It was like eating when I wasn't hungry.

She was really putting some "work" into that kiss too – stuck her tongue out, closed her eyes, held me close, and everything, but eventually, I pushed her away. She looked at me and asked, "So, I'll see you tomorrow?"

I looked at her, carefully thinking about what I was going to say next. I didn't care that I had gotten the one person that every guy at school wanted. I didn't want to have anything to do with her. Finally, I said, "Naw, I'm good…" When I walked away, I looked back to find her still standing on her porch staring at me. I didn't wave or anything. I just walked away.

The next day, I didn't even have to look for her. I didn't have to because she was on me like air. Every time I looked up, I was looking in her face. Now, she was the one paying me compliments. Now, she was the one buying me gifts. Then, after a month of ignoring her ass, she decided to up her "game."

Chapter 15

The next day, she passed me a note that said that she wanted me to come over to her house after school. I looked at the piece of paper long and hard before sending it back to her with a big fat "No" written across it. She looked at it and then mouthed, "Please." I never had a girl say, "Please," to me before, so I looked at her and nodded "Yes."

After school, I went home. I wasn't in any rush to see her. I ate a bowl of cereal. I laid in my bed for a while and did some homework before going over there and I hated doing homework. But on this day, I was wishing that I had more, so that I would have an excuse for not going over there. As I was walking over there, I wondered what she wanted to see me for. When I approached the door, I rang the doorbell. Her sister answered the door.

"She's in her room," she said, before walking out into the front yard. "Down the hall to your right."

I looked at her and then slowly walked in. I looked around as I wandered through the house. They had a beautiful home – something that you would see in a magazine. It was so perfect, I was scared to touch anything. I looked down and decided to remove my shoes. Carrying them under my arm, I continued to walk through the house until I found a room with the door slightly cracked. "Trey?" she purred.

Slowly, I opened the door. Suddenly, I dropped my shoes. Yvonne was sitting on the edge of the bed – wearing nothing but a pair of panties. I looked around to make sure that she wasn't setting me up, but there was no one there but us. I walked over to the bed and said, "What is this about?"

"Well, I like you, Trey and…you've been really nice to my sister…"

"So you wanna pay me with pussy?" I asked.

She grabbed my hand. "No, I really do like you."

"Ohhhhhh, you like a brotha, huh?" I asked.

"Yes…of course…," she said. She started unbuttoning my shirt.

I grabbed her hand. "Stop…I don't want to do this."

She began to pout. "You don't want me?"

I started to re-button my shirt. I made up a lie. "Look, I didn't bring a condom."

"Don't worry…I'm on the pill," she said, rubbing me between my legs.

I grabbed her hand and said, "No, really I can't do this."

"Why? What's wrong with me?" she asked, now looking around the room for her clothing.

"Look, I don't want to be responsible for popping your cherry. You are cute and all, but...and this might sound stupid...but I ain't feeling you."

She pulled her shirt over her head and said, "What?"

I started laughing. "I'm really not feeling you."

Frustrated, she said, "What do you mean...you're not feeling me?"

I frowned. "It's interesting...when I was chasing you...treating you like a lady...you treated me like a motherfucker with an STD, but when a "mug" stop sweating yo' ass, then you wanna play your pussy card."

"That's not what happened..." she said.

"Oh, yes, it is...who do you think you playing with? I know the truth. That's why you can't be nice to motherfuckers."

"You're damn right," she huffed.

I took a deep breath and continued. "You know…in the beginning, I thought you were cute, but then I realized that you were no better than the rest of them. Now, look at you. You're a fucking fake just like the rest of those knuckleheads."

"What did you call me?"

"K-n-u-c-k-l-e-h-e-a-d…"

She was in shock.

"Now, that I think about it, you don't deserve this dick."

"What?" she asked.

"You heard me…you ain't worthy of this dick."

Her eyes widened and her mouth fell wide-open. I looked at her mouth and began to unzip my pants.

She frowned and asked, "What are you doing?"

"Oh…I thought that you was about to give me a blowjob…'cause I'll take one of those from anybody."

Her eyes widened. "You piece of shit…get the fuck out!!!!"

"Not a problem," I said, walking towards the door.

Suddenly, I felt something hit me in the back of the head, hard, before shattering and falling onto the floor. I grabbed the back of my head. When I looked at my hand, it was covered in blood. Before I knew it, I turned and ran towards her. I raised my hand in the air. I was going to hit her, but then I stopped. "Mannnnnnnn, you better be glad that I was raised not to hit women or your face would be on fire right now."

"Do it…do it with your punk ass," she said.

I stepped back and said, "Wow…" I shook my head. "See…so glad that you exposed your crazy-side…you would have had a brotha all jammed-up with

144

your bullshit." I paused and continued, "Now, find your pants and your dignity and get your shit together and tomorrow when we get to school, I better not hear anything about this or I'm coming back over here to finish what you started."

She started screaming. I turned and left her sitting there.

≈

The first couple of days, she gave me the "evil-eye", then when she realized that I wasn't bothered by it, she decided that she would try to hurt me by hooking-up with one of my boys. Later, I found out that she allowed him to take her virginity, and nine months later she was saying "goodbye" to all of her hopes and dreams and "hello" to diapers and a baby-daddy.

Chapter 16

When I was younger, I used to watch a TV show that used puppets to educate children. I was fascinated with those guys who used strings and rods to control the movements of the dolls. Sometimes, they would control the dolls by sticking their arm up the doll's ass. While it was on, I could not look away. I did not move from that spot until the show was off, because I was so fascinated with it. I learned so much.

No, I didn't learn that if I stick my hand up someone's ass, I can get them to do whatever I want them to do. Even though I believe that if someone had their hand up your ass, you will do whatever they want you to do…but what I learned, by sitting there watching it, is that once you control a person's mind, their body will follow.

I never really quite understood this until I went to church one day. You see, for years, we suspected that the pastor of our church had been sleeping with a few of the women in the congregation. Now, I've already described his wife to you, so I understood why he did it, but people were pissed when the news hit the fan. They felt like he should have known better, that he should have been stronger than that, and that he never should have succumbed to the trappings of the flesh. And maybe he shouldn't have, but here's the big problem with this kind of thinking. First thing, everyone that claims to be "called" weren't "chosen" at least, not by God. Second, people tend to hold preachers to a higher standard than everyone else – like all of a sudden, once they take the "oath" they become sinless.

Preachers are men before they are anything else and men commit sins.

They are victims of their "senses" or the lack thereof. We all have seven of them. We've been taught that we only have five – see, touch, taste, smell, and hearing, but no one likes to talk about the other two. One is called, "Proprioception" and the other sense is called, "Common". The lack of the latter is what gets most people in trouble.

One day, after choir rehearsal, he and one of the choir members went into his office. He thought that everyone was gone, but one of the members had forgotten something, so one of the deacons let her in. When they walked in, they heard moaning sounds coming from one of the back rooms. They followed the sound to the office and then placed their ears against the door. I guess when they realized that that wasn't the sound of someone praying, they opened the door. They walked in to find a woman bent over the desk and the pastor hitting "it" from the back. Of course, he was shocked when they walked in, but he didn't stop what he was doing until he was done. They actually stood there and watched him until he finished.

Now, you know that some folks can't hold cold or hot water, so that following Sunday, the pastor decided to get out in front of the shit storm that was coming his way. With his wife by his side, he stood in front of the congregation, quoted a few scriptures, started crying, and said, "I know that there are rumors circling around about me sleeping with another woman…I want you to know that those rumors are true. On Wednesday, after rehearsal, a member told me that she needed to talk to me….and I was going to leave, but she was troubled and in need of prayer, so…" he paused and looked at his wife, who was looking down at the ring on her finger. "Well, she seduced me…like the Devil tempted Eve with that apple…God placed that woman in my path to test me. I failed the test, miserably…over and over and over and over and over again…and for that I have asked God for His forgiveness…"

My father looked at me and said, "Get the fuck out of here with that bullshit. I heard that he didn't even stop when they walked in. He was tearing that ass up…"

I laughed.

The pastor continued. "I pray for God's forgiveness. I pray for your forgiveness…"

"So the Devil prays too…who would have thought…" my father said.

"I pray for my wife's forgiveness…" and before he could finish, a woman stood and said, "Who in the hell were you fucking in your office?"

The congregation gasped. Then another woman stood and said, "And who the hell are you?"

The other woman turned and said, "I'm his woman."

Then a pregnant girl stood and said, "I'm his damn woman and I'm carrying his baby."

The whole congregation went up in an uproar. Woman after woman began to stand up. Soon, my mother stood-up.

My father looked at her and said, "What the hell are you standing up for? You better sit down."

She frowned and said, "Get up…let's go."

My father said, "No way, this shit is getting too good."

"We can't watch this…" she said.

"Says you…" He leaned forward to make sure that he didn't miss anything. "If you gon' leave, could you stop, get me some popcorn, a can of pop, and one of those candy bars with the nuts in it? I love those nuts…"

My mother frowned and then put her hands on her hips. "We have to get our kids out of here."

My father said, "Okay…get the kids out of here, but I paid my tithes…I'm not going nowhere."

My mother said, "We will be waiting for you in the van."

"Suit yourself," he said. "But don't be trying to get the scoop later."

My mother huffed and said, "God is not the author of confusion…"

My father laughed and said, "You say that He ain't the author, but somebody wrote this shit…now, go…I'm missing the action."

As we were being escorted out of the church, I looked back and looked at the chaos going on in the pulpit. The interesting thing is, the First Lady hadn't budged. She just sat there – staring at her ring.

≈

And the following Sunday, like nothing happened, we all had our asses back in those pews, listening to his bullshit, with our money in our hands. I wouldn't have believed it if my mama hadn't made us all get up and go ourselves. Matter fact, people who'd stopped coming to church were there and there were a lot of new people too. It was freakin' amazing and service went forward without one mention that our pastor was a hoe. My mother explained that God forgives those who repent and want to be forgiven. She explained that it was not our place to judge the pastor because he had to account for his sins.

"Ain't none of us so clean, we squeak...we all have dirt under our fingernails," she said.

And while she tried to distract us from his cheating ways, I couldn't help but notice that the First Lady was looking real good in that diamond necklace and that there was a new BMW in the parking lot with vanity plates that say, "1st Lady."

Chapter 17

After I graduated, my parents called a "family meeting." What is the "family meeting", you ask? It is when everyone comes together to discuss what the hell Trey should be doing with his life. You see, while I was in high school, my parents blamed my messed-up decisions on the fact that I was young. I got a "pass" because I was too immature to be held accountable for anything that I said or did, but once I graduated, after they put that diploma in my hand, now, I'm a man and I had to get my shit together and get the hell out.

Please note: that once you become a teenager, your parents will pull out their calendars and begin counting-down the days when they will be free of your butt – like a prisoner counting down days to his release date. Matter of fact, they plan a holiday around it. Now, the reason that many parents don't kick you out before then, is because if they wait until you graduate, then they can keep the "state" out of their ass. They hate words like run-away, child neglect, child endangerment, and prison time, but if they wait until you graduate to put your ass out, then the state won't mess with them. Then, when they finally throw you out, you can use your diploma as a pillow when you find yourself sleeping under the stars.

Things finally came to a head one Sunday morning. Normally, the house is noisy, but today, I woke up to complete silence. I thought that I was alone, but I should have known better. Anyway, I decided to watch one of my favorite porn videos – get some girl-on-girl action before we went to praise the Lord. They were really going at each other and I was starting to get horny. I was starting to feel a tingle between my legs. I thought about it for only a second before I leaned over and grabbed a bottle of lotion off of my nightstand. I slid my pajama pants down and then began to pour lotion all over my hands. Slowly, I began to rub it all over my dick. Still looking at the video, watching the two ladies go down on each other, I began to stroke myself. This went on for a couple of seconds before I began to feel my balls filling-up. Seconds later, my back arched and then I "came" all over the place. I kicked my legs a few times and I collapsed, back, onto the bed. I was still holding my dick when my mother walked into my room.

"Boy!!!! What are you doing?"

I couldn't move. I hadn't cum that hard in a long time. I was so weak that I didn't respond. I needed a minute to regain my composure and for the blood to return to my head – both of them. I could hear her screaming, but I couldn't hear what she was saying because my pillow was calling me. Slowly, I pulled up my pants, wiped my hands on the sheets, and turned the video off.

"Answer me, boy!!!!! What are you doing?" she insisted.

Dizzy, I said, "Ma, please."

"Don't 'please' me, boy," she said. "Now, I want you to tell me what you were doing."

"Do you really want to know?" I asked, curling-up in my bed and pulling the blankets up to my neck.

"Yes, I want to know," she said.

Now, here's the problem. When a man cums, he only wants to do one thing and arguing with his mama ain't it, so her questions were really starting to piss me off. "Well…since it's not obvious…I was jagging off," I said.

She walked towards me. "Boy, what did you say?"

"Ma, don't make me say it again. You know what I was doing," I said.

"I know and why are you doing that on the Lord's Day?" she asked.

"Is there a better day to do it?" I asked.

"Boy, if your grandmother was here..." she said.

I looked out of my bedroom window and said, "But she ain't."

She looked at me and said, "What did you say?"

"Ma...please...I'm a grown man. What do you expect me to do? At least, there's no girl in here."

"Boy, that's a sin and watching that smut is a sin...you trying to go to hell?"

"At least, if I go there, I don't have to worry about you busting into my room," I said. "And jagging..." I paused when I saw her eyebrow go up. "I mean...masturbation is not a sin..."

"Yes, it is and if you keep doing it then you're going to go blind."

I sighed and shook my head. "No, it's not a sin...now, watching those videos... that's another story..."

She interrupted me. "In for a penny...in for a pound..."

"What?" I asked, scratching my head.

"Proverbs 6:16-19 says 'There are six things that the Lord hates, seven that are an abomination to him: haughty eyes, a lying tongue, and hands that shed innocent blood, a heart that devises wicked plans, feet that make haste to run to evil, a false witness who breathes out lies, and one who sows discord among brothers.'"

"I didn't hear the word, 'masturbation.'"

"Boy..." She paused, "It don't have to say the word, specifically..."

"So now, we're reinterpreting the Bible...reading God's mind?"

160

She couldn't say anything because she knew that I was right. With her hands on her hips, she continued, "You're always talking about being a man...a man don't have to do that mess in his mama's house...he could grab his wee-wee in his own house."

"Then, that's what I need to do," I said.

"And how do you plan to do it? You ain't got a pot to piss in or a window to throw it out off," she said.

If I had any blood in my head, I would have argued the notion of people pissing in pots and throwing it out of windows and how unsanitary the suggestion was, but I couldn't.

"Instead of playing with yourself, you need to get your butt ready for church," she said, before walking out, and slamming the door behind her.

Waiting until she left the room, I mumbled, "What I need to do is get the hell up out of here."

≈

All the way to church, she stared at me from the mirror on the back of the sun-visor. I wasn't sure if she was staring at me because she was still pissed, if she wanted to kill me, or she was making sure that I wasn't masturbating in the back seat. Whatever the reason, she kept her eyes on me – scowling all the way to church, but as soon as we pulled into the church's parking lot, she put on her "church face." Now, you may be asking yourself, "What is the 'church face'?" This is the face of the pious, perfect, and the sanctimonious. Church folk throw it on to give the impression that their lives are "blemish-free" when it isn't. They throw on that face to hide the lies, the truth, all of their bullshit, and their pain. The interesting thing is, sinners and liars have the same skill – the ability to put on a "mask" for the public.

My mother was so good at throwing that face on. She could be right in the middle of going-off on us about something and as soon as one of her church friends walked up, she would stop, and act like everything was all rainbows and sunshine, but as soon as that person walked away, the storm would immediately return.

≈

During the entire service, she stared at the side of my head. I'm surprised that her staring didn't leave a hole in it - she was staring so hard. After all of the singing and the four "pass-thrus" of the collection plate, the preacher finally called for people to come up to be prayed for. My mother, stood, grabbed my arm and then began to pull on me.

"Let's go," she said.

I didn't budge. "Mama stop…"

"Let's go," she said, still pulling on me.

"No," I said.

"NOW!!!!!" she shouted. The whole congregation turned and looked at us. My father grabbed her hand and said, "Stop."

She turned and looked at him like she was going to hurt him. He looked back and said, "Sit down and stop making a fool of yourself."

"Don't tell me what to do."

"You better control your emotions. Don't let them control you. Now, sit down."

She looked around the room, threw her "church face" back on, and then slowly returned to her seat. She remained quiet during the rest of the service.

She didn't say a word all the way home, but when we walked into the house, all hell broke loose. "GET YOUR SHIT AND GET THE HELL OUT!!!!" she spat.

We were in shock. Not because she yelled, because we were used to that, but because she used the words 'shit' and 'hell'. My brother and sisters ran to their room because they thought that they were experiencing one of the signs of the apocalypse. I waited, in the hallway, to see what was going to happen.

My father said, "Who in the hell do you think you're talking to?"

With her eyes bulging out of her head she said, "You embarrassed me in front of my church...you have lost your God-damn mind."

"One, it ain't your GOD-damn church. I don't care how much of MY MONEY that you give to them...that church ain't yours. Two, I don't give a damn about what those folks in that church think about you or me. Three, you were making an ass of yourself before I even said anything to you. Four, this is my damn house too."

"You shouldn't have done that..."

"Yes, I did...you got a problem at home...you fix it at home...and not at church..."

"Well…" She took a deep breath and then said, "I caught that boy playing with himself while looking at porn…and on a Sunday…"

My father looked at her. "Is that all? You're ready to end our marriage over that?"

"What?"

He shook his head. "You can't control a man's urges. What do you expect that boy to do? Get blue balls? If a man ain't having sex, what do you think he's doing? Dreaming about it? A man has to take care of that or his shit will explode. Do you want that boy's dick to explode? If men don't masturbate there would be dicks exploding all over the place. Do you want that?"

My mother was speechless.

"I jag-off almost every day and you and I have sex. Sometimes, a man just needs to do what a man do without having to romance a motherfucker to get it. That boy ain't bringing no girls in here…you want him to go out and mess with these little girls and end-up with a baby that he can't take care of or mess around and get one of those diseases that'll make his dick fall off? So he masturbates? Leave that boy alone."

My mother was in shock. She didn't say a word. I don't know if it was the fact that he didn't agree with her or that he'd just admitted that he masturbates too.

Then, my father called me into the room.

"Yes..." I said.

"Look boy, don't jag-off on the Sabbath...okay?" he said.

I smiled and said, "Okay dad," before looking at my mother who was still in shock. I left the room.

≈

Things changed immediately after that. I felt like she was always looking over my shoulder making sure that I wasn't touching myself. It became her own personal mission - popping in and out of my room and popping in and out of the bathroom. It was making me crazy. I could only use lotion in front of her. She was checking my laptop every day. It was out of control. So one day, she gave me the, "This is my house…my rules…it's my way or the highway speech" and I chose the highway.

Chapter 18

I moved in with one of my brothers. As I mentioned earlier, there are ten of us. All of my siblings either moved out or were kicked out of my parent's home. Now, I have to preface this part of my story by telling you that we didn't all turn-out right. Three of my brothers, got out and went to college. One of my other brothers is a serial baby-maker and a dead-beat dad. One of my sisters went to bed one night as Brenda and then woke-up the next day as Bobby. My other sister, is a "pot-head" and is married to a woman-beater. One of my brothers is doing "time" and the rest of my brothers are among "America's Most Wanted." They were notorious. You would think that growing up in a home like mine would make people run from crime – instead, it pushed them to it.

My oldest brother, the one that I was staying with, was one of the biggest drug dealers in Chicago. When I told him that mama was trippin', he didn't hesitate to take me in. In the beginning, he didn't ask anything of me. I sat around all day, ate, and played video games. Until one day, he pulled a "mama" on me.

"Hmmmmmm? What are you doing?"

"Chilling…" I said.

"Naw Son…everybody has to pull their own weight. We ain't husband and wife…I work all day and come home to you sitting on your ass…"

Turning the TV off, I said, "Why don't you tell me what you want me to do…"

"You need to go to work or put in some work."

"Okay…I'll go and look for a job."

"Sure…tell me how that works out. Here's some money…"

"Thanks," I took the money and began to walk down the hall to my bedroom. Something said, "Turn around," and I found him staring at me. "What?"

He smiled and said, "Nothing."

I shook my head as I walked into my room. I turned on my laptop and began to do a search. I saw that a few companies were hiring, so I decided to submit a resume. Everything was good until I got to the spot that asked for job experience. Unless, shitting my life away qualifies as job experience, I had to leave the spot blank. Becoming frustrated, I closed my laptop and fell back onto the bed. Realizing that the jobs weren't going to fall out of the sky, I decided to get dressed and beat the pavement.

I walked around for hours, going from door to door, but no one was hiring. My feet were hurting and my stomach began to speak to me. I pulled out the money that my brother had given to me and decided to grab a bite to eat. I was walking out of the restaurant when I heard someone say, "Hey Shorty…what cha' doing?"

I looked around and then pointed to myself. "Who…me?"

"Yeah, you…what cha' doing?" he asked.

"I'm about to get my 'eat' on…"

"You wanna make some money?"

I looked him up and down and said, "Naw, I'm good."

"You sure? You ain't looking too good," he said, doing inventory of my clothes.

I frowned. "Naw, I'm good."

"Well, if you want to come-up…come back and see me."

"Sure…whatever..." I said, before walking away.

When I walked into the apartment, my brother was waiting for me. "How did things go?"

Flopping onto the couch, I said, "I put in some applications…just waiting for a call."

He looked at me and said, "Really?"

"Yeah…they're going to be calling me any day now."

My brother laughed. "Sure, and while we wait for that call…I'm going to take you for a little ride."

"Where are we going?"

"I wanna show you something."

When I climbed into his Benz, I couldn't help but enjoy how the leather seats hugged my butt. I inhaled, deeply. The car still smelled new. Before pulling off, he said, "You're going to like this." He flicked a button to turn on the massager and the heated seats. It felt so good that for a moment, I actually felt my dick get hard. "This is nice, Bruh…real nice," but he couldn't hear me of the booming sound of the music. As we drove around Chicago, his phone rang several times. He said, "Yep…nope…" and then he hung-up. Every call was the same thing. "Yep…nope…" then he hung up.

He turned down the music and looked at me. "You see this shit? Look at these motherfuckers," he said, pointing at the people waiting to cross the street on Lake Shore Drive. "I should run their asses over…"

My eyes widened.

He smiled. "Naw, I won't kill them…these people are the reason why I'm in business…they are the reason why I'm rich…with their stressful jobs and fucked-up lives…they need me." The light turned green and then he pulled off.

"Where are we going?" I asked.

"I'm going to take you to a party."

I became excited. "A party…?"

"Yeah…a party…" he confirmed.

We drove around for another twenty minutes before we arrived at a gentlemen's club. When we pulled-up, a man walked over and opened my door. I stepped out of the car. He did the same thing for my brother before he handed him the keys and a fifty. "Take care of my shit."

The young man said, "Gotcha…" before pulling away.

We walked up to the door. My brother handed the man at the door a fifty and we walked in. The smell of stale-ass greeted us. The music was loud and there were naked women everywhere. I grabbed and adjusted "myself." My brother smiled. "You still a virgin?"

Lying, I said, "Naw Bruh…why you say that?"

He smiled and said, "Your hand don't count."

I frowned.

A woman walked up to us and said, "Hey Pleasure." She kissed him on the cheek and then walked away.

"Who is she talking about? Your name ain't Pleasure."

Walking to a chair that sat in the middle of the room, he said, "That's what they call me on the streets. I'm Pleasure…" Then he pulled up his shirt and continued, "And this is pain." He smiled and sat down.

The light from the gun caught my eye. "Do mama know that you have that?"

He laughed. "Boy…get the fuck out of here…do mama know…Hell naw, she don't know." He continued to laugh.

The women walked-up to him. He whispered something in one of their ears. She walked away and when she returned, she had two glasses. He handed one to me. "Drink this."

"What is this?"

"It'll help you relax…"

I took the glass and smelled the contents of it. "This smells like instant death…"

My brother laughed. "Drink that shit and stop acting like a bitch…"

"I'm no bitch…"

"Then, man-up…"

I stared at him and the glass.

"Trust me…" he said.

For a moment, I looked at him and then I looked at the glass. Suddenly, I lifted it to my mouth and with one gulp it was gone. When it entered my mouth, I didn't feel anything, but by the time it made it to my throat, I was regretting my decision. It burned as it entered my chest, burned as it traveled passed my heart, and then burned as it entered my stomach. I gasped for air.

He smiled and said, "Keep them coming."

I sipped the second one as a woman danced in front of me. I drank the third one as she sat in my lap and placed my hand on her breast. I drank the fourth one as she unzipped my pants. After the fifth one, I closed my eyes as she placed her mouth on the zipper of my pants.

Suddenly, I wasn't feeling well. The room began to spin. My mouth began to fill with spit. The next thing I knew, I was throwing up all over the girl's head. She screamed. I would have said, "Sorry," but every time I opened my mouth, my words were replaced with vomit. I threw-up food until there was nothing left but air. My brother laughed and said, "Newbie…" He handed the girl some money and said, "Sorry about that."

She looked at the money and said, "Thank you…I'll clean this up."

Finally, I caught my breath and said, "Sorry," before passing out.

I woke-up the next day with something heavy sitting on my chest. When I was able to focus, I looked down to find a naked woman lying next to me. She started to move. She looked up at me. "You want some more?"

Confused, I asked, "More of what?"

She smiled and pulled the blanket over her head. I watched her head until her mouth found the spot between my legs. I closed my eyes as she took my virginity, again.

Chapter 19

That afternoon, I was on cloud-nine. I'd never felt so good. Even after my brother paid her, she stuck around to give me some more. If she wouldn't have been paid to get me off, I would swear that I was in love. I was still thinking about her as me and my boys sat in the park and talked.

"Man...get out of here with that shit."

"Bruh, I'm telling you. Candy fucked and sucked the shit out of me."

Hustle and Money laughed. "Your hand got a name now?" Money asked.

"Fuck you, man...I'm telling the truth."

"Yeah, right and my face is on the million dollar bill."

"Ain't no million dollar bill," I said.

"Exactly…"

I knew that no matter what I said I wouldn't be able to convince them, so I changed the subject. "So what y'all 'no sex having asses' been up to?"

While Money talked about getting enrolled in a HBCU and Hustle spoke about getting "scouted" – maybe getting a basketball scholarship, my thoughts were back on Candy and on finding a way to get paid.

I interrupted all of the boring shit that they were talking about and said, "You know what? While y'all doing that dumb-shit, I'm going to get me some hoes and sit back and kick-it for a while." They stopped and looked at me like I was wearing a clown costume. The air filled with laughter.

"What's so damn funny?" I asked.

"You," Hustle said, still laughing.

"That pussy must have been laced with LSD, because you have lost your damn mind," Money said.

Hustle said, "And when you're done kicking it with some hoes...what do you plan on doing?"

I looked at him and said, "Shit, I haven't thought that far. The average life-span for a Black man is twenty-five years...shit, after I'm done with all of that and stacking my paper, I might get shot...so, why stress a brotha out by forcing him to think about fairy-tales..."

Money shook his head. "You know...I've heard some dumbshit...but by far, that is the dumbest shit I've ever heard."

"Look...y'all have dreams and I ain't knocking them, but that 'suit and tie' shit is for people who wanna spend their lives wearing a suit and tie and I ain't one of them. Life is too short to be working for somebody who's already rich - busting your butt everyday just so you can afford to pay some bills and buy some food. You might even get lucky and be able to take your family to the show every once in a while…I ain't trying to do that shit."

Money started to laugh. "Boy, you been looking at too many reality TV shows…"

I didn't respond.

He stopped laughing and said, "You know what? You should be a gang-banger or better yet…you should be a drug-dealer."

"Being in the drug game is too hectic. Plus, my dad did that shit. He didn't make a lot of money," I said.

"Well, maybe you can do better?" Hustle said.

"Naw, I don't want to be responsible with turning my people into zombies," I said.

"Then, shit…why don't you become a pimp. You good with the ladies. You said that you want some hoes. I'm sure that they wouldn't mind selling their bodies for you," Money said, sarcastically.

"You mock a motherfucker, but I could be a damn good pimp," I said.

"Yeah, I bet. Get you one of those big fancy cars and a few flashy suits and you in the game," he said. "Maybe you could get you some of those gold-teeth?"

I frowned.

"Or better yet...to make sure that your pimp-game is tight, you can go to pimp school, graduate with your Master's in dumb-shit, and your PhD in mo' dumb-shit and you set." Money paused and then shook his head. "Man, who the hell grows up and becomes a pimp?"

I looked at him for a second before saying, "Me."

$$\approx$$

So the seeds were planted. They were right. No one with an ounce of decency wakes-up one day and says, "Damn, I wanna be a pimp." I've been raised to see them as vampires who feed off of the blood of our communities. They are one step above pond-scum and one step below the stuff that you find on the bottom of your shoe. They were frowned-upon, but feared. People respected them as much as they respected politicians. They weren't liked, but they were understood, and there's something about their lifestyle that makes young men want to be like them.

And there was power in the pussy. There was a lot of money to be made if you do the shit right. Sure, the shit is illegal, but folks weren't tripping over themselves to hire a motherfucker with no job experience and no college education. A brotha needed to consider his options.

Chapter 20

For months, I watched everything he did - how he carried himself, the way that he walked, talked, and the way that he treated people. He was a business man who was about taking care of his business. He worked all day and he kept his business in the streets. He never brought anything home. The two worlds never crossed.

Sometimes, he took me on a run. Each transaction, was quick – fluid. He did what he had to do and then he was gone. On any given day, we were driving around with at least $50,000 in the trunk of the car. As soon as he picked it up, we would drive to various places to drop it off. He was real careful about making sure that he got rid of the shit quick, just in case he was pulled over.

When we pulled up to our "stops", they were waiting to either give or receive, but on one of his trips the "giver" was late. We were about to pull off when, suddenly, the young man pulled up.

"You're late."

"I'm sorry," he said.

My brother got out of the car and then walked-up on him. "You're sorry?"

Nervously, he said, "Look, I got caught by a train." He handed my brother a large duffle-bag.

My brother laughed and said, "You got caught by a train?" He looked at me and said it again. "He got caught by a train."

I laughed and said, "That's what he said...he got caught by a train."

Suddenly, the smile disappeared from my brother's face. He pulled out a razor and with one swing, he'd drawn a smile on the young man's face.

The young man screamed and then grabbed his face. Blood poured through his fingers.

"When you're late, you leave me open to dumbshit and I hate dumbshit. Now, today, it was your face...the next time, it's your throat."

The young man cried and nodded his head. My brother removed a roll of bills from his pocket and said, "Get your shit fixed and I'll see you tomorrow."

When he jumped into the car, he looked at me. "So...what did we learn today?"

Not knowing that I was going to be quizzed, I guessed at an answer and said, "Ummmm...you don't like dumb..." I hesitated to say the second part of that word.

"Say it..."

I looked at him and said, "You don't like dumbshit…" I smiled.

He smiled back. "No tolerance for it…none. In this business, you can't leave room for it."

I nodded my head as we pulled off.

≈

For months, everything went smoothly. There was nothing, but women and money. I was having sex every day and always with somebody new. I never got drunk again, but I couldn't say "No" to the pussy.

One night, he'd purchased the company of two girls for me. I didn't know what to do with one girl let alone two, but I didn't have to do anything. They did all of the work. After they finished playing with each other, they turned and let me play. It was amazing watching them take turns satisfying me. I was on my way to

Heaven, but my "trip" was interrupted by screams coming from my brother's room. I stopped and listened for a moment and heard a loud smack, and another scream. I stood and ran to his room. I knocked on his door. "Bruh...is everything okay in there?" A minute passed before he said," Everything is just fine..." I heard another loud smack and a scream. I knocked again and before I could say anything, the door flew open. "Unless you're about to take care of this..." he pointed at his hard dick. "...I advise you to stay away from this door." Then, he slammed the door in my face.

I was on my way to the bathroom when one of the girls exited his room. She looked at me. Her eyes were bruised, swollen, and her mouth was split open. I was about to say something when my brother shouted. "Get your ass back in here!"

She looked at me before turning and going back into the room. I could see my brother standing by the bed with a belt in his hand. "Get over here," he ordered. She looked back at me before closing the door. Suddenly, I heard a "whipping" sound and a scream and it continued until the sun came up.

When I woke up, the next morning, they were all gone. He was in the kitchen reading the newspaper. He looked up and said, "Another motherfucker got shot last night."

I poured myself a bowl of cereal and then said, "What did she do to you?"

My brother looked over the edge of the paper. "Who?"

Wiping milk from my mouth, I said, "That girl that you beat-up."

"First, it may do you some good to mind your own business, but since you're my brother, I'm going to give you a pass." My brother folded the paper and sat it down in front of him. "I was stressed and needed to relieve some tension."

"But you hit a girl…"

"I hit a hoe," he said.

"But she's a girl…"

He took a deep breath and said, "I didn't do anything that she didn't want done to her."

"She wanted you to beat her up?" I asked.

"Yep…"

"Why would somebody want that?"

"What the fuck I look like? A therapist? Some women are just into that shit…sure, I might have gotten a little rough, but she got paid…"

Confused, I shook my head. "And that makes it okay?"

"You're over-thinking this shit. These girls are in business…this is what they do. She could have stopped me at any time, but she didn't. I ain't the type of man that go around beating-up women. She knew what I wanted before she got here. It wasn't like I asked for a blowjob and she ended-up with my fist in her face. This is her 'thing.' Every girl has their specialty. You'd be amazed what they are willing to do for money and if I'm paying for it, I wanna get my money's worth. Shit, because of me, her rent is going to get paid this month. That ass-whooping was not cheap..."

"But her face...?"

"Again...if that's what she's selling and that's what I'm buying...what more can I say? Her face will heal...now, eat your breakfast. I have some runs to make."

I looked, deeply, into my bowl of cereal as I thought about what he said.

≈

We'd been riding around all day, doing what we did every day – picking-up and dropping-off. I was tired so, I turned on the massager and the heated seats and settled in to take a nap. We pulled down an alley for our last pick-up when the young man stepped out of the shadows. His face was covered in bandages. I glanced at him for a second before closing my eyes. I heard my brother say, "Punctual...I like that shit." The young man mumbled something back. Then my brother said, "What the fuck you gon' do with that?"

Groggily, I looked up. As I turned to see what was going on, I heard a loud, *POP!!!* I saw my brother's body fall to the ground. The young man pointed the gun at me, he mumble something and then I heard another *POP!!!* I closed my eyes, waiting for the bullet to hit my face, but nothing happened. Suddenly, I opened my eyes and didn't see anyone. I heard the sound again. *POP!!!* I waited a second and then crawled over to the driver's side of the car. I looked out of the window and saw my brother's body slumped against the door. I jumped out of the car and ran to his side. He was still pointing the gun at him.

"Nooooooooo…noooooooooo!!!!" I screamed.

He rested his arm and said, "Did I get him?"

With tears in my eyes, I looked over at the other guy. With his eyes wide open, he stared at me. I was turning my head when I saw something out of the corner of my eye – a smile. I looked back at him and he was actually smiling - not through the smile that my brother had cut on his face, but an actual smile. Without thinking, I grabbed my brother's gun and pointed it at him. I pulled the trigger three more times. The young man's body twitched before his eyes rolled into the back of his head.

"He's dead…" I said.

He looked down at his bloody shirt. "Damn…this is kinda fucked-up." He placed his hand on his chest. He looked at his blood-soaked hand. "What did I tell you about these Niggas?"

"You said, 'Don't trust them…'"

"Exactly." He laughed as he coughed-up blood.

Crying, I grabbed him and held him in my arms. "Don't die…don't die…" I begged.

He looked up at me. "I'm not going to die. I'm just going to sleep…." He coughed a few more times before saying, "Goodnight, Little Bruh…see you on the other side."

"NOOOOOOOO!!!! NOOOOOOO!!!!" Then suddenly there was nothing. The only noise was coming from my heart beating, loudly, against my chest. I held him until his body turned cold. Gently, I rested his head against the concrete. I grabbed his gun and climbed into the driver's seat. I looked out of the window one last time. "See you on the other side," I said, before pulling off.

I took Lake Shore Drive back to his apartment. I walked in. I didn't turn on any of the lights. Instead, I sat in the darkness. In the darkness, I couldn't see it, but when the sun crept through his living room window, the next morning, I saw it. I was covered in it – my brother's blood. I stripped out of my clothing and walked down the hall to the bathroom. As I walked, the images, of last night, replayed themselves in my mind. When I turned on the water, I thought about my parents and how I was going to tell them that their baby was dead. It was too much to process. As I stepped in the shower and watched the blood go down the drain, I realized that I'd just witnessed my first murder, and that I'd just killed a man.

Chapter 21

I removed anything, from his apartment, that I thought would shine a negative light on him, and packed it into his car. Then, I drove around until the red-light on the 'dash' began to blink. I pulled over and parked the car. I sat there. Suddenly, I could feel him again, lying in my arms. I closed my eyes and started to cry. I began to bang my head on the steering wheel. "Why?" I continued to cry. "Not him…what am I going to tell my mama?" I cried until finally I fell asleep.

Tap, Tap, Tap.

I opened my eyes to a girl knocking on my window. "Get away from my car," I said.

She was about to walk away when she turned and said, "You look like you could use a friend."

"GET THE FUCK AWAY FROM MY CAR!!!!!" I pointed the gun at the window.

She threw her hands in the air. "Okay…okay…" She was walking away when I began to bang my head again against the steering wheel.

When I stopped, I looked-up to find her staring at me. "You want to get shot?" I asked.

"I'm walking away," she said.

I started crying again. This time, it wasn't about my brother. I was so overwhelmed with emotion that I felt terrible about the way that I treated her. Suddenly, I rolled down the window and said, "Look…do you have a minute?"

She turned and said, "Who me?"

"Look, I'm sorry…I need to talk to somebody."

"Are you going to shoot me?"

"Naw…please…I really need to talk to somebody." Slowly, she walked over to the car. I popped the locks. She opened the door and climbed into the passenger seat.

She didn't say anything. I was staring out into the street when I said, "He's dead."

"Who?" she asked.

"My brother," I said – no longer able to cry.

"What happened?" she asked.

"He got shot."

"So sorry for your loss…"

I didn't respond.

She took a deep breath and said, "I usually get paid for my time."

I looked at her. I reached into the backseat, into one of the bags and grabbed a twenty. She reached for it, but then pushed my hand away. "This one's on me."

We sat there for a while in silence. She looked in the backseat. "You got anywhere to go?"

I looked at her and said, "No…I guess I better get a room."

"You look like you shouldn't be alone….where's your family?"

"I can't talk to them right now…"

"Oh…I understand…" She looked me up and down before saying, "I got a spare room if you got some money."

I looked into the backseat and said, "Why would you let a stranger move in with you?"

"It ain't no different than you going to a motel…plus, strangers are my business."

I thought about it for a second and said, "I don't have any energy for any psycho-bullshit…so if you're one of those crazy-bitches, just know that I'm not above putting a bullet in your ass."

She laughed. "Right now, you're the one acting crazy..."

"And that's what I want...I want you to know that it's possible..."

"As long as you keep that shit in the closet, we're good..."

I yawned. "Okay..."

"You will have access to everything in the apartment, but this pussy. You want some of this...you gotta pay like everybody else."

I looked at her and said, "You ain't gotta worry about that...now where's home?" I asked, trying to start the car.

She frowned. "First, let's get your crazy-ass some gas..."

Chapter 22

And so it began. A partnership was formed. I had no idea what the hell I was doing. I didn't know anything about being a pussy-wholesaler. I wasn't nothing, but a young man with a gun, a pocket full of money, a car, and a girl who liked to fuck men for money.

The first week, I just drove Trisha around. She handled her "business" and when she was done, she gave me some gas money. At first I was okay with it, but then I started to feel like she was taking advantage of me. So one night, I climbed in my bed and wondered how my brother would handle this situation. I thought about the things that he did, the things that he said, and then decided that things needed to change. Not because I needed the money, because I didn't. No, this was about something else. It was about being treated fairly and about respect. So the next night, after she was done, I flipped the script on her ass.

"Whew…I didn't think he was gon' ever cum," she said, reaching into her purse. She handed me a twenty dollar bill. "Thanks for the ride."

I looked at the bill and said, "We need to talk."

"About what, Sweetie?"

Hearing her say "Sweetie" made me think of my mother, I frowned. "What am I to you?"

She smiled and said, "You're my ride." She reached over and touched my hand.

I looked at her hand. She removed it. "So all I am is some glorified cab driver?"

"No...you're more than that. When these tricks know that I got somebody waiting on me, they don't try no funny business..."

"So I give you a ride...I watch your back...seems like I should be getting a little more than gas money..."

"Why? I do all of the work?"

"True, but my time is money...just like yours...you ain't gon' fuck them while fucking over me...now, I'm gonna take care of you, but you got to take care of me too..."

"Shit...I was able to do this for a long time without a pimp...I don't need one now..."

"Okay...well, it's been good then...no hard feelings..."

"That's it?"

"That's it..." I confirmed.

She was about to get out of the car, but then turned and said, "The shit can get scary sometimes…"

"Well….good luck with that…"

She frowned. "I can't believe that you would leave me out here like that…"

"Hey…like you said, 'You were able to do this a long time without a pimp…"

She took a deep breath, reached into her purse and said, "Here…" She removed all of the money and handed it to me.

"Why did you hand me all of your money?"

"Because that's what I'm supposed to do…right?"

Confused, I looked at her. *It can't be that easy.* I thought to myself.

Then she said, "That rent thing…forget about it."

I didn't say anything. Then, she said, "Am I done for the night…daddy?"

I had no idea what to say to her. My dumbass looked at her and said, "Well…what do you wanna do?"

She looked at me and said, "Whatever you want me to do."

Feeling cocky, I said, "Do a few more and then let's call it a night."

"Okay, daddy," she said, before getting out of the car.

As I watched her crossed the street, I thought about what'd just happened. The shit was so easy that it didn't seem real. When I saw a car pull-up next to her, and she jumped in, I realized that I'd just graduated to pimp.

≈

I'd heard through the grapevine about my brother's funeral. At first, I didn't want to go, but I needed to go and say my "Goodbyes." When I arrived at the church, I decided that it was better for me to sit in the back – away from everyone else. It was beautiful. His casket was silver, lined in white satin, and trimmed in gold. The flowers were yellow and white. I loved when they played a video of his time here on earth. It was weird seeing him as a kid. I'd almost forgotten those times. When they asked everyone to go up and see him for the last time, before they closed his casket, I couldn't bring myself to do it. I wanted to remember him as he was when he was alive – not as a hollow empty shell covered in makeup.

When the service began to let out, they rolled his casket passed me. I reached out and touched it. I felt its coldness against my fingertips. As my family proceeded down the aisle, my mother saw me and smiled. I stepped out of the pews to greet her. She grabbed me and said, "I'm glad that you were there for him." I looked at her and said, "I'm sorry, mama."

She wiped her eyes and said, "Why? That man was trying to rob him...you're a hero."

"A hero?"

"Yes, a hero..."

My father touched her shoulder and said, "We're holding up the line."

She looked over her shoulder. "Oh...okay...good to see you, son... come by the house later, I cooked."

"Okay mama..." I said, smiling. "I'll try." She smiled and followed his casket out of the door.

My father walked up to me and wrapped his arms around me. He whispered in my ear. "I know what you're doing..."

I pushed away from him. With tears in his eyes, he continued, "I lost one to the streets...I won't lose another one." Then he turned and walked away.

212

Chapter 23

After a while, Trisha was promoted to Bottom Bitch. Now, I know that you're thinking that being a Bottom Bitch is a bad thing, but it isn't. You have to sell a lot of pussy to move up to that position. It's kinda weird to think that a position that is called, "Bottom Bitch" is actually considered a promotion, but in this line of business it is. If someone called, "Bottom" is the one on the top then it makes you think about how the industry feels about the girls that come in after her.

She grew to become a shrewd business woman. I watched her go from twenty dollar blow-jobs to becoming one of the "baddest" hoes on the south-side. Men traveled far and wide for that warm spot between her legs and they paid heavily for it. They were so happy and excited to tap that ass. Most of her clients acted like they hadn't seen a pussy since the day that they came out of one. They gave her cars, jewelry, fur coats – tricks were dipping into their kid's college fund for that ass and she loved it. A few of them left their wives for her, but she wasn't the marrying type. She knew what she was worth and she wasn't accepting anything less than that. That ass kept us both living comfortably for a long time.

I was known as a "Chili Pimp" or what some people call a "Popcorn Pimp". I was very new to the game and only had one girl working for me. At that time, one girl was all that I needed. Even though, Trisha was a prostitute, she was a woman first and she had needs. For some bizarre reason, people seem to think that hoes don't have dreams, needs, emotions, or feelings. Folks seem to think that most hoes are just some junkie who's doped-up most of the time and who has no clue as to what's happening to them. They are wrong. Now, don't get me wrong, I'm sure that some of them exist, but Trisha wasn't one of them. Trisha is no different than any other human being. She whines, bitches, and moans just like the rest of us and that can be hard on a person. Especially, a pimp.

Now, I could be like one of those pimps who slap his girls when they start making a lot of noise, but when you hit somebody, it's only a matter time before they hit your ass back – in one way or another. So when she's having one of her "moments", I just sit and listen.

"You know…it was never my dream to suck strange dick for a living," Trisha said.

"No? But you do it so well, Bottom," I said, smiling.

"I know…I know…but there was a time when…" she said, but then paused.

"Go on," I said.

"Well, I wanted to be a doctor," she said.

At first, I wanted to laugh, but something told me that it probably wouldn't be a good idea, so I said, "Yeah? A doctor?"

"Yep, I wanted to heal and treat people," she said, smiling.

"But isn't that kinda what you do?"

Confused, she asked, "What do you mean?"

"You 'heal' a lot of sick men and women and don't you examine them before you put your mouth on them?" I said, being sarcastic.

Not catching my sarcasm, she said, "I do, but I want to do more with my life...I want to give more."

"You want to save the world, Bottom...one dick at a time?"

"I'm being serious..."

"I know, Bottom..."

"I don't know about other hoes, but this one wanted to be somebody."

"And you are…you are the best hoe on the South-side…"

She frowned.

"Well…think of it this way…what you do makes the world a better place. Because of you, there are a lot of happy men and women in the world. If it wasn't for you, they would be forced to masturbate and who gets rich off of that? The lubrication companies? Naw, Bottom, you are right where you're supposed to be."

"How do you know?"

"My mama always told me that what God has for you, is for you and that God doesn't make any mistakes…"

Frowning, she said, "So you think that God wants me to fuck strangers?"

"Well…probably not, but he used prostitutes and other sinners all of the time to complete His plan…and because of their obedience, He eventually forgave them and washed away their sins." I said.

"Really?"

"Yep...so it may be God's will...who knows...other than the Man...or Woman upstairs."

"Interesting..."

Yep...and think about this...He controls life and death. Do you think that He would have woke you up this morning if He wasn't pleased with what you were doing?"

"Wow...I never thought about it that way," she said.

"Man can't do no more than what God allows him to do."

"Really?"

"Would I lie to you?" I asked.

She thought about it for a second before saying, "Well...."

"Look, if it'll make you feel better...go 'trick' and when you're done, go and repent...ask for forgiveness and you should be good," I said. "People do it every day."

"Won't that piss God off...me tricking and apologizing...only to trick some more?"

"He forgives all sins," I said. "And really...I don't think there's a cap on how many times you can say, 'I'm sorry.'"

"Really?"

"Yep...in the end, it's between you and the Man upstairs...there are no perfect people in the world...even those claiming to be perfect and righteous are the most imperfect and unrighteous."

"Thanks Miller..."

"Not a problem, Sweetie...remember God loves you like He loves everyone else."

How do you know all of this stuff?" she asked.

"I grew-up in a church…" I said, smiling.

Chapter 24

Prostitution is like any other type of relationship that you may have. You have to treat the people in your life, well, or they will walk away from you. There is nothing worse than feeling like you've been cheated on or rejected – even by one of your "girls." It's a terrible feeling knowing that you dropped the ball and lost something important to you, whether it's replaceable or not. Now, in real life, if you lose your woman to another man, you can try to get her back, you can go out and get you another one, or you can cry like a bitch until everybody get sick of listening to your ass. But in the game, you cannot lose your woman to another pimp. It can be a matter of life and death – for you and your business. .

As I was making a name for myself, I scouted an area for a few months and noticed that there was some heavy traffic in this one particular spot. It looked like the pimp was making a lot of money, and I decided that I wanted some of it. So one night, I decided that I was going to take one of his girls just to test his strength and to show him mine.

I saw my "tool." She was a sweet little young thing – didn't look like she'd been on the "tracks" for long. She was wearing some thigh-high boots and a very short skirt. She had on a cut-off shirt that exposed her belly-button. She had her hair in a ponytail and her lips were covered in lip-gloss. She was the perfect person for the job.

I pulled-up along-side of her. I rolled my window down. She walked over.

"What can I do for you?" she asked.

"Why don't you get in and let's talk about it?" I said.

She looked around before walking around to the passenger side of the car. I pulled off. She pointed towards an alley and then said, "Pull into there."

I pulled in and turned the car off. She looked me up and down and asked, "Are you vice?"

"You probably should have asked me that before you got in my car...I could be a serial killer."

"Are you a serial killer?"

"Do serial killers get discounts?" I asked, smiling.

She didn't smile at first, but something about me must have made her feel comfortable. "No, you have to pay the same price as everyone else."

"And what are those prices?"

"Well, a blow-job is $20 and if you want a 'happy-ending', that'll cost you $50," she said.

Confused, I asked, "A happy-ending? Your blow-jobs don't end with a customer being happy?"

"Of course, they are, but if you want to cum in my mouth…" she said, looking in the mirror and applying more lip-gloss. "…It's going to cost you extra."

"Oh…and you don't do that for free?"

"Ummmmmmm….no…and if you want to have sex…that's going to cost you $50 or $100 for anal," she said, puckering and making sure that her lips were completely layered.

"Why so much for anal? Isn't a hole a hole?"

"Not mine, so you have to pay extra if you want to get in this ass…" She paused and continued, "If you like, I could fuck you in the ass, that'll be $150."

"Fuck me with what? You got a dick too?"

"No, but I can get one…"

I didn't even want to know how she was going to accomplish that, so I laughed and said, "Nobody touches this ass…"

"Don't knock it 'til you try it…"

"Oh, I'm 'knocking' it…"

"Suit yourself…so what will it be?"

"What if I just want to talk?"

"You still have to pay," she said.

I reached into my pocket and pulled out a one hundred dollar bill. "Here," I said.

"Ummmmmm…I don't have any change."

"I don't want any," I confirmed.

She smiled, stuffed the bill inside of her top, and said, "What do you want to talk about?"

"I want to talk about you."

225

Looking me up and down, she said, "I thought that you said that you wasn't vice."

"I'm not…now, I'm sure that that hundred dollars will buy me at least thirty minutes, so start talking."

"Well, I'm going to have to put my head in your lap to do that."

"Why?"

"Because we're being watched…"

I looked in my rearview mirror at the man standing on the corner. "Ummmm… okay…" *Perfect.* I thought to myself.

She placed her head in my lap and then looked up at me. "There's nothing to tell…I'm a prostitute…"

"Okay, Ms. Obvious…what brought you into the game?"

She didn't answer. She just stared at the ceiling.

I decided to ask her a different question. "Are you a happy hoe?"

She started laughing. "Are you fucking kidding me?" she asked. "You have to be joking, right?"

"That was a stupid question, huh?"

"Yep…"

"Do you love your pimp?"

She sat up and looked out of the window "Yes…yes…I love him…I would do anything for him," she said, nervously.

I smiled. "Did he have to beat that into you?"

"No, no…I do…I do love him."

I grabbed her arm. There were marks where she'd been injecting drugs. "Are you sure that you love him or is that the monkey on your back talking?"

"No…I mean…yes…I mean no…" she said.

I smiled and looked at my watch. "Look my time is almost up. What would you like to do for the last few minutes?"

227

She began to pull at my zipper. I grabbed her hand. "Look, I'm good...tell your man what you have to...but we are good." I reached into my pocket and pulled out another hundred dollar bill. "Tell him that you gave me a blowjob and you keep the rest for yourself."

She sat back and said, "Are you sure? I do this thing with my tongue that drives my tricks crazy."

I smiled. "I bet...but we're good."

She smiled and then said, "Okay... well...thank you."

"You can 'thank' me later. Now, go before you get in trouble."

She jumped out of the car pretending to wipe her mouth. She looked back, smiled, and waved 'goodbye.'

≈

We did this for a month. I would find her on the tracks, pick her up, pay her to talk to me, and every night, her pimp was there – watching her.

Then, on the last night, I noticed that he wasn't on the corner.

"Can I trust you?" she asked, looking over her shoulder.

"Sure…what's up?"

"I'm so scared…"

"Scared of what?"

"Him…" she replied.

"Why?"

For a moment, she didn't say anything. She took a deep breath and said, "I don't want to do this. I want to go home to my mama." She began to cry.

"I can get you to your mother," I said

She wiped her eyes and asked, "How?"

"By just taking you to her…"

"He'll kill us both."

"I'm not worried about that…"

"Why not?"

"Cause I'm not…"

"You should…"

"Probably, but I'm not…" I waited a second and continued, "I'm not going to lie to you. I'm a pimp too," I said.

"I should have known…" she said, turning to get out of the car.

"Wait…I'm not recruiting…I just want to help you."

"Why do you want to help me?" she asked.

"I just do…don't try to understand it…"

"So…you're just running around saving hoes?"

"Not really…"

"So why do you want to help me?"

"Cause I do…"

"WHY?" she insisted.

"Sometimes, people do that…they just help people."

"But you're a pimp…"

"Again, I'm willing to help you, but you need to make up your mind before he rolls-up on us…" I knew that time was of the essence. I needed to get out of there. I didn't want him showing-up and seeing me pulling off with his girl. I wanted the element of surprise. I wanted him to wake-up and find his shit missing like it'd been repossessed.

"But what about the contract?" she said.

"He made you sign a Slave Contract?"

"We all have to…"

I grabbed her hand. "You don't have to worry about that either…I will take care of that."

She looked at me for a long time, because she knew what this meant. It was a dangerous move, but she thought about the alternative and said, "What do I have to do?"

"Just put on your seat-belt..." I started my car and pulled off.

Once at the stable, I told Bottom to take care of her.

"I thought that we talked about you bringing in strays?" she said, opening the door wearing nothing but a robe.

"And I thought that I told you that I don't ever want to see you naked?"

"Fuck you, Miller," Trisha said.

"Maybe later."

She frowned.

"I need you to clean her up and take her home."

"Take her home? The fuck I look like, Benson?"

"Well, you do have that five o'clock shadow thing going on..."

"Fuck you..."

"I told you 'later'…"

"Shit, she could bring in a lot of money. You know that the 'johns' like 'em young," she said, examining the girl.

I stared at her.

"Okay…" Trisha looked her up and down and said, "Go and take that shit off…you smell like a hoe."

"Bottom…be nice," I said.

She walked away mumbling. "Now, I have to put on some damn drawers and play cab driver for your ass."

Chapter 25

The next day, I was walking up to my car when someone ran up behind me. He wrapped his arm around my neck. I felt something hard pressing against my back. "If that's your dick...be easy...I'm still a virgin."

"Let's talk," he said.

I put my hands in the air and said, "You wanna talk under these street lights or do you wanna go somewhere private?"

"Open the door and get your ass in the car," he demanded.

"If that's your idea of foreplay...then we're off to a bad start."

"Get your ass in the fucking car," he said, pressing the gun harder into my back.

"Okay…" Now, I could have easily taken his gun and pistol-whipped him with it, but I was too amused by the fact that he didn't search me for any hardware. He'd just made a rookie-mistake or he just underestimated me. Either way, things were going exactly as planned. I opened the doors and we jumped in.

"You got something that belongs to me."

"I do?" I asked, acting like I didn't know what he was talking about.

"Don't play with me…now, where is she?"

"I don't know what you're talking about."

He placed the barrel of the gun up against my head. "I'm not going to ask you again."

I looked into my rearview mirror. He was looking around, checking to make sure that we were alone. Slowly, I pulled the gun out of my waistband, placed it under my arm, and pointed it towards the backseat.

"Where is she?" he asked, again.

"I thought that you said that you weren't going to ask me again?"

"Motherfucker are you playing with me?"

"Do you feel me caressing your balls? Then, I'm not playing with you...that's just wishful thinking."

"You're a funny motherfucker...aren't you?"

"I'm a lot of things, but funny ain't one of them."

"Well...we've played this game long enough...since you won't return my shit..."

I saw his reflection in the mirror and fired a shot. His hand flinched causing him to pull the trigger. The sound was deafening as a bullet grazed my head. I turned and saw him holding his stomach. He pointed the gun at me, again. I turned and reached over the seat, grabbed his hand and while holding his hand, I fired off two more shots. The second bullet opened his head like a cantaloupe and splattered it against the back window.

"Shit," I said, wiping blood off of my face. I jumped out of the car and looked around the parking lot – making sure that no one saw what happened. Then, I turned and looked into the backseat of my car. "Damn," I mumbled to myself.

I walked back into the stable. Bottom ran up to me. "What happened to you? Are you hurt?"

I wasn't in the mood to answer her questions. "Call my boys and tell them that I got a clean-up in aisle 9," I said, removing my shirt. "They'll know what to do."

"Got it," she said.

Chapter 26

B*OOM! BOOM! BOOM!*

The noise startled me. Getting caught-up in the covers, I rolled over and fell out of the bed.

BOOM! BOOM! BOOM! BOOM!

After frantically releasing myself from the blankets, I reached up on the nightstand and grabbed my gun. Out of breath, because I'd just lost the fight with my covers, I stomped down the hall to my door – ready to shoot whoever was standing on the other side of it. I looked through the peephole. It was Bottom. I opened the door. She flew passed me –

closing all of the blinds and curtains in the room.

Rubbing my eyes, I said, "Good morning, Bottom."

"Have you seen the news?" she asked, pacing the floor.

My head was killing me. "Naw, why don't you fill me in?" I said, walking towards the kitchen to make an ice pack.

"Well, while you were sleeping, the police was at the hotel investigating that murder."

"Really?" I asked, nonchalantly.

"Yes, really," she said, peeking out of the window.

"Well, did they talk to you or the girls?"

"No."

"Did the boys stop by and clean it up?"

"Yeah…but it was hard getting his brains out of the back speakers."

"Remind me to replace them…you know how I am about my music."

Trisha peeked out of the blinds.

"Trisha, get away from the window and come sit down….you're making me nervous."

She walked over and sat down. "I'm not trying to go to jail, Miller."

"Nobody's going to jail, Bottom…we did the community a solid by killing his ass. You saw that girl. After they do their investigation, they are going to find out that he was kidnapping little girls, getting them hooked, and making them work. Believe me…I will look like a hero when it's all over…the heat will cool soon."

"It better…"

"It's the nature of the business… sometimes, somebody's head needs to be blown off, so that other people know and understand who you are…kinda like sending out a group text, but instead of using the phone, I used a gun."

"Did this have anything to do with that girl?"

"In the end, it's always about some girl."

"If you gon' kill people, can you please do that shit somewhere else?"

Holding the ice against my head, I said, "First, I didn't plan on killing him. He snuck up behind me and rubbed his gun against my back. I thought he was a pervert, so…"

She laughed. "No, you didn't…"

"Hey, that's my story and I'm sticking to it…" I smiled and continued, "…and somehow he fell on my gun…three times."

She laughed. "He fell on your gun? That's new…"

"Yeah, happens all of the time. You haven't heard of folks falling on guns?"

"Sure, he zigged when he should have zagged…" she joked.

"Exactly…"

She frowned. "I saw your car…the man had no head."

"That's what happens when you zig."

She looked at me. We both began to laugh.

"Miller, you're crazy."

"But you're right…I do need to be more careful. I can't tell the police that a motherfucker fell on my gun. That might not be a good defense…"

"Yeah, that might work with me, but that shit will get you thrown under a jail…"

I smiled. "You're probably right."

"I know I'm right."

Chapter 27

When we were younger, my boys and I did everything together. When you found one, you found the other. We were always competing against each other; trying to see who had the best "game" and who had the most girls. We competed in everything except school. Who cared who got the best grades? That shit was corny, but if there was a competition, I would have won, because I was the smartest one among us.

But eventually, we grew-up, and drifted apart. Life is like that. You can have people in your life, but then something happens and you find yourself going in different directions. Doesn't mean that you stop being friends. You're just waiting for life or a set of certain circumstances to bring you back together.

I ran into one of them, one day. He was selling boot-leg movies in a parking lot.

"I got those movies…movies…movies," he said.

I looked at him and asked, "Money? Is that you?"

He stepped back and looked at me. "Trey, is that you? Look at you 'G'. Damn, you looking good…real good."

I got out of my car and hugged him. "Man, what are you doing…selling CDs?"

"Bruh, it's a hustle," he said.

"I see…boot-leg too? I could have been the police. That's a fucked up reason to end-up in jail."

"I know, man, but when you have to pay child support and you're trying to eat, you have to do what you gotta do."

"What happened to the HBCU?"

"You know what happened... Yvonne's ass got pregnant..."

"She had some help...didn't she?"

"Yeah, she did..." He paused and sighed, "My ass should have known better. When that little head start making decisions for you...shit is always bound to get fucked-up..."

"And how is our little beauty queen?"

He sighed. "That bitch is trying to get blood from a turnip, and you know how hard that shit is...how am I going to feed someone else when I can't even feed myself?"

"That's why you think, before you stick it in..."

He dropped his head and said, "But it felt so good..."

"How's it feeling now?"

"Fucked-up…"

"I bet…" I stopped and looked at the box in his hand. "How much are you selling them for?" I asked.

"Five a piece or three for twelve."

I pulled out a roll of money, pulled out five Bens, and handed them to him.

He stared at the money. "Damn, I should be calling you, Money…what you want for this?" he asked.

"Nothing…"

"Look, man, I can't pay you back," he said.

"Throw the box in the trunk…"

"Shit is hard, but I'm no charity case…I'm willing to work for mines…"

"Good…then let's go for a ride," I said, reaching into the car and popping the trunk.

He looked at me for a second, looked at the money in his hand, and then looked at the box of CDs. He threw the box in the trunk so fast, they went flying all over the place. He walked around to the other side of the car. When he jumped in, I heard his butt squeak as it slid against the leather seats.

"Man, this shit is nice," he said, touching the woodgrain on the door.

"Thanks…" I paused for a second and said, "You like selling CDs?"

"Yeah, one day I woke-up and said, 'Fuck college…When I grow up, I want to be a boot-leg CD peddler."

"That's what being impulsive would do…one day, you're on your way to college, then a nice piece of ass walks by, and now, you're a baby-daddy. You have to learn how to say 'No.'"

"You ain't got to tell me no more…my shit gets double-wrapped. I wear so many condoms, I don't even know what I'm sticking my shit in."

"That's a smart move…a shame that you didn't think of it sooner."

"True that, but you seem to be doing good."

"I'm okay…but I could be doing better," I said.

"Better than this?" he asked.

"Bruh, this shit ain't nothing. I'm talking about cornering the market on some shit…make some bank and retiring on that shit."

"That sounds good, but how do you plan on doing that?" he asked.

"I'm already doing it…I just need somebody that I can trust who will watch my back."

Money looked at the money that I'd given him. "What do I have to do?"

"First, let's find Hustle," I said, pulling off.

We drove around for an hour in our old stomping grounds. Driving through the neighborhood brought back a lot of memories. Now, it looked like a ghost town. There was garbage all over the streets, most of the buildings were boarded-up, and if it wasn't for the churches, the beauty supply stores, and the liquor stores, I would swear that no one lived there anymore.

We had almost given up looking for him, when we drove passed an alley where we saw someone holding another person in a choke-hold.

Money pointed. "There's your boy."

I smiled and slowly pulled into the alley.

Hustle didn't even release the guy. I rolled down the window. "Hey Hustle…"

Hustle walked up to the car, still holding the man by the neck. "Damn motherfucker…what's up…where have you been?"

I looked at the man. He was struggling to breathe. "So, ummmmmmm, what you got there, Hustle?"

Hustle looked down. "This Bitch-ass Nigga was trying to pay me for some shit that I did for him in food stamps."

Still looking at the man, I asked, "How much does he owe you?"

"Forty dollars..." he said.

"You're choking the shit out of a man for forty dollars?"

He smiled. "I will choke the shit out of a motherfucker for a boloney sandwich."

I pulled my roll out again and pulled out another five Ben's, and handed them to him. Hustle looked at the money and then looked at the man. He took the money and said, "Say thank you to my boy."

The man looked up at me. "Thanks Bruh."

"If you let him go, I can show you how you can get some more of that." I smiled and said, "Let's go for a ride."

Hustle released his grip from around the man's neck and said, "Run."

The man looked confused at first, but then turned and ran. Hustle looked at me and smiled. He was about to climb into the backseat, but stopped and picked-up a brick that was sitting by a dumpster. Before I knew it, he reached back and swung the brick at the man who was running down the alley. The next thing I know, he hit him in the back of his head – so hard that his feet flew up into the air. He landed face-forward onto the concrete.

Hustle started laughing. "Motherfuckers have to know not to fuck with me and my money."

I smiled and said, "Perfect," before backing out of the alley.

≈

When I told them what I was doing, they jumped at the opportunity. They didn't ask any questions or consider the risks. They strapped-up and never looked back.

And things were really working out for us.
Until, she knocked on my door.

Chapter 28

The "Board of Directors" consisted of me and my two boys, Hustle and Big Money. Having them along made things run like a well-oiled machine. The more money that I made, the more that I had to watch my back. I couldn't do that while watching my money and my girls too. That's how people end-up dead. They get distracted and wind-up with a bullet in the chest.

Big Money, real name Brian, was the neighborhood bully. He shook-down kids for their lunch money. Everyone was afraid of his big ass, but me. Poverty would do that to you – make you think your ass is invincible until "life" proves otherwise.

The story behind our meeting, is the urban version of the story of David and Goliath. One day, he caught me on a bad day. My mother had just purchased me a pair of Converse. Don't laugh, 'cause back in the day, they were more than a collector's item – they were a status symbol. If you had a pair, guys respected you and pretty girls gave you a second look. And my ass was strutting. I was walking down the street in my favorite black jeans. You knew that they were my favorite because I'd ironed them so much, they shined.

Money and his boys were waiting for me. I don't think they were waiting for me, specifically. They were waiting for a "mark" and my ass showed-up at the wrong place and at the wrong time. I was almost passed them when Money said, "Give me some money."

Shaking, I said, "I don't have any money."

"Yes, you do," he said, as he searched my pockets.

"I don't, man…stop feeling on me."

His friends laughed.

"Bitch…ain't nobody feeling on you."

"I'm telling you…I don't have any money."

Then, Money picked me up. Holding me upside down by one leg, he said, "Give me some money."

As the blood rushed to my head, I said, "I don't have any money."

Holding me by my ankle, he stopped and said, "Well, look what we have here."

With the blood still rushing to my head, I looked up. "No…wait."

He slipped the shoe off of my foot and said, "Damn…these are hot…" He sniffed them. "Shit, they still smell new." He dropped me on my head.

"OUCH!!!!"

"Man, these are nice…"

Rubbing my head, I said, "Please…give that back to me."

"Bruh, I need some shoes."

Standing on my feet, I tried to get my shoe back. Money stopped and looked at me. His eyes had become dark. "I SAID…I need these shoes."

My heart was racing. I was breathing heavily. I thought about how long I waited for those shoes, how much I needed my shoes, and how long I would have to hear my mama's mouth if I went back home without them. So, I had to make a decision. Give him my shoes and end-up barefoot for the rest of my life or beat his ass, now, and put an end to this shit. And believe me, if you let a man take your shoes, he will always take your shoes. Once he gets those, he's coming back for your manhood and I couldn't have that. So slowly, I kneeled down to take off the other shoe.

On my way down, I was face to face with his balls. I slid my hand into my shoe and on my way back up, I put that shoe all up into his nuts. He hit the ground, landing in the fetal position. While he was down, I took my shoe and beat him in his face - blow after blow, he stayed down. During all of this, his boys did nothing, but laugh. I looked down to find the word "Converse" imbedded in the blood on his forehead. When I was done, I took my shoes and ran.

The next day, he was standing in the same spot. This time, he was alone. I was going to run across the street, but I knew that if I ran, I was going to be running for the rest of my life. So, I clenched my butt-cheeks together, balled my fists, bit my bottom lip, and went to face my "giant." As I approached him, I could see that he was badly beaten. His mouth and eyes were swollen. He looked a mess.

"What's-up G?" he said.

When he said it, I was so scared, I almost pee'd on myself. "Ummmmm… nothing…what about you?"

"Nothing…" he responded.

There was a moment of silence. I was still waiting for him to bust my head wide-open, but he didn't do anything. Suddenly, I said, "Well…ummmmm …okay then."

He nodded and said, "See you later, G."

And that was it. It took a while, but we eventually became friends.

Then there was Hustle, real name Jimmy. Hustle and I were like brothers. His mother used to drop him off every day so my mother could babysit him while she went to school. Most of the time, he spent all day with us, because his mother wouldn't pick him up. She would say that she had detention or some after school project, but we knew what was really going on. She hated his ass, because he represented all of the pain and trauma that she'd experienced in her life.

Hustle was the result of an unwanted pregnancy and a botched abortion. His mother got pregnant very young. After the "Baby-daddy" got what he wanted from her, he didn't want to have anything to do with her or the kid. According to my mother, "She was a "fast" little girl and "Too hot for her own britches." When she found out that she was pregnant, she had one of those "Back-Alley" abortions; no doctor, no sanitizer, no nurse, and no idea what the hell she was doing. It was just her, a bottle of liquor and a coat hanger. Nine months later, she still gave birth to a little boy.

As soon as she made 18, she left him – just left his ass in an empty apartment. Just so happen that one day the landlord was getting ready to show the apartment to another family and they found him lying in his own waste, filthy, and starving to death. My mother fought hard to get custody of him. I'm not sure if they ever found his mother, but it didn't matter because we took care of him.

But Hustle ended-up having a lot of problems. His mama fucked him up. He was always getting into trouble, because there was something wrong with his head. A normal person would think before they do crazy shit, but not Hustle. "Crazy shit" was his middle name. He would lie about things and steal shit just for the hell of it – for no other reason than the fact that he could. I used to just look at him and wonder what was wrong with him, but I knew.

My parents fought hard to keep him. He was so bad, they couldn't do anything with him and my mother's charitable nature only went so far. So after having him medicated and prayed for and that didn't work – they gave-up and threw him in the "system."

I never knew how crazy he was, until one day, we were just sitting around, just hanging out, on top of a building's rooftop, when he said, "I wonder what it's like to Bungee jump."

When he said it I blew it off, because there's a few things that Black folks don't do – ever. We don't go in the woods after dark. We don't stay in haunted houses that tell us to get the fuck out and we don't Bungee Jump. Black folks ain't too keen on ropes, not even for fun, so I knew that he had to be trippin'.

"You ever wonder what it would be like to jump from a really high place with only a rope that is tied around your ankle to save you?" he asked, playing with a rope that was sitting nearby.

"Bro…if I want to have a near-death experience, I could get that just walking to the grocery store. Shit, I ain't doing that crazy shit," I said.

For a moment, he didn't say anything. He just stared over the edge of the building. What that fool did next blew my mind. He tied a rope to one of those plumbing vent pipes that was sticking out of the roof. As he was tying the rope to his ankle, I thought that I should stop him, but I actually thought that he was bluffing. Then, he started counting.

"1,2,3…" he began.

The next thing I knew, he was going over the side of the building and then *SPLAT!* His ass hit the side of the wall like an egg hitting the floor. I ran and looked over the side of the building. "What the hell is wrong with you, man?"

He was laughing so hard. "Motherfucker, just help me get up."

When I pulled him back up to the roof, he had the strangest look on his face. I was hoping that the impact would knock some sense in his ass, but it didn't and of course, I blew it off. Consequently, what I will learn later is that when someone shows you their crazy- side, pay attention.

Chapter 29

One day, Trisha came rushing into the house dragging a girl in behind her. We all drew our guns because we thought that we were being raided. "Put that shit up and help me," she said, pushing passed us.

We put our guns up and walked into the kitchen where she took the girl. When I walked in, she was filling a plastic bag up with ice. I looked at the girl who was holding her eye.

"What happened?" I asked.

The girl did not respond. Trisha trained them not to speak to me. Everything came directly through her unless she wasn't around.

Trisha responded. "The bastard stuck his dick in her eye."

"I looked at Money and Hustle who had just entered the room and asked, "What did you say?"

"That piece of shit stuck his dick in her eye," she confirmed.

"And what's wrong with that?"

Trisha walked over to the girl and pulled her hand away from her face. We looked at her and said, "DAMN!!!!!!!!"

Money spoke. "Gad-damn…are you sure he used his dick?"

Trisha handed the girl the bag of ice and then walked over to the counter and grabbed a handful of paper-towels. "Yes…that's what she told me." She reached into her purse, pulled out a glass jar, and placed it on the table.

I walked over and examined her. "Naw, she got FUCKED in the eye...he didn't just stick her...that eye took a pounding...unless he hit her and didn't want to pay extra for beating the shit out of her."

Trisha handed the girl the paper-towels and then walked back over to the freezer for more ice. She stuck her hand in the freezer. "That motherfucker paid for it, alright."

We all leaned-in and looked at the jar on the table. "Bottom...what is that?"

"That's his dick," she said.

We all jumped back and grabbed our "junk." "DAMN!!!!!! You cut off his shit?" I asked.

"I cut that shit straight the fuck off...," she said, turning up her mouth.

Frowning, I said. "Bottom...get that shit off of my table."

She picked up the jar and put it back into her purse.

"Bottom, it ain't your place to be disciplining tricks. You should have called me."

"And that bastard shouldn't be sticking his dick in folk's eye…eye-fucking ain't on the menu. Sick-ass…some of these motherfuckers don't know how to act. So they got to be taught…"

I examined the girl closely.

Bottom continued, "How she gon' work with one eye?" she asked. "Who gon' fuck a one-eyed-hoe?"

Money responded. "I wonder if she saw it cumming. Get it? Cumming…Not coming…" When we didn't laugh, he frowned. "Fuck y'all…that was some funny shit."

Hustle frowned and looked at him. "Shut your ass up…" He walked over to the girl and started playing with her hair. "I'll fuck her."

Money frowned and said, "You'll fuck a can of pop."

Hustle grabbed his crotch and said, "Naw, what I got won't fit in a can of pop."

Trisha looked him up and down and said, "I don't know about that."

"Know your place, hoe," Hustle said.

"Fuck you," Trisha said. "I got yo' hoe."

"Naw, I won't fuck you…that ass got so many miles on it, it's lost some of its tread, but I WILL fuck her." Hustle turned his attention back to the girl. We all thought that he was playing until he began to unzip his pants.

"She don't want your nasty ass," Bottom said, standing between them. "Get away from her."

"She can lick the salt off of these nuts…" he said, trying to get around her.

Bottom whipped-out a switchblade. "One more step and you're going to be able to lick your own nuts."

He leaned into her face.

She leaned back. "You're in my personal space…now, back that shit up."

"Get out of my way, bitch," he said, pushing her.

She regained her balance and said, "I'm warning you…touch me again and they are going to make a movie after my ass called, '50 ways to Cut a Nigga'…Now, do that shit again."

I looked at him. "Hustle, what the fuck are you doing?"

"I'm going to fuck her," he said, now pulling at the girl. "We don't want no pussy going to waste."

"You better get this fool before I cut his ass," Bottom said, waving the blade at him.

I walked over and then pushed him. "What the fuck is wrong with you?"

Hustle caught his balance and said to the girl, "Go in the back…I'll be back there in a minute."

The girl looked at me, but she didn't move. Bottom kept the blade pointing at him.

"MOVE HOE!" he ordered.

I looked at everyone and said, "Give us a minute." Money was leaving the room when I stopped him. "I'm going to need your help for this."

Money walked back in and sat at the table.

I pulled my gun out and placed it on the table.

Hustle looked at the gun. "You 'drawing' on me over some pussy?"

"First, I'm not drawing on you. I don't draw my gun unless I plan to use it. Second, I think that we need to have a fucking discussion."

Fixing his clothes, he said, "You don't have to explain shit to me."

"Oh, but I do."

"I would have paid her...if that's the issue."

"It ain't about the money."

"You said that it's always about the money."

"It is, but right now it's about nigga-shit and how it must stop."

"We're talking about hoes, Trey…" he said.

"We're talking about my hoes…they work for me…you work for me…nobody…I mean NOBODY gives orders other than me."

"We got all of this ass around us and you're saying that we can't touch it?"

"We don't touch our own product. You want to fuck somebody…go fuck yourself."

"Now, why would I do that?" he asked.

"For the same reason you thought that you was gon' fuck one of my girls…MY GIRLS!"

Money looked at him and shook his head.

Hustle looked at him. "The fuck you shaking your head for?"

He took a deep breath and said, "Man, you're a loser."

Hustle frowned. "Fuck you...you're the loser."

Money shook his head, again. "And that's exactly what losers do...say dumb-loser-shit...you been a loser for so long, you don't even know that you're a loser and that's what makes you a gad-damn loser...loser."

Hustle opened his mouth to say something, but I interrupted him. "Before you open your mouth...let me warn you...if it ain't, 'Yes, Boss,' I'm going to cut your dick off and shove it down your throat."

He hesitated, but then said, "Yes, boss."

I looked at the gun on the table and said, "Only one person runs this shit and it's me."

274

Chapter 30

I have to admit that it was starting to get to me. Every aspect of the "game" is challenging - except for the money part. I love the money, but spending most of my time looking over my shoulder is becoming exhausting. Sometimes, I wish I could do like that little girl - click my heels three times and go back to that moment before it all began, but it was too late for that now, because this wasn't Kansas and my name ain't Dorothy.

It's in my down-time, that I sometimes find myself regretting my career choice. It's not easy being a wanted man – wanted by your girls, wanted by other pimps, and wanted by the police. As I sat there, having a "crisis of consciousness", my thoughts were disturbed by the vibration of my phone against my crotch. Bottom was calling to check on things and to give me a status on today's receipts. We were about to wrap-up our call when she said, "We're shutting it down early tonight. The police are all over the place. Plus, the girls could use a little rest."

"That's fine with me...I think I'm going to call it a night too."

"Why? You're not feeling good?" she asked.

"Naw, I think it's just that I'm tired...you know when the weather changes, folks start to feel sluggish..."

"Believe me I know..."

I laughed. "What do you know about being sluggish?"

"Look...I work as hard as you...probably harder. Dealing with these bitches day-in and day-out, takes a toll on you..."

"I bet…"

"You know it does…that's why you left the job for me…"

"And I'm so grateful…"

"Yeah right…after the last girl check-in, I'm going to bed. I hate having to pick these girls up in the middle of the night…it's not safe out. It's some crazy people out there."

I laughed so hard, I almost hurt myself. "Says the crazy lady who just cut off a man's dick."

"That's 'work-product', Miller…I don't just run around cutting off dicks…"

"Well, speaking for all of the men in the world, we 'thank you'…" I laughed.

"Whatever…"

"Anyway…where is she at? I'll go and get her."

"Are you sure?"

"Sure…I'm out. I will drop her off on my way home."

"She's   at   our   place   on 22nd…Chinatown…you   know   that place?"

"Yep, I know the place."

"Yeah…she's going to be a while. She's servicing a preacher. You know how those motherfuckers are…have your ass tied-up all day…talking 'bout nothing."

Something snapped in me. "Did you say, preacher?"

"Yeah…you probably know him…you church folks all know each other…y'all run in the same circles…"

"Ummmmm…I gotta go, Bottom. Don't worry about the girl…I got her."

"Is everything okay?" she asked.

"Everything is just fine," I said, before hanging up. I didn't know what was happening to me, but anger rose up inside of me. Something about hearing that one

278

of my girls was servicing a man of God made me want to hurt somebody – mainly the Man of God. I don't know why, but it did. I drove over there so fast – slow-rolling through every red light and stop sign until I arrived at the hotel. I parked my car and ran inside because I wanted to catch them in the act. It's one thing to hear about preachers who sin, but it's another to witness it for yourself.

I knocked on the door like a motherfucker who was about to catch his girl cheating on him. My girl didn't answer, but the preacher did. "Who is it?" he asked.

Look at this motherfucker. "Open this door!" I demanded. My girl opened the door. They were finishing up. He had already paid her. "You answered that door like you live here."

"Naw, that was just out of habit," he said.

"Habit? The kind of habit that you developed being at home or the one that you developed from answering doors at the 'No-Tell' hotels and motels?"

"Look, I'mma just get out of here."

I stopped him and locked the door behind me. "Where are you going, Mr. Preacher?"

Curious, he asked, "How do you know that I'm a preacher?"

"You in my house with one of my girls...Daddy knows all of his girl's friends." I looked over to where she was standing. She smiled.

He looked down at his watch. "Boy, look at the time..." he stopped to yawn. "I gotta get up early tomorrow morning."

"Got some souls to save?" I asked.

"Hey...you know how we do..."

"No, why don't you tell me...better yet, let's have my girl tell me." I looked at her. "Did he save your soul tonight?"

She laughed so hard, she spit her gum clear across the room.

"What did y'all do tonight?" I asked.

She paused before speaking – not really sure if she should. In a soft voice she said, "We fucked…he gave me a blowjob…"

Shocked, I said, "He gave you a WHAT? He gave YOU a blowjob! Damn preacher…you dared to walk through the valley of the shadow of death?'" I paused and shook my head. "Damn, I wouldn't put my mouth on that and I pay for her to go to the clinic."

The pastor looked embarrassed.

I looked at the girl. "Damn…no offense, but that bowl has seen a lot of spoons…again, no offense."

She smiled.

"And you're going to go home and kiss your wife and kids with that mouth." I shook my head.

He dropped his head.

"Was that all?" I asked her.

In a soft voice she said, "He spanked me."

I smiled. "You are a freak...a preacher that likes a little S&M...wasn't no sparing the rod tonight, huh? Did you like it?"

He began to answer, but I interrupted him. "The question was for her." I looked in her direction. "Did you like it?"

She lifted her skirt to expose the welts on her legs. "It hurt a little."

"Did he pay you for that?"

"Yes," she said, pulling her skirt down.

I looked at him. The room was silent until he said, "You know...I think that this is going to be my last time..."

I leaned towards him and smacked him in the mouth. "Shut, your lying-freaky-praying-ass, up."

He grabbed his mouth. "I just want to go home."

I thought about this for a second before saying, "Why? When we're having so much fun."

"But I really need to go..."

"Sure, but let's play a game first."

He frowned. "A what?"

"A game...you like games...don't you, Mr. Preacher-man?"

He looked at me and realized the seriousness of this situation, so you could tell that he wanted to cooperate. "Yes...I love games."

"Good...my mama used to force us to read the Bible...I want to test my knowledge..." I looked over at the girl and said, "Cut that cord off of that lamp and hand it to me."

His eyes widened. "Wait...what?"

"You should know all of the answers to these questions...this shit is Bible Study 101...you'll be out of here in no time." I watched my girl remove a "blade" from her purse and with one swipe, she cut the cord. She handed it to me. I looped it around my hand and said, "I'm going to be Pat and you be Vanna..."

She smiled and began to prance around the room.

"Here are the rules of the game. I'm going to ask you some questions...for every wrong answer, I'm going to hit you...for every right answer...I'm going to hit you..."

"Wait...what?" he asked.

"Yeah, I know...it's one of those 'damned if you do, damned if you don't' kind of games."

Nervously, he looked around the room.

"Now, I want you to pull your pants down..."

"What?" he asked.

"You never had your ass-whipped before?" I paused. "Yeah...you look like a person who's been whooped a lot."

He began to beg. "Please....please...I promise...I will never do this again."

"Come on…this is going to be fun… matter of fact, I'm going to be nice. Since you hit her, I'm going to let her hit you."

"Oh my God…" he began.

"Don't call on Him now," I said, laughing.

"Jesus please…"

I placed my hand over my ear and pretended to listen to see if someone was coming. "I don't think they're coming."

"I will give you anything that you want…"

"Okay…What I want is your pants down."

"But…but…"

"You SAID that you would give me what I want and THAT'S what I want."

The preacher stood and slowly began to pull down his pants.

I smiled. "I love that…a man of his word…not God's word, but his word...Now, I'm going to need you to assume the position..." He placed his hands on the bed and stuck his ass in the air. "You sure that you've never played this before...you look like a natural."

He began to cry.

"Good boy...now...the first question... 'What did the Serpent temp Eve with in the Garden of Eden?'"

He looked at me and smiled; thinking that his freedom was only a few questions away. "That's easy...it was an apple."

I handed the girl the cord. "Nope...hit his ass."

He put his hands up. "Yes, it is...the serpent offered her an apple."

"Nope...there is no mention of an apple in the Book of Genesis and the type of fruit was never specified..." I turned to the young lady and said, "Vanna, what did he win?"

Her hand went up in the air and when the cord came down, he screamed like a girl.

"Aaaaaaaaaahhhhhh!!!!!" She swung so hard that I felt a breeze. He collapsed onto the bed and began to rub his ass.

I looked at the girl. "Dang…remind me not to piss you off."

She smiled.

"Jesus, please…Jesus, please….have mercy," he begged.

"Jesus is busy, but I'm here…how can I help you?"

The preacher cried.

"Now, the next question…who was the serpent?"

"The serpent was the Devil…" he replied.

I shook my head. "Unless you're reading the Bible backwards…the fall of Satan happened later…there is no mention of Him until then. Which makes you wonder about the 'whole-talking-snake-thing', doesn't it…?"

The preacher whimpered. "Hit him again."

She swung and he screamed again. I began to laugh. "Dude, you gon' need to get some bass in your voice if you don't want me to laugh at you."

He continued to whimper.

"Okay...Adam and Eve had several children...and those children had children...who were the mothers of Cain, Abel, and Seth's children?"

"Ummmmm...ummmm...Eve?"

"That's sick...hit his ass..."

"Wait!!!!!"

She swung again, so hard that this time she drew blood.

"First, according to the book that you read every Sunday...Adam and Eve were the first and the original people...they had children and in order for their children to have children, somebody had to have sex with a sister or a niece...and since we are all descendants of Adam and Eve and all of 'one blood'...you probably just fucked your sister."

The preacher couldn't hear me because he was crying so loud.

"Okay…okay…ummmmm…this is an easy one…"Is money the root of all evil?"

Whimpering, he said, "Yes…money is the root of all evil…"

"WRONG!!!! Hit his ass…" As she swung to hit him, I quoted the scripture. 'For the LOVE of money is a root of all kinds of evil…' 1 Timothy 6:10….it's the love…it's the love…"

He was crying uncontrollably. "It's almost over. Here's a good one…'What's the Sixth Commandment?"

Through tears, he said, "'Thou shalt not kill…"

I shook my head. *Sigh.* "Hit his ass again…"

"Noooooooo…wait!!!!!"

She swung and hit him again. "Ahhhhhhhhh!!!!"

"The Sixth Commandment is 'Thou shalt not murder'...not kill...two different things...If you shoot a man who has a gun pointing at you...and to defend yourself, you take his life...that's killing, but if you shoot an unarmed man...that's murder... see the difference?"

The preacher continued to whimper.

I saw the blood dripping from the cord. "Okay...here's the last one...True or False...is there a scripture that says, 'Spare the rod, and spoil the child?'"

Trying to block his ass from another blow, he said, "No...the scripture actually reads...'Whoever spares the rod hates their children, but the one who loves their children is careful to discipline them.'"

The girl looked at me; waiting for my instruction.

"Bruh...you got that right...I'm so proud of you...I was starting to worry about you for a minute..."

The preacher began to smile. "Thank you…"

"Hit is ass…"

"NOOOOOOO WAIT!!!!" he yelled, before she swung again.

"I told you the rules before we started…if nothing else…I'm a man of my word."

Slowly, he stood to pull up his pants. He grimaced from the pain. "Thank you…I promise…I'm never going to do this again."

"Last thing…what are the wages of sin?"

"I thought that we were done…"

"We are…but humor me…"

"Death," he mumbled.

I smiled. "Look at you…you got another one right…"

"Are you going to hit me again?"

"No, not this time…" I pointed my gun at him.

With his hands in the air, he said, "NOOOOOOO WAIT!!!"

I pulled the trigger. *Bang!!!* The bullet hit him in the chest. The girl grabbed her ears. The preacher's eyes widened and when his body realized that he'd just got shot, he closed them before his body went limp and fell onto the floor. I stared at him as the smell of gun powder filled the room. The girl looked at me – afraid to say anything. I smiled, and said, "He should have saw that coming."

Chapter 31

The seasons were starting to change. I loved the colors of autumn, but I hated the cool air. We had to start taking it all indoors. The girls liked walking the tracks, but it's hard to be sexy when you're freezing your ass off. Luckily, we had a lucrative online business too. The good thing about marketing sex online is that a john can order a pizza and some pussy without even getting out of his bed. The problem with the internet is that you never know who's going to answer the door.

We had this one trick who ordered the services of one of my girls online.

Usually, the prices have to go up a little to cover service and maintenance fees for using the internet, but the services don't change. Johns seem to think that they are entitled to a little something "extra" because they were forced to pay a convenience fee, but that's not how it works.

Now, I've seen this trick before. He's requested services from the same girl on several occasions, so he wasn't unfamiliar with the rules, but tonight I get a call from Bottom because the trick didn't want to act right. I didn't get the whole story, because you have to be careful about what you say over the phone, so when she called me and said that he wanted to play in the rain without a raincoat, I knew exactly what she was talking about.

"I'm on my way," I said, before hanging up.

When I arrived at the hotel, I went to the room and noticed that the door was slightly open. I walked in to find my girl, arguing with the john. She looked up at me, but the john was unaware that I'd entered the room.

"You need to pay me...you have taken-up thirty minutes of my time. I need to get paid," I heard her say.

"We go bareback or I go home," he said.

"No," she insisted. "I don't know you," she said.

The trick began laughing. "How many times have you sucked my dick or fucked me? And now, you need to know me? Bitch, you got a lot of damn nerve." He continued laughing.

She frowned. "All I'm saying is...I have to protect myself..."

He interrupted her. "YOU ARE A WHORE!!!!!"

"So," she said, turning to get her purse. "There are too many diseases out there."

"You are a disease...Bitch, if you don't take your fucking clothes off..." Suddenly, the trick stood up, walked over to her, balled-up his fist, and then swung. He swung so hard that the girl went flying against the wall. I pulled my gun out, walked up behind him, grabbed him by his shirt, and hit him with the butt of my gun. I looked at the girl and said, "Turn the TV up."

She scrambled to her feet and ran over to the TV.

"Who the fuck are you?" he asked, grabbing the back of his head.

"Don't matter..."

"You better get out of here and mind your own business..."

"Her business is my business..."

"What is this? A shakedown? I should have known..."

"No, I'm here to give you what you want."

"You can't give me shit..."

"Yes, I can...I heard that you wanted it raw...I'm here to give it to you raw."

"I ain't fucking no man…"

"Me neither…"

He threw his hands in the air. "Okay…okay…there has clearly been some confusion…you think that I'm gay. I'm sorry, but I'm not…"

I started to laugh. "You flatter yourself…I wouldn't give you any of this dick…even if I had a spare one…"

"Well, then…look, I'm sorry," he said. "Let me just get out of here."

I looked at him and then hit him again. "You said that you want it bareback…then bareback is what you're going to get. Turn your bitch-ass over and spread 'em." I grabbed him and flipped him onto his stomach.

"Huh??" he asked, turning to look at me and trying to protect his butthole.

"If you flip back over again, I'm going to kill you," I said.

Looking at my gun, he said, "You're going to kill me for hitting a hoe?" he asked.

"No one has to die...today...I want to make sure that you get what you asked for...the rest depends on you. Now, enough foreplay...let's get this over with..." I said, looking over at the girl. "Help me with his pants."

Holding her face, she walked towards me. The side of her face was swollen. I looked at him and said, "You're going to pay extra for that."

"Please...please...don't kill me...Look in my wallet...you can have it all. There's at least a thousand dollars in there," he said, pleadingly.

"No...no...I run an honest business...we don't take any money until services are rendered."

The girl unbuckled and unzipped his pants. She pulled his pants down around his knees. I forced him on all fours, looked at her, and said, "Spit on this."

She smiled and then spit on the barrel of the gun. I turned back to him. "If you sneeze, cough, scream, fart, look at me hard, any sudden moves, and that's your ass…I mean that literally…."

He interrupted me. "The gun??? You're going to use the gun?"

"You have something else in mind?"

He thought about it for a second and said, "No…"

"Then shut the fuck up…" I handed the girl the gun. She took it and slid the cold, hard, barrel of my gun up his ass. He let out a "yelp" and started to squirm. "It's a little tight and painful in the beginning, but once that ass loosens up, you're going to thank me."

"Okay…" he whimpered.

"Is it good?"

"Huh?" he asked.

"Tell her how good it feels…"

"Huh?" he asked, again.

"You don't want to hurt her feelings…now, tell her how good it feels…"

The man began to cry. "It…it…it feels good."

The girl smiled. She was really enjoying herself. She slid the gun in and out – forcing it deeper and deeper into his ass until all you could see was the handle.

"Tell her how much you like it."

Through tears, he said, "I like it…"

"You're going to hurt her feelings…"

She shoved it in harder. "I LOVE IT! I…LOVE…IT!!!"

"Good boy…"

Blood began to stain his boxers. She continued until suddenly, he "came". He moaned a little and then his body relaxed and went limp. She pulled the barrel out and handed the gun to me.

He climbed onto the bed, into the fetal position, and mumbled, "Thank you."

"Ahhhhhhh…you're welcome…see…I told you that you would like it…just took a little convincing…" I looked at my gun and said, "Now, open your mouth and get this shit off of my gun." Through tears, he slowly opened his mouth and began to suck the barrel of my gun. I looked at the girl, who was now smiling, as she emptied his wallet.

I looked back down at him. "Same time next week?"

The man nodded, "Yes."

"This is a referral business…don't forget to tell your friends," I said, before leaving the room.

He didn't respond.

We left the room and locked the door behind us.

302

Chapter 32

This time of the year is hard. People hate working during the holidays - even prostitutes and pimps. While most folks heard, "Ho, ho, ho," I was knee-deep in "Hoe, hoe, hoes" and I was tired. I needed a break. This time of the year, brings out the worst in people. I never understood how we could go from a holiday where we give thanks for all of the things that we have, just to turn around on "His birthday", and go buy shit that we don't need. Watching the news during the holidays is better than watching Pay-per-view. It is so entertaining watching people kick each other's ass while preparing to celebrate Christ's birthday.

It gets crazy in my world too. Bottom has this one client who treats himself to a little "strange" every year for Christmas. She used to tell me about all of the funny shit that he used to do and the crazy shit that she used to do to him, but I didn't believe her. I used to laugh and blow-it off, because sometimes Bottom's imagination can get the best of her. She has a unique way of stretching the truth, but after seeing what I saw, I will never doubt her again.

One night, Bottom needed to make a "drop", but was in the middle of a session, so I agreed to pick it up on my way to my mama's house for dinner. I didn't mind doing it, because I was in the "festive" mood.

I was walking down the hall of the hotel, when I heard a barking sound. As I approached the door, I heard it again. *Woof, Woof, Woof!* I knocked on the door. Next, I heard Bottom say, "Heel."

She opened the door. She was handing me the bag when I looked down at her other hand to find a leash dangling from it. She saw the look on my face. Slowly, I pushed the door back to see what it was attached to, to find a grown-man on the other end of it. I looked up at her and she smiled.

I was turning to walk away when she said, "Don't leave…I want you to meet my pet."

Bottom knew that I didn't want to be a part of this crazy shit, but when she said that, the man crawled over to me and sat at my feet. "You have to rub his head," she said, fighting back laughter.

I looked at her and then down at him. He was panting, anxiously. Now, NORMALLY, no man is going to rub another man's head unless that's something that he's into, but he looked up at me with the saddest "puppy-dog" eyes and I did it. I rubbed his head. That made him so happy that he rolled over so that I could rub his stomach, but I wasn't doing that shit. He can pretend to be a dog, but I was still a man, so I said, "Heel" and he quickly returned to all fours.

After I rubbed his head, I rubbed my hands on my shirt like doing that was going to wipe away the experience.

"Come on in and sit for a moment. We were about to wrap this up," she said.

I looked around to make sure that no one was around to see me join them. As we sat and talked about "nothing", I noticed that he followed her every command - sit, kneel, roll-over, and when he did what he was told, she gave him a treat. She rolled a ball and he chased it all around the room – all of this, he did, while we talked. It was the strangest thing that I'd ever seen. After a while of playing, I noticed that he was crawling around the room, sniffing things. "Bottom, it looks like your dog needs to go for a walk." Now, mind you, I was joking when I said that, but then she walked over and whispered in my ear, "It's a part of the game." She sat back down as he lifted his leg and pissed all over the floor.

She walked up to him and shouted, "Bad dog…bad dog…" She slapped him on the nose and he loved it.

Suddenly, she walked over to her bag and removed a black belt with a dildo strapped to it. She put it on. Her pet climbed-up on the bed and rested on all fours. She poured lubricant on the tip of it and said, "You might not want to see this."

I stood and said, "Yeah…my mama's waiting on me."

"Tell her that I said 'Merry Christmas,'" she said, as she entered him.

The man howled.

"Ummmmmm, sure…I'll tell her," I said, as I tried to forget what'd just happened.

308

Chapter 33

Things were slowing down. That's the interesting thing about this business, it's all about supply and demand, but when there's more supply than demand, you have to start considering other means of revenue. When you saturate a community with ass, drugs, liquor stores, clubs, churches, and beauty supply stores – it can start to make a brother's pockets thin, but there's only so many ways to keep your pockets 'fat' in a Black community. Now, back in the day, you could control demand by taking out the other "pimps," but you can't just run around eliminating the competition. So I was considering other ventures.

One of our regular tricks, who was a big-time drug dealer, who only wanted to party with clean honest girls, was trying to hook me up. Every-time, he was done "tricking", he would talk to me about getting into the drug game and every time, my answer was, "No." You see, being a pimp was easy, because all of the work is done by someone else, but dealing drugs would force me into a world that my father escaped from and one that took the life of my brother.

But after much convincing and wearing me down, he hooked me up with someone who got me into the "game." I received my "drug dealer's starter kit" and I was on my way. I started out slow. At first, I was dealing locally, but after word got out about my product, I had yuppies skateboarding from the suburbs for my shit. When their buzz vanished, and life came back to kick them in the ass, I was right here waiting for them, so that they could give me some more of their money.

≈

The drug game is serious business, and every once in a while, you will find yourself dealing with some crazy random shit. The shit would be so crazy that even the hardest motherfucker in the world would be at a loss for words. This one time, I had to meet a guy to discuss some business. I was looking to buy some product from him. We're talking heavy weight and a lot of money, so before deciding to go over there, I thought that it would be a good idea to take Money with me for protection. Because of the unpredictable nature of the drug game - shit can go sour fast, so you need to be prepared.

All the way to the meeting, Money and I discussed what we were going to do because I wanted to keep things "fluid" – in and out. And I have to admit, I was a little nervous, because I wasn't meeting no regular dealer. This guy has been in the game for a long time. He had a reputation on the streets as being hardcore. He'd just got out of prison after doing time for a murder that he'd committed, so I was very apprehensive about meeting him.

Now, let me preface the rest of this story by saying this…in this business, you have to understand the mentality of the people that you're dealing with. Men who serve time in State prison are accustomed to watching TV without sound. Not because they want to, but the State didn't have enough headphones to go around. The ones that they had, many were broken, so most of the time the inmates, spent years, just staring at the TV screen. Now, imagine a person who has been conditioned to stare at a TV screen with no sound for eighteen years. That ain't no regular motherfucker.

So when I walked in, I looked around and I noticed that he had the TV on, but the volume had been turned off. Now, you would think that a man who has been forced to live in silence for eighteen years would want to hear the voices of other people, but he didn't. That's what conditioning does or what being institutionalized does to a human being. He had access to sound, but denied himself of it, because he'd been trained to live without it. Even though he was physically free, he was still a prisoner in his own mind. So when I saw it, I didn't think a lot about it, until I saw what was playing on the screen. He was watching porno. Now, I like to watch porn like the next man, but a lot of what keeps me interested, is the moaning, screaming, and the heavy breathing. Clearly, he didn't need the sound effects, but most people do. But, that's not the crazy or the random part.

We also noticed that he had one of his boys there too – to provide protection; which was cool. He didn't inquire about my boy and I didn't inquire about his, because, again, I was keeping it fluid. We were all sitting around, discussing business, and getting into the dollars and cents of things, while the movie was still playing in the background. Then, out of the blue, his boy shouted, "DAMN, look at how big his dick is!!! Do you see how big his dick is?"

What the fuck did he just say? Now, this may not seem weird to a lot of people, but when four men are having a meeting about drugs and one of them interrupts the meeting to discuss another man's dick, that's a problem. Before I got there, I'd prepared for certain possibilities. I'd prepared for the possibility of getting shot. I'd prepared for the possibility of getting robbed. I'd even prepared for the possibility of getting locked-up, but what I did not prepare for was a motherfucker falling out of the "closet" in the middle of a drug deal. *NEVER.*

Suddenly, things became uncomfortable. The room fell silent. We stopped and stared at him. My 'hook-up' was so embarrassed by his boy's outburst that he suggested that we end the meeting and talk at a later time.

I knew that I had to get out of there. When me and Money got outside, he looked at me and said, "What the hell was that?"

I shook my head and said, "Man, I don't know, but I need to go and find me some pussy after that."

"Me too," he said. "How about we call it a day?"

"Yeah, let's do that," I said, looking over my shoulder.

Chapter 34

So, I had it all. Business was so good I could have setup a drive-thru window – one window for sex and another for drugs - your regular "One-stop Shop." Anything you needed to make you feel good, I had it and it was the best that the "Chi" had to offer. I was sitting on money. I had so much of it that I moved my family out of the "hood" and into the "burbs". I could have moved my business out there, but doing business in small communities can be very hazardous. People in smaller communities don't want to see a hoe or a drug dealer standing on their corners. They take Neighborhood Watch very seriously and will call the police on you if you look at them wrong. Not only that, and this may sound terrible, but I didn't want to see that shit either. That's why most pimps work in the city and live in the suburbs. After looking at that degradation all day, you want a peaceful "clean" place to rest your head. Being a criminal, is like being forced to stand in shit all day. People would like to make you think that you'd get used to the smell, but if you know what it's like to smell fresh air, smelling shit will start to get on your nerves. Also, crime-rates are lower in the suburbs and there's nothing that a criminal loves more than living in a crime-free community.

When my parents asked me how I made the money that I used to move them out of the neighborhood, I told them that I won the lottery. It was easier to convince them that I won the money on a "scratch-off", then by working at a job that paid me a high salary. My father knew that it was bullshit, but my mother never questioned it, because to hear the truth, would mean that she would have to accept it or move back to the "hood" and she wasn't going to do that. My mama was real good at avoiding and not accepting the truth. She knew that I didn't have no damn job and she knew damn well that I didn't win the lottery, but her selective blindness allowed her to have something that made her look good to those church folks that she was trying to impress every Sunday. It was funny watching Mrs. "I am Blind, and Wanna Stay That Way," pick out the furniture for her new home. When I purchased a Benz for them, she didn't ask not one question.

My dad asked, "Is it stolen?"

I said, "No."

"Is it paid for?" he asked.

"Yes," I replied.

"That's all that I want to know," he said, taking the keys.

My mama on the other hand, said, "God works in mysterious ways…huh, son?"

I looked at her and said, "Yep...and imagine what He'll think of you when he sees you riding around in that car? I bet He'll say, 'Ooooooooweeeee, look at Sis. Miller driving around in that blessing that I bestowed upon her."

She faked a smile because she knew that I was full of shit, but admitting it wouldn't allow her butt-cheeks to enjoy those nappa-leather heated seats.

She loved inviting the church ladies to her home for tea. She enjoyed flaunting her new home in their faces. Even though, she hated most of the women in the church, she loved showing them how good God is, how prayer works, and how blessed she was. If only those women knew the truth – that I was the one doing all of the "blessing."

The cool thing is that now, I didn't have to worry about her busting into my room anymore. This was my house and she had to follow my rules.

Chapter 35

When I made a half of million, I poured it out all over my bed and told my boys to come in the room to see it. They stood at the door for several minutes before moving. They were in shock. I smiled and said, "Come on in…it's cool." They walked in, but they seemed confused as to what to do next, so I said, "It's fine…go ahead."

They looked at each other and then they both ran and jumped on the bed, throwing money up into the air – something that we've only seen done in the movies. They were so happy.

"Some of this belongs to you," I smiled and said.

They stopped and said, "What?"

"Yeah...I want to share it with you."

"Are you serious?" Hustle asked.

"Yes, I'm serious, so Money you can finally take your mama to get a pedicure...cause her feet are jacked up," I joked.

"Why you gotta talk about my mama?" he asked.

"Cause everybody talks about your mama..."

We laughed.

"Some of this is ours? But you already pay us," Hustle said.

I answered. "Yeah, I want you to know that I appreciate what y'all do for me, so I'm going to give you a little extra...maybe you can go on a trip...Money you can buy your mama some new teeth."

Money shouted, "Now, it's her teeth…fuck you, man."

"Naw, I don't 'swing' that way, but thanks for the offer." I laughed and continued. "What's mine is yours."

Hustle asked, "What's yours is ours?"

I confirmed. "Yeah, what's mine is yours."

He smiled.

I watched them handle the money. What they didn't realize is that they were being tested. They watched all of my comings and goings. I would be a fool to assume that they didn't know what I was bringing in. Money would turn a person that you once called your boy into a person who would kill you in a heartbeat.

So I watched them as they counted and rolled around in my money – watched their eyes and wondered what they were really thinking. As the cold steel of my gun pressed against my skin, I wondered which one of them would turn on me first, but they seemed cool – at least, for now.

I've learned a very important lesson being in this business. "Do unto others as you have them do unto you…" You treat people well and they will do the same to you. So the next morning, I kept my word. I gave my boys $30,000 each. My thinking behind this gift was that if they feel like I valued them then I won't have to worry about waking up with a knife in my back.

Money was so shocked and happy that he began to cry.

"Man, I don't know what to say," he said, wiping tears from his eyes.

"You don't have to say anything…" I said.

"No man…I don't think you know or understand how much this means to me…"

"The tears say it all…"

He wiped his face. "Anything…I mean anything…just ask…and it's done."

I smiled. "Thanks man."

"I mean that shit…anything…anytime."

"That's good to know…"

He smiled as he looked at the gift. "Man, look at you…I don't know how you did it…"

I laughed. "My last name should be O'Malley, 'cause I got the 'Luck of the Irish' on my side…except that my Black ass ain't Irish." Money and I were laughing, but I noticed that Hustle was unusually quiet. I looked over to find him staring at me.

"What's going on Hustle?"

He didn't respond.

Money looked at him and screamed, "HUSTLE!!!!"

He finally blinked. He didn't respond at first. It was like he was searching for something to say. Then, suddenly, he looked at me and said, "We good." But I could tell that something else was going on with him. What, exactly? I didn't know, but it didn't look good.

≈

There were moments when he did shit that really got on my nerves. Now, I know that living with people can be hard and living with all men can, at times, be harder, but sometimes, I felt like he went out of his way to piss me off. Every day, I had to say something to him about something. He was always leaving stuff on, leaving stuff out, or not replacing stuff. I didn't want to say anything to him because then, I would look like the bitch, and no man wants to do that.

And I wasn't used to nasty shit. I was raised by my mother and grandmother, I learned to keep things clean. We were taught that "Cleanliness is next to Godliness." We didn't eat until we cleaned our rooms. We didn't go outside until we cleaned our rooms. And because there were women in the house, the bathroom had to be left spotless and the "top" of the toilet seat had to be left up. My mother had a strange habit of using the bathroom at night without the light on. If she ended-up putting her ass on the toilet-lid and not on the toilet seat, all hell was going to break loose, and that was minor. Well, there's nothing minor about thinking that the top is up, you start pissing only to realize that it is down, and you end-up pissing all over the floor, but you get my point.

So one day, I came home after a long day of hustling. I was looking forward to putting my ass on my own toilet. This may sound cliché, but it's true. "A man's home is his castle" and his toilet is his throne. After a long day, we look forward to putting our asses on our own toilets. We like to read a magazine, drink a cup of tea, watch a little TV on our phones, and get caught-up on current events. It is our time to gather ourselves and our thoughts before dealing with the shit that is waiting for us on the other side of the door.

When I walked in, I didn't even speak to them, I walked right passed them and went straight into the bathroom, but I was stopped in my tracks by a toilet full of shit.

"WHO IN THE HELL…?" I asked, dancing in the middle of the floor. I walked back into the living room where they were playing video games. I looked at Money.

"Man, don't look at me. I haven't been to the bathroom all day," he said.

I looked over at Hustle.

He smiled. "My bad, Bruh…I must have forgot," he said, putting down the remote control.

"How do you forget to flush the damn toilet?" I asked, still dancing. "You shit, you wipe your ass, and you flush the toilet…how do you mess that up?"

He stopped and looked at me. "Calm down before you shit on yourself." He turned and continued down the hall.

Holding my 'shit', I said, "Don't tell me what to do in my house. I don't want to walk in here and see a toilet full of shit. I don't want to see piss, ass crumbs, sweaty balls' streaks or pieces of toilet paper on the seat, shit stains on the toilet bowl, or shit in my toilet. We are not fucking animals. Now, clean that toilet and hurry the hell up."

"Get one of the hoes to clean it," he said, flushing the toilet.

"They are not supposed to clean-up behind your grown nasty ass," I said. "What I look like making them clean your shit? They are not your mama."

He frowned and said, "They too good to clean toilets?"

I stopped dancing and became extremely serious. "Clean the damn toilet and don't question me about my girls. They got one job...you got one job...and right now, that job includes cleaning this damn toilet."

He stopped and looked me up and down. His eyes grew dark. He looked like he wanted to do something. I wasn't sure what he wanted to do, but at that moment, I wasn't above whooping his ass. A man standing in the middle of the floor, with his butt-cheeks clenched, trying to hold his shit, is probably capable of killing a motherfucker. I was ready to do it too, but then he finally asked, "Where's the cleanser?"

I unclenched my 'cheeks' and said, "Under the sink."

When he was done, he bumped me as he walked out.

"Is there a problem?"

"No," he said, smiling.

As soon as he walked away, I sat down to relieve myself. I closed my eyes because it felt so good to be home. Then suddenly the bathroom door opened. I opened my eyes to find Hustle standing in the door.

"Ummmmm, can I help you?"

"We're leaving…" he said.

"You could have said that shit on the other side of the door," I said, frowning.

"I could have, but I didn't…" He pause for a moment and stared at me before closing the door.

≈

After that, things were tense between us. I know that it may sound stupid, but as I look back on it, I should have broken ties with him then. When people show you their 'crazy', you have to believe it, but who walks away from a life-long friend over silly shit like bathroom etiquette? So I tried to put it behind us. Now, I wish that I hadn't.

Chapter 36

We were hanging-out, playing video games, when there was a knock at the door. When I first looked out, I didn't see anyone standing there, but as I began to walk away, there was another knock at the door. Again, I looked out, but this time there was a pipe-head, "tweeking," on my front porch. I grabbed my gun and slowly opened the door. "What do you need?" I asked, looking around and making sure that she hadn't brought any "company" with her.

"You selling?" she asked.

I took inventory of her. She was a mess. Her hair was matted, her clothes were dirty, and she smelled like shit. She could have been a decoy, but no one could fake this stench. "You buying?"

"Do you have any primo?" she asked, scratching her arms.

"How much do you need?" I asked.

She held-up one finger.

"Okay, where's your money?" I asked, because something about her was "off". She looked like a "snatch and run". I wasn't in the mood for chasing a hype. If a hype gets a hold of your stuff, you might as well say, "Goodbye" to it, because those motherfuckers can run.

After staring at me for a few minutes, she finally confessed. "Look...I don't have any money."

I knew it. "Stop wasting my time," I said, trying to close the door.

She stuck her foot inside of the door. "Wait...please...don't do that...look, look, look...I was wondering...maybe I could work it off."

"What do you think this is?"

"Look…Look…I need it so bad," she begged. "I will do anything."

"You have to pay to play…now, move your foot before I cut it off…"

"Please…please…" she begged.

Hustle must have heard what was going on. He walked up to the door. "You need me to take care of this?"

"Naw, I got it…" Before I could say anything else, Hustle had grabbed the girl by her hair.

"Please…let me go…let me go…" she pled.

"Hustle, what are you doing? Let her go…"

"You need to make an example out of these roaches," he said. "They need to know that you ain't running no charity."

"Oh my God…I'm sorry…I won't do it again…I promise," she said, trying to get his hand out of her hair.

335

Still holding her by the head, he said, "Every time, you think of running game on a brotha…choose another brotha…you hear me?"

"Yes…yes…" she said.

He let her go and walked passed me. She stood, wiped her face, and began to walk down the driveway. I closed the door and walked into the living room where Hustle was sitting. I walked up and smacked him in the back of his head.

"Damn…why did you do that?"

"I told you that I had it."

Rubbing his head, he said, "You pay me to protect you."

"I don't need protection from a hype…"

"Shiiiittttt…those are the motherfuckers you need protection from. That bitch is desperate…she would have offered you some head in exchange for a bag, and right when you start to cum…right when your defenses are down, that bitch will cut your throat…then the police will find you with a dumbass look on your face and your pants wrapped around your ankles."

"That wasn't going to happen…I had the shit…"

"Yeah…while you were running your mouth. You know how many people get stabbed in the middle of a conversation? She ain't got no money, close the damn door…"

Money paused the game and said, "You have to be tough on them, Boss…"

"Finally, he speaks…"

Money continued. "I'm just saying…be nice to their asses and the next thing you know, they are following you around like a stray alley cat…"

I was about to respond when there was another knock on the door. I opened it to find her standing back on my porch.

"Please, please…beat my ass…whatever you have to do…the pain will feel better than what I'm feeling right now."

I sighed. "And how do you plan to work it off?"

"I can…I can…I can give you some head," she said, through teeth that hadn't been brushed in weeks.

"TOLD YOU!!!!!" Hustle shouted from across the room.

"I don't need my dick sucked." I looked over her shoulder. My door had been open for too long. I wanted to make sure that we weren't drawing any attention to ourselves.

She grabbed my hand. "I know, but…but…I'm begging you. I'm in so much pain. I'm dying on the inside. Please….PLEASE…"

Before I could say anything else, she was on her knees and pulling at my zipper. I reached down to stop her when she looked up at me, her eyes were full of tears, but behind those tears were the most beautiful eyes that I'd ever seen. I made her stand up. I signaled for my boys to come and remove her, when suddenly I looked into her eyes, again, and saw it - something that I've never seen in the eyes of a 'hype' before. I saw life, where in others, I only saw death. They were pulling her away, when she began to beg again. "Please…I'm begging you."

"Bring her over here, so that I can look at her." They pulled her close. I examined her.

I thought about it for a second and then said, "I can make you feel better."

"You're going to fix me up?" she asked.

I smiled and said, "Yep…fix you right up." I looked at Hustle and said, "Take her to the back."

As she walked down the hall, she kept looking over her shoulder at us. Once we all entered the room, she said, "Where's the drugs?"

Hustle reached into his pocket. I looked at him and said, "Put that up."

Hustle waved the bag in her face. She tried grabbing it like a rabbit chasing a carrot. Hustle laughed, amused by her desperation.

"I said, 'Put that shit up.'"

He stopped. "Sure, Boss." He turned and looked at her. "Now…if you still want to work it off…"

"Get out and tell Bottom that I need her."

He smiled and said, "Sure…" While still holding the bag in his hand, Hustle grabbed his crotch and slowly walked out of the room.

I turned and looked at her. Suspiciously, she looked back.

"What the hell is this?"

"We're waiting on a friend."

"That friend got drugs?"

"No, she got something better."

"She got something better? I can't wait to see what she got…" She smiled. "I hope she hurries up."

"Oh…she'll be here soon."

While we waited, we didn't speak. She rocked back and forth while talking to herself. I watched her. From the look of her, she didn't look like she had anywhere to go. She was a throwaway. Families didn't care about them and the city wanted them to disappear. They were a stain on the city's beautiful skyline, so if one of them came-up missing no one would care.

Suddenly, I heard my door open. I listened as her heels clicked all the way down the hall. She walked into the room. I nodded for her to come towards me. She leaned in. After I whispered in her ear, she turned and left the room. Seconds later, Money and Hustle walked into the room. "Take her," Bottom said.

"Take me where? Wait...what the fuck are you doing?" They grabbed her and began to drag her down the hall towards the bathroom. She struggled. "What are you doing? What the fuck are you doing?"

When they were in the bathroom, Hustle tried to remove her clothes, "No

341

way…don't touch me…" she began fighting him. "Get him off of me."

"Get off of her and let Bottom handle this," I instructed.

"Who the fuck is Bottom?" she asked, frantically.

Bottom looked at her and said, "Before the night is over, you're going to know all about her…don't worry."

She became so hysterical that I had to promise her a "bag" if she would quiet down, and climb into the shower.

"No…keep your drugs," she insisted.

We all stopped and stared at her. "What kind of freaky sick shit do y'all have going on here?"

Bottom spoke. "Bitch, you stink. You should be knocking us down trying to get to some damn soap and water."

"No, I want out of here," she said, trying to push passed us.

I looked at Bottom. "Take care of this."

Me, Money, and Hustle walked out of the room and closed the door. We heard them struggle for a minute, she screamed a couple of times, and then there was nothing, but silence. Moments later, we heard the water running, then thirty minutes later, the water stopped. Suddenly, we heard another struggle, she screamed again, and then there was silence. The bathroom door opened. She yelled down the hall, "Can I get some help with this?"

Money and Hustle walked down the hall. When they came out of the bathroom, they were carrying a wet-limp body. "Is she dead?" I asked.

"Naw," Bottom said as she dried her hands. "The bitch just needed a nap."

Money looked at me and said, "What do you want us to do with her?"

"Shiiiittt, I have a few ideas," Hustle said.

I ignored him. "Take her to the room."

They laid her down in the bed and then locked the door.

We all walked to the front of the house. I sat down across from them. Bottom spoke first. "Ummmm…what was that all about?"

"Nothing…" I said.

"Are you aware that you have an unconscious naked girl in the room?"

"Yes, I am…"

"Ummmmmm…do she owe you money?"

"Nope…"

"Ummmmm…did she steal anything?"

"Nope…"

"Ummmmm…she gon' be a hoe?"

"Not sure, yet…"

"Okay…I give…so why is there a strange naked…unconscious girl in the house?"

"She has nice eyes…" I said.

There was a moment of silence before the room erupted in laughter.

"Da fuck, Miller? What? She has nice eyes?" Money asked.

"Look…I know that you don't understand."

"You damn, right…" Bottom said. "The fuck…you kidnapped a motherfucker cause she got nice eyes? What kind of crazy shit is that?"

I listened to them.

She continued. "That bitch is going to wake-up and scream 'Holy Hell!!!'"

"I'm not worried about that…"

"Really…you ain't worried? That's beautiful…glad you ain't worried. I told you that you have to stop doing this shit so close to home," she said. "Now, we gon' all go to jail cause she got nice eyes."

"Look…go and pick up some clothes and soup and I will take care of the rest."

"I'm going to get your ass some petroleum jelly and one of those 'Bump and Grind' CDs…'cause you gon' need it when Bubba, the Booty-Bandit, comes to pop your cherry."

"I got this…ain't nobody popping nothing."

"I hope so," she said, grabbing her purse and walking out of the house. "Cause I'm too cute for jail…"

"Says you…" Hustle said.

"Fuck you, you dirty bastard…" she said.

"Fuck you, you nasty hoe…" he retorted.

While they argued, Money looked at me and asked, "We okay?"

"We're good." I turned and looked at Hustle who was staring down the hall. "We good, Hustle?"

He didn't answer. He just stared down the hall.

That night, we were awakened to the sound of someone trying to kick a door down. I knew where the sound was coming from, so before going to the room, I called Bottom.

Groggily, she said, "I'm on my way."

Thirty minutes later, she walked into the house. "So I take it that she woke-up, found that her dirt and funk was missing, and she went crazy."

"Yeah...she's not happy."

Bottom went into the kitchen and warmed-up a can of soup. "I hope you know what you're doing."

I didn't respond. As we walked down the hall, Hustle yelled, "You better shut that bitch up before I shut her up."

I opened the door to his room and looked at him. He threw the blankets over his head and went back to sleep.

347

Bottom and I unlocked the door and entered the room. Bottom threw the clothes at her. "Put this on and shut up."

"I won't…now, give me my old clothes so that I can get out of here."

Bottom looked at me. "Hold this bowl…looks like someone wants to go back to sleep."

The girl stopped fighting and proceeded to put on the clothes.

"I thought so…"

Bottom tried to feed her. She filled her mouth with food and spit it in Bottom's face. Bottom put the bowl down and slapped her. As she wiped the noodles and pieces of chicken out of her eyes, she said, "Let's get an understanding…the first time, I slap you…the second time, I cut your face up so bad, you gon' need a new driver's license photo, cause motherfuckers ain't gon' be able to recognize you…you understand?"

She nodded, "Yes."

Bottom lifted the spoon again. The girl took the food and swallowed.

"Good girl…" she said, dipping the spoon back into the bowl.

"Look…I'll finish it," I said, taking the bowl from her.

Bottom walked out wiping her face and mumbling under her breath.

I dipped the spoon into the bowl. "Are you going to finish this?"

"Please…I just want to go home?"

I handed her the spoon and bowl. "Where is home?"

She dipped the spoon into the bowl and said, "I don't have one."

"Well, let's make a deal. You finish this soup, get some rest, and let's talk in the morning?"

"Why are you doing this?"

"You said that you wanted me to help you, so I'm going to help you."

"Okay, I will stay the night, but I really need 'something' or I'm not going to be able to get through the night."

"You'll be fine…I'll check back on you…"

"No, really…I can't do this…"

I looked at her. Under all of that filth was a beautiful woman. I would have told her that, but my words would have fallen on deaf ears. The only thing she wanted was some drugs, but she wouldn't be getting any of that tonight.

"You get some rest. Let's talk in the morning?"

"You can't do this. This is kidnapping. You can go to jail," she protested.

"That's true, but I don't think anyone is looking for you."

She turned to look away.

"Now, I'll be back. I promise. I'm going to have some boys over in a little bit. Unless you want to be tricked-out, I'd

350

advise you to keep it down. I'll check on you later."

She never turned to look at me. As I exited the room, I thought about something that my daddy once said to me. "Son, some of the most beautiful things are found in some of the darkest places." There was a reason why this young lady knocked on my door and I wanted to know why.

Chapter 37

The next three days were hard for her. Each day, she threw-up, screamed, and cried.

"Why are y'all doing this to me?" she asked, as I handed her a bowl of soup. "I asked you a question...why are you doing this to me?"

I didn't answer. I just closed the door. When I walked back into the living room, Money looked at me and asked, "Why are you doing this?"

I decided to tell him. I needed to trust someone. I looked around to make sure that we were alone before answering.

"Money…have you ever looked at someone and just knew that they had something important to give to you?"

He looked down the hall and said, "The only thing she looks like she has to give are crabs…"

I shook my head and said, "No Money…I mean…sometimes, you do so much inhumane shit, that something or someone walks in your life, and makes you want to be human again…you know what I mean?"

"Man, I don't even think you know what you mean…"

"Okay…we sell drugs, right?"

Curious, he said, "Ummmmm, yeah…"

"Usually when they come to get the shit, we just take the money and keep it moving, but every once in a while…that one hype walks up to you and…"

"And you want to kidnap them, give them a bath, and then force them to get clean?" He asked, with a raised eyebrow.

I smiled. "Yeah…"

He frowned and then said, "Are you smoking any of that shit?"

"No…of course not…look at it this way…this is our way of giving back…"

"By cleaning-up our customers…you wanna go out of business Trey the Saint?"

"No…I just want to clean-up this one…"

He shook his head and said, "I hope you know what you're doing."

"I don't, but we will see, right?"

Money patted my back and said, "We'll see…"

On the fourth day, there was a calm in her that I bet she hadn't seen in a really long time. She looked good…a little pale, but good. She sat up in the bed and said, "Thanks."

I looked at her. "Get up and shower. I'm going to show you something."

This time she went without a fight. After she was done, she walked up front to where me and my boys were watching a game. "Are you hungry?"

She hesitated, but then said, "Yes, I'm starving."

She followed me into the kitchen. I poured her a bowl of cereal. She ate it like she'd never eaten before. As milk was flying everywhere, I asked her for her name. For a second, she pulled her face away from the bowl, just long enough to say, "Sarah."

Sarah, I thought to myself. "I'm Miller."

"That sounds like a last name, not a first name," she said.

"That's what the streets call me and that's what you're going to call me." I stood to walk back into the other room. Before walking away, I said, "You can leave if you want to. I won't keep you here any longer."

She looked confused. "Ummmmm...I thought that you had something to show me?"

"Okay..." I grabbed a set of keys off of the coffee table. "Let's ride." When we were close to the door, I looked back to find Hustle staring at us. I nodded to signal that all was okay and then we left.

When she walked outside, she shielded her eyes as if she was seeing the sun for the very first time. When she got in the car, I could tell that she was still weak from the detox. I asked her what she would like to eat. She hesitated for a moment, but then said, "Tacos."

"Tacos?" I asked.

"Yeah, tacos...what's wrong with tacos?"

"Not a damn thing..." I laughed, because she could have asked for steak, or for a lobster, but she asked for tacos. "Okay...let's get you some tacos." We drove around, found a fast food restaurant that sold tacos, ordered a few, and ate them in the car. Every time she took a bite, she licked her fingers.

"Are they good?"

"Delicious," she said, licking her mouth.

"I'm glad…"

When she was done, she looked over and noticed that I hadn't finished mine. "Do you want that?"

"Ummmmm no…"

She took my remaining tacos and finished them in two bites. She licked her fingers, took a swig from her cup of soda, swallowed, and said, "I can't remember the last time that I had tacos."

"Well, what if I told you that you could eat tacos every day?"

Picking her teeth, she said, "Who eats tacos every day?"

"A person who likes tacos…"

She smiled.

I laughed. "Anyway…what I'm saying is….I don't know how, what, or where you used to get your meals, but you're clean now…you don't have to go back to that life."

She didn't respond.

I looked at the clothes that she was wearing. Even though they were clean, they were more of a hooker's uniform, so I decided to get her a few things. We drove to the mall to get her some gear. We purchased five pair of jeans, a pair of shoes, a few tops, and some underwear. We stopped by a nail shop and got her nails done. I ran her by the "house" and let one of the girls do something with her hair. When we were done, she got in the car. She was happy, probably happier than she's been in a long time, but now it was time for her to make a decision about her life. "Look around you. What do you see?"

She smiled and said, "Is that a trick question?"

"No, what do you see?"

"I see some grass…some cars….some kids on the streets…"

I interrupted her. "Those streets are your home, right?"

She dropped her head as reality hit her. "Yes, it is."

"You have a choice. You can leave those streets and come and stay with me at the house."

"You mean…become a hoe?" she asked.

"No, you don't have to trick if you don't want to…I could use a woman at the 'house'…keep things clean and tidy…maybe cook every once in a while."

She thought about it for a moment and said, "And I wouldn't have to screw nobody?"

"Nope…"

"You're going to pay me…with drugs?"

"Do you want drugs?"

She paused for a second before saying, "No...I don't."

"I'm going to put a roof over your head and feed you...If you need some ...ummmm...lady stuff...I will get that for you too."

"And what if I don't want to?"

"No harm no foul...Sarah...we will break our ties here."

"And I get to keep everything?"

"I can't wear that shit, even though I know that I'd probably look good in those jeans and heels..." I laughed. "But yeah, you get to keep it."

She paused for a moment and opened the car door to get out. She stopped and then climbed back into the car.

"Oh and there's one more thing...you have to stay clean."

She looked at me for what seemed like forever and then looked outside into the streets. She dropped her head and said, "I can't lie to you. I've been doing this shit for a long time. I can't remember what it's like to be clean."

As she said that, I'd thought about how long I've been hustling…been doing it for so long that I didn't know what it was like not to do it.

She continued. "The streets are what I know. Drugs are what I know."

I thought about what she was saying and said, "My mama used to tell me that 'all good things must come to an end.'"

Sarah laughed. "Ain't nothing good 'bout the streets or drugs."

I looked at her and said, "Exactly."

We both sat for a while, quietly, as we stared out into the streets.

Chapter 38

Things were good for a while. She did exactly what we agreed upon. She kept the house clean. She cooked. She did laundry. She was really trying to better herself. It felt good to have a woman around. All we had to do was bring in the money and she took care of the house. I would say that it was like she had three children but it was more like she had three husbands; we all started to get close to her. She was pretty and once she got used to taking care of herself, she wanted everything around us to be "pretty." She purchased curtains and took down the blinds. She even bought table mats and cup holders. Our 'house' started to feel like a home. It was almost too good to deal drugs out of it, but business was business. Somebody had to pay for the table mats.

She wore this perfume that stunk up the whole house. I don't mean "stunk" like it smelled bad, because it smelled good – almost covered the smell of weed that we smoked all day, but she wore so much of it, like she was trying to cover up the stench of the bad decisions that she'd made in her life. We were suffocating on that shit, but I didn't say anything, because I didn't want to discourage her.

Learning to be sober had its challenges for her. Being clean, Sarah was like a fish out of water. She wanted to please me so bad that she never complained about anything. She just ran around pampering our asses all day. I was starting to get spoiled. I have to admit that being away from my mama made me long for the 'gentleness' that only a woman could provide. Sitting around these "hard-legs" all day can get rough on a brother.

We all started to get comfortable around her – started to act like gentlemen around her; everyone except for Hustle. He was an asshole to everyone and she was no exception. I think that the fact that his mother left him, made him bitter, because no matter what Sarah did or tried to do, he was always on her back.

She made breakfast for us one morning and she went out of her way to make it nice – had some flowers on the table and everything – almost looked like a restaurant. She put the food on the table: grits, eggs, bacon, and toast. Hustle's ass started complaining right away.

"Where did you learn how to make grits?" Hustle asked.

"My mama used to make them for us every day," she said, sweetly.

"Well, you should get her ass over here to make us some grits because this shit is hard as a rock. Look like one big-ass grit."

I didn't laugh, but Money fell on the floor laughing. "One big grit...that's some funny shit."

Sarah ignored him.

But then things got ugly. "Did you hear me, Bitch? Take this shit and cook it over," he said.

She took a deep breath and said, "I thought..."

Hustle threw the bowl of hot grits at her. "BITCH...YOU DON'T THINK!"

Sarah ran out of the room, crying.

I looked at him. "Man, she didn't deserve that shit."

Hustle frowned. "Man, you getting soft on that chick? I swear that if I didn't know any better I would swear that you was 'whipped'. Don't you know that you can't turn a hoe into a housewife?"

Money interrupted, "I don't know what you're talking about...hoes make the best housewives...who don't want a woman who would suck your dick while making you some pancakes?"

I looked at him and frowned.

He threw his hands in the air and said, "I'm just saying."

I looked at Hustle. I stood up and then pushed him out of the chair. "You are out of line. This is why you can't be nice to motherfuckers..."

Hitting the floor, he said, "What was that for?" He stood and adjusted his clothes. "She's trying to fool yo' dumbass? Bitch got your nose so wide-open...twisting that little butt around here and got you sprung. You better open yo' eyes to what's happening before you get caught-up."

I walked up to him, and with the palm of my hand, I slapped the shit out of him. Yes, I slap his ass like a woman would slap his ass. At an early age, I saw what a slap in the face does to a man. It humbles him. It takes him to a strange place – for a second, he is reminded of his mother, his grandmother, or the crazy-psychotic bitch that he has at home.

Stunned, he grabbed his face and asked, "Did you just slap me?"

"Do you feel like a bitch right now?" I asked.

He didn't respond.

"Because that's what I do to motherfuckers who act like a bitch...I bitch-slap their asses."

"I can't believe you did that shit...you should have slapped her ass. She's the one who can't cook grits."

Frustrated, I called her back into the room. "Sarah, come in here!"

She walked into the room – drying her face with the hem of her t-shirt. "Yes," she said.

"Sit down in Hustle's seat," I said, turning to look at him. "He's going to make you breakfast. He wants to show you how to make grits."

He stood. "I don't know how to make no damn grits."

I sat down at the table. "And yet, you're making the most fucking noise about some shit that you can't even do yourself. That's what separates men from boys – what separates you from me."

The room fell silent. Then, Hustle spoke. "I ain't fixing that bitch shit."

Sarah interrupted. "He doesn't have to make me anything...matter of fact, I prefer that he didn't."

I moved next to her, smiled, and said, "Hustle is going to make your breakfast and he's going to do that shit with a fucking smile on his face. Ain't he?" I turned to look at him.

Hustle looked at me and Sarah, and then turned and looked at Money.

"Don't look at me. I don't want your nasty-ass making me shit."

Hustle frowned, but then quickly replaced his frown with a smile. "What would you like?" he asked.

Sarah looked at him and said, "I would like some grits."

Frustrated, he frowned and began to fumble around the kitchen – looking for a pot to put them in. When he finally found one, he grabbed the container and began to read the cooking instructions. Sarah laughed as she watched him, but I didn't. I just stared at him. When he was done, he walked over and began to pour them into a bowl. He looked at me.

I turned to Sarah, who was staring at the bowl. I turned to see the grits that Hustle had thrown at Sarah earlier. I picked-up the hot bowl of grits and threw them at him.

He screamed. "What the fuck, man????!!!! You burned my fucking arm!!!"

I stood. "Clean that shit up...clean all of this shit up...don't ever throw some shit that I paid for...in my house."

"You got me doing that hoe's work. I didn't sign-up for this shit," he said, looking at the burns on his arm.

Sarah stood and ran out of the room.

"This is my house. You don't like the way that I run shit, get your own. Now, I'm going to walk in the back. If I come back and this shit is still on the floor, your ass better be gon'."

Hustle looked confused. I left him, standing in the middle of the floor with that stupid look on his face.

When I walked down the hall to Sarah's room, she was lying across the bed, crying. I sat down beside her.

"Don't pay that boy no attention. He's just mad that you're not on the streets."

She looked up and frowned. "What?"

"I'm just saying that he's hating on your progress…he don't want to see you come-up. That's all. Ignore his ass."

She sat up and looked at me. "I'm really trying.

"I know that you are," I said.

"And…and…I want you to be happy," she said.

I smiled.

"And…and you know that it's not easy being around drugs all day and not want it, but I fight the urge every day."

"I know."

"I didn't like being in the streets, but once you out there, the streets are the only thing that'll take you…not judge you."

I didn't respond.

"You look at me and see a hype…Hustle looks at me and see a piece of meat, but I'm good people…I just got lost for a while…" She paused and continued. "I wasn't always like this…I had a good family, went to school, got good grades…I didn't have it bad…I had a good life…then one night, I was at a house party and somebody put something in my drink. The next thing I know, I woke-up in a room with my clothes off." She started to cry again. "I don't know what happened, who touched me or how many…there were rumors that four boys did 'it' to me, but I don't know…" She paused for a moment and continued, "We were both devastated. My mama took it so hard. I hated myself for putting myself in that position….I was saving myself…I was still a virgin when that happened, and to lose my virginity to a bunch of strangers…I just couldn't cope…the doctor gave me some painkillers, and from there it just got out of control. My mother was so ashamed of me, she threw me out of the house…I was only sixteen."

"That's messed-up," I said.

"Now, my mama wouldn't throw steaks on my ass if I was on fire," she said.

"Now, look at me…I have a chance to fix things…"

"Look…I know that I may not be in the position to say this, but…you shouldn't blame yourself…a man who has to take pussy is a sad and pathetic piece of shit. A real man don't have to do that…they're dogs, and I know that people like to call us that, but we're not all animals…"

She smiled.

"So you became a victim twice…by the hands of those men and then by the hands of your mother…it's amazing to me that your mother took something that happened to you, so personally…she took your pain and turned it into her own personal tragedy…kinda ass-backwards if you ask me…she should have been there for you, but she threw you out on the streets…alone…so fuck your mother and fuck the bastards who raped you…because the shit that doesn't kill you will only make you stronger."

She smiled. "God sent me to you and you saved me."

I laughed. "God sent you to a drug dealing pimp to get saved?"

"I'm saved aren't I? He uses people all of the time. You never know who gon' do it. You just have to be open to receive it," she said.

"I guess you're right."

"I know that I'm right," she said.

We sat there looking at each other. She leaned in to kiss me when Money walked into the room. "Boss, can you come and look at this?"

I hesitated, but then said, "Duty calls."

She took her hand and touched the side of my face. Her fingers were so soft. I closed my eyes and when I opened them, she was smiling. We stared at each other for a moment, but then I stood to walk out of the room. I stopped to look at her again. She waved. I paused for a second and then waved back. I took a deep breath and proceeded down the hall. When I entered the living room, I almost fell-out laughing.

"What the hell you got on, girl?" I asked.

She started modeling the school girl uniform that she was wearing. "I'm gon' make all of the girls start wearing this."

I dropped my head and said, "Why?"

"Cause this is what the men want…they want them young, so since I can't turn the clock back on some of those hoes, I can at least create the delusion."

"Illusion…" I said.

"Huh?" She asked.

"Not delusion…illusion," I clarified.

"Naw, I meant 'delusion'…have you seen some of those hoes?" We all started laughing.

"Bottom, you're crazy," Money said.

Suddenly, Sarah entered the room. Bottom started circling her and licking her lips like a coyote who'd just spotted a deer. "Look what we got here...you looking good girl...and all it took was some soap, water, and a little detox. Damn, you look good enough to put on the tracks. That ass would definitely bring in some new clientele. What do you think, Miller?"

I walked over and plopped down on the couch. "Naw, she's not for sale."

Everyone in the room looked at me. "You heard me...she's not for sale," I clarified.

Bottom put her hand on her hips. "What? She too good to fuck?"

"I didn't say that...I just got something else planned for her."

"What is that?" Hustle asked.

"Don't worry about it...when you need to know, you'll know."

"Humph," Bottom said. "Why can't she multi-task like the rest of us? She can hoe and still do what you need her to do. She'd be good for business."

I looked at her. The look on my face indicated that I was done talking about this. She pouted and started to walk towards the door.

"You know what'll be good for business? You taking that shit off!" I shouted.

She huffed and then walked out of the house.

Hustle looked at me. "Boss, the hoes ain't bringing in the money that they used to...don't you think..."

I interrupted him. "Then we need to have a talk with the girls. Putting her out there ain't gon' do nothing. You expect her to make up a shortfall created by twenty other women. That's not good business"

Hustle interrupted, "But she..."

"No, you have to look at it this way. If you got a car with four bad tires...based on your logic, we should just replace one tire and the car would be fine. Sure, the car is going to run, but that one tire has to work harder to make up for what the other three ain't doing…if anything, you replace all four. Now, the car will run fine."

"How did we start talking about tires?" he said.

Money looked at me and said, "That's why you're the Boss."

I could tell that Hustle didn't like my response. He wanted me to agree with him, but like I said, I was saving Sarah for something special and I meant that.

"Now, you and Money can go and find out what's going on, and if we need to start replacing some tires."

Money started laughing but Hustle just stared at me. "Should we knock them around a little?" Hustle asked.

"Don't put your hands on them. You only raise your hand to your enemy. You don't hit no woman or no child, you got that?"

Hustle frowned. "I hear ya'…loud and clear."

Chapter 39

We were together every day. I started to take her around and introduced her to a couple of my 'connects.' For some odd reason, I felt like I could trust her. She was indebted to me. She wanted to make me happy, and I wanted to do the same for her. She was a good woman, so when she came to me and told me that she wanted to go to school, I didn't hesitate. I gave her some money and she started taking some accounting classes. When she got her certification, I allowed her to get more involved in the business. I liked where things were headed, but there were a couple of people in the organization that weren't too happy about me letting her handle the money.

"Boss, do you know what you're doing?" asked Hustle.

"Why do you ask?" I said.

"You got this chick counting our money," he said.

"Our money?" I asked.

"Your money, Boss. You know what I mean…but a little of it is mine's too. I work hard too."

"I know that you work hard, Hustle, but there's nothing wrong with letting her count the money. I'm still keeping an eye on things."

"I'm just saying, Boss…we can't let that 'skirt' get all up in our business. They have their place."

I thought about that statement for a second. I didn't like him telling me how to run my business. "Look, the reason why things are the way they are is because

382

of me. You work for me, not the other way around. You've trusted me this far don't start doubting me now. But if you're uncomfortable with the direction that things are going in…"

He began to stutter, "Naw, Boss…I trust you…I'm just saying…"

"Then, we're done talking." Sarah entered the room. She had a calculator in her hands.

"Oh, I'm sorry." She turned to leave the room.

"You can stay…he's leaving."

Money stood and grabbed Hustle by the arm. "Let's go."

I could tell that he didn't like that, but he'll get over it. He left the door lightly cracked. I knew that he did that to keep an eye on me – to protect me, but I didn't need protection from her. She wanted to be something and I wanted to help her. She was so pleased with what she was doing with her life.

"Miller, I was looking at some numbers and I was wondering if you thought about investing some of your money?"

"You want a brotha to diversify? I thought I did that already by offering drugs and hoes." I laughed, but she didn't find it funny. She was serious. "Okay, keep talking."

"I'm just saying. You got a lot of money coming in here."

"Yes…it's illegal money. I can't setup a mutual fund account with drug money."

She grabbed my hand. "I can do it for you. Right now, your money is just sitting…let your money make you some money."

I liked what she was saying. "And this won't bring me any heat?"

"No, it'll be under my name."

"My money in your name?" I asked.

"It doesn't have to be all of it. Just a little…" She looked down and then looked back up. "You have to trust me like I trusted you."

I thought about it for a minute and then said, "I'll give you a couple of dollars and see what happens. If things go well, I'll give you a little bit more."

"Really?" She said, jumping up and down. "Thank you, thank you, thank you…you won't regret this."

In a moment of happiness, she reached over and grabbed me around the neck and kissed me. Caught off guard, I almost pushed her off of me, but in the moment, I surrendered. It was nice, soft, and different. It wasn't what I'd grown accustomed to. I was used to the "stunt-doubles." What they offered was satisfying, but it wasn't this. Before I knew it, we were holding each other and kissing, passionately. What happened next, neither one of us expected. She pulled my shirt over my head. My heart began to beat so fast and so hard, you could hear it. I felt like a virgin. I was fumbling, like an amateur, trying to get her clothes off. She pushed me back onto the chair, unbuckled my pants, removed her jeans, and then straddled me. I was shaking. I've never felt this way before. She rode me until we both "came." She collapsed into my arms and I held her until my heartrate slowed down. Suddenly, I heard the door close behind us. I looked back, but then turned my attention back to her.

≈

Things around the house became even more tense and awkward after that. Sarah and I were starting to act like a couple. Hustle hated that shit. He was always making comments and doing shit to get on my nerves, but I ignored him, because I liked what Sarah and I had. Every chance that he got, he tried to plant "seeds" to try to destroy what me and Sarah had, but our bond was strong and getting stronger every day. As my love for her grew, I was starting to love my boy less.

Chapter 40

The next day, I decided to have a barbeque at my place. There was a lot of people in and out of my home. We were drinking, 'smoking', dancing, playing cards, and talking shit. The music was "thumping", and when a woman yelled, "That's my shit!!!!" I decided that it was time to restock the alcohol. When I walked into the kitchen, I had a sudden need to use the bathroom. I emptied my pockets on the kitchen counter and went into the back. When I came back, my money was gone. Now, everybody at the party were people that I dealt with all of the time, so I knew that none of them took it. It wasn't because they were upstanding individuals, because they weren't. I wasn't worried about them, because they knew how crazy I was, and it wouldn't be shit for me to turn a barbeque into a crime scene.

I was looking around when Hustle walked up to me and whispered, "Have you checked your girl's room?"

Immediately, I knew something was up. I knew that she wouldn't cross me like that. She had it good here. She wouldn't fuck that up and risk being thrown back on the street. I just shook my head with disappointment as I walked down the hall to her room. When I got to her door, I didn't knock, I just walked in. She was sleeping. I searched her whole room. I was about to leave, when he said, "Look under her pillow."

I walked over, lifted her pillow and there it was. When I moved it, I woke her. "Hey Miller, is everything okay?"

I smiled and said, "Everything is good...go back to sleep."

As I left the room, I ran into Hustle who was still standing in the hallway. "Did you find it?" he asked.

I looked at him. I couldn't believe that he would try to set that girl up. It pissed me off so bad, but I couldn't let it show. This wasn't the time to deal with dumbshit, so I decided to table-it until tomorrow. I smiled through the corner of my mouth and said, "Yeah…I found it."

"Soooooooooo…I don't hear her screaming," Hustle said.

Confused, I asked, "And why should she be screaming?"

"That thieving-bitch took your money… we need to handle her."

"We?"

"Yeah, we…we need to go in there and peel that bitch's cap back."

"Is that what we should do?"

"Yep…" Hustle remained outside of her door. "I'm telling you…we should go in

391

there and tag-team that ass...beat that head-in until she never does it again."

I turned and looked at him. "Is that how I should handle the thief?"

"Yeah...you have to keep these hoes in check, man, or they will walk all over you. Today, it's your money, tomorrow? No telling what that bitch will do," he said.

"That's some good advice...I'll have to remember that."

"You should, man," he said.

"I will."

≈

Later that evening, I walked into the living room and had just turned on the TV to watch the evening news when there was a knock at the door. I turned down the volume, walked over to the door with my hand on the handle of my gun, and looked through the "peep-hole." It was Bottom and one of my girls. I opened the door. She walked passed me, dragging the girl behind her. She pulled the girl until she was standing in front of me.

"Where's your key?" I asked.

She waved it at me. "Look at this shit," she said, throwing her purse on the couch. "Look at this bullshit."

I looked at the young lady. "Okay, I give…what am I looking at?"

"Look at her stomach," Bottom said.

I did as she said. "Umm…Bottom…how long are we going to play this game?"

Frustrated, she said, "She's pregnant."

I threw my hands in the air. "I didn't do it."

She frowned. "I know you didn't."

"Whew…for a second there I thought that you were blaming me," I said, trying to lighten the moment.

"Miller...what the fuck am I going to do with a pregnant hoe?" Bottom asked.

"What do we normally do with pregnant hoes, Bottom?"

"Well, first, they shouldn't be getting pregnant...second, they know what happens if they get knocked-up..."

"And why are you talking to me about this?"

"Because she works for you..."

This is one of those moments when a man wishes he could be anywhere on the planet, but where he is right now. "So...okay...I'm going to go out on a limb here and ask this question...they're having sex, right?"

"Right..."

"And as a result of having sex, they get pregnant...right?"

"Well...right..."

"Okay...I'm just trying to understand... so we know from the Bible, the Science books, and our health and Anatomy classes…that when people fuck… somebody might get pregnant, right?"

"Right…"

"So…what happened was supposed to happen? Right?"

"No…" she said.

"Okay…I'm still confused…help me understand…"

"We take all of the necessary measures to prevent that from happening…" she said.

"Did she stop having sex?"

"No…"

"Then, not ALL measures were taken…right?" I scratched my head and continued, "Isn't that kinda like walking on ice and not expecting to fall. If I don't break my ass…that's a good thing, but I have to still assume the possibility… right?"

"Miller, I don't have time to explain this shit to you…that baby will be still in her womb and twenty years old before you understand it…"

"Bottom, you storm in here in the middle of the night with a pregnant girl hanging off of your arm…you ask me what to do like I know what to do…"

"I should have expected this from a man…"

I frowned. "First, a man knows his place…and second, a real man knows what to do to avoid getting a phone call nine months later."

"Well, somebody didn't get the memo."

"Clearly…"

"Well, he's not around, so we need to handle this…"

"An abortion?"

She nodded, "Yes."

"That's interesting…" I paused for a second and said, "What if she fucked somebody and got a disease…one of those permanent ones…what would she do then…cut it out?"

"You're talking apples and oranges, Miller…"

"Probably…but most people practice fire prevention to avoid getting burned. They don't wait until they are knee-deep in flames, before they realize that the shit is hot….I'm just saying."

"Miller…there are risks in this job and we all know the risks and we have to take protective measures to keep certain things from happening…"

"Certain things we have no control over…we can do everything that we can, and shit will still happen…people who drive carefully still have accidents… healthy people, who eat right, and exercise still die…people who dodge birds still get shitted on, and people who have sex get pregnant…even those who use protection…"

"But…"

"But...For every action there's an equal reaction...if I know that shooting someone is going to possibly kill them, and I got a problem with that, then maybe I shouldn't shoot people...that's all I'm saying...just like she made a choice to have sex...for whatever reason...this is going to have to be her choice too...the consequences of her actions are hers...not mine....but when her decisions start to affect me...then we need to talk." Suddenly, I realized that everyone was talking, but the person who was pregnant. I looked at her and said, "What do you want to do?"

The young lady looked at Bottom, looked at her stomach, and said, "I don't want to kill my baby. I ain't getting no younger and this might be my only chance to be somebody's mama."

"Okay...problem solved." I said. "She made her decision."

"OKAY?" Bottom asked, in shock. "Problem solved?"

"Yep...it's okay," I said. "All I know is...I can't control what she does with her pussy and her body...just like she can't control what I do with this dick and these nuts...I don't know why you asked me in the first place...I didn't have sex with her..."

"But she works for you..."

"And that's it...I don't own her..."

"I don't mean to be a problem, and I know that this will cost you some money, but I'll find a way to make it up to you," the young lady said.

Bottom responded. "Yeah...you damn right you gon' make it up to him. You gon' keep hoeing."

This statement bothered me. I would never forget this girl who used to stand on the corner. She was young and very pretty, and she was selling herself. Every day, we would see her standing there, holding the hand of a little boy. I don't know if she was doing it to feed the kid or to feed a habit, but she was out there – letting those men take her in the alley to do whatever they wanted to do to her, while the little boy watched. One after another, from sun-up to sun-down, they did that to her. As a kid, it made me angry and sick to my stomach to watch that shit, and that feeling hasn't changed. "Not on my watch…"

"Then, what is she gon' do…"

"Ask her…I have enough shit to think about…"

Bottom spoke to her. "You need to be thankful…because if it was up to me…"

I interrupted her. "I guess it's a good thing that it ain't up to you."

She frowned. "A pimp with a damn conscious."

I shook my head. "Naw, we all have crosses to bear…I just choose to carry my own."

Chapter 41

He had me looking over my shoulder. My boy was acting out and what was, at first trivial, was becoming something that could be harmful to my health. I know that we made a pact, "bros before hos", but every once in a while someone special comes along, and makes you rethink how you do things.

And Sarah is that girl…It feels weird even saying that. I've been with a lot of women in my short lifetime, but this was the first time that a woman qualified for "couple status", and it actually felt good. I didn't realize how lonely I was, until I met her. She was making changes in me that I really started to like. I was starting to get tired of the game. I wanted to take what I had, settle down, and I wanted to do it with her, but my people didn't like that. I didn't realize how much, until today.

Earlier that morning, I woke up and noticed that Sarah wasn't lying next to me. I rubbed the crust from my eyes and looked again, but she was gone. I stretched and then climbed out of bed. I was walking down the hall when I heard two people talking to each other. As I got closer, I realized that it was Sarah and Hustle. I heard the word, "sex" and then stopped to hear what they were talking about.

Sarah said, "No, you are not my type."

"…the fuck is your type?" he asked.

"Not you," she confirmed.

"So Trey is your type?"

"Yes…he is…" she confirmed.

I heard this and smiled.

"Look…I'm not trying to love you…I just want to fuck you…you don't have to tell Trey nothing."

Ain't that some shit…that back-stabbing motherfucker.

"Why would I do that? Trey is a good man. I love him."

"We share everything…" he said.

"Well, you won't be sharing me."

I heard her walking towards the door. I was about to walk away when I heard a chair slide across the floor. Suddenly, I heard her scream. "Get off of me!!!"

I ran into the room. He'd just ripped her shirt off. "Please…help me!!!" She screamed.

"What are you doing? Get off of her!!!" I said, pulling at him.

"You said what's yours is mine…you said what's yours is mine," he said, unzipping his pants.

"Get off of her!!!" I yelled, again. I pulled him off and then Sarah ran screaming down the hall. He started to push me.

"Man, it's just pussy, right?" he said, zipping up his pants.

I walked over to the breadbox and pulled the gun that I kept hidden there. I looked at him and before I knew it, I hit him in the face and knocked him out cold. I was so mad that I continued to hit him until my hands and my gun were covered in blood. Then, I ran down the hall to find Sarah hiding in her closet.

"He tried to rape me," she said, putting on another shirt.

"I don't know what's wrong with him," I said, turning to look at the door. "I'll be back."

I walked back down the hall and into the kitchen. I filled a glass with cold water and then walked over to Hustle who was still out cold. I poured the water on his face.

Waking up, he said, "Wha....what? What's happening?"

"Get your ass up," I instructed.

"What?" He grabbed his face which was now covered in blood. "What the fuck? Are you fucking serious?"

"Get your ass up!" I said, again. I looked over at Money who was watching the whole situation from a distance. "Help this Nigga to his feet."

Money walked over and grabbed Hustle, who snatched his arm away from him. Rubbing his face, he said, "I can't believe you hit me...especially over some hoe."

At this point, I was pacing and thinking. I wanted to kill his ass, but I needed to think it through. Killing him would be emotional, and while his actions were a violation of trust, I didn't want to kill a man over a piece of ass - even one that I felt belonged to me.

"Sit your ass down," I said.

"Man, you hit me over some pussy," he said.

"Sit down or get put down," I said.

He hesitated for a second, but then sat down.

"I don't know what the fuck is going on with you, but you don't touch shit in my house."

"But you said..." he paused and then said, "But I thought..."

"Why are you fucking thinking? Only one motherfucker thinks in my house and that's me," I said. "You don't touch my shit."

"So she's yours?"

"Everything in this bitch is mine...even you."

Money and Hustle looked at me.

I continued. "I don't know why I have to explain basic shit to non-basic Niggas. I protect and take care of mine...you are my boys...we go way back...and

Sarah…" I paused for a second and said, "You don't touch her. Do you understand?"

Money looked at me. "Bruh, I ain't got to touch your shit."

I looked at Hustle. "Do you understand?"

Hustle looked at me, stood, and then walked out of the house.

"Do you want me to take care of him?" he asked.

Breathing heavily, I looked at Money. To think that he would kill Hustle, a homeboy, for me, made me feel special - for a second. His loyalty would have been appreciated if I didn't think that he would do the same thing to me – if the opportunity presented itself.

"Naw, his ass needs a time-out…he'll be back. Until then, I need to think…go and do a pick-up, and we can meet later," I said.

Money looked at me and said, "Got you, Boss."

I bet, I mumbled to myself.

≈

"I can't stay here if he's going to stay here," she said, sitting on the edge of the bed.

I sighed. They were both putting me in a bad situation, trying to force me to choose between the two of them. She was my girl, somebody that I wanted to be a part of my life. He was someone that I've known most of my life, but he was becoming a liability. I thought about it for a moment, but this was a no-brainer. I knew what I needed to do.

"I will take care of it," I said.

She looked at me. "I'm not trying to come between you and your boys."

I looked at her and said, "I said that I will take care of him."

"Something is wrong with him."

I didn't respond, but I knew that she was right.

She touched my hand. "Trey...I know that this is hard and probably not my place to say, but some people have to be let go..."

I didn't respond.

She continued, "I know that he's your boy, but if the pain that you feel now is the same pain you will feel when they are gone, then they are not worth holding on to."

I looked at her and then said, "It'll be over soon...get some rest."

"Please leave the light on and...please lock the door."

I did as she asked before leaving the room.

≈

After taking care of the day's receipts, Money and I took a trip over to the playground where we knew that Hustle liked to hang-out at. He was sitting in a car, drinking, and watching some little girls jumping rope. We pulled up next to his car and then rolled down the window. I looked at him. His face was still swollen from being pistol-whipped.

"What ya' doing, Hustle?" I asked.

He didn't look at me. He kept his eyes on the little girls. "I'm just sitting here thinking."

"Get in the car, Hustle," I said.

He turned to look at me. "Why? So you can kill me?"

"Get in the car, Hustle…we need to talk."

"So you want to talk?"

"Don't make me ask you again."

He locked his car up and then jumped into the backseat. Money started the car and pulled out of the parking lot.

"Where are we going?" he asked.

I was looking out of the window, thinking, while holding my gun in my hand.

He looked around and asked, again, "Where are we going?"

"We're just taking a ride," I said. I looked at Money who was driving and keeping his eyes on the road.

Hustle tried pulling on the door-handle. "Let me out of here."

I turned and looked over my shoulder. "Stop pulling on that door before your ass fall out on the street – bringing attention to my car."

"But I don't want to go…I got something to do," he said.

"Me too…now, sit back and enjoy the ride…while you can."

I looked back again to find him looking around, nervously. Beads of sweat rolled down his face. We drove for another thirty minutes before we pulled into an open field. Without looking back, I said, "Get out." Money and I got out. When I looked back, I saw that Hustle was still sitting in the car. I signaled for him to get out.

For a moment, none of us said anything. I was thinking about this moment – trying to come up with a few good reasons to kill or to spare my best friend's life. There are three reasons why a man dies – women, money, and power. He'd violated two out of the three. I was really deep in thought, when Money decided to break the silence.

"Who is your favorite Super Hero?"

"Huh?" I asked.

"Your favorite Super Hero? Who is it?" he asked, again.

"Ummmm…Money…really?" I asked.

"Shit, we ain't doing nothing else, but standing here looking stupid."

Nervously, Hustle said, "Mighty Mouse."

We both looked at him. "Who?"

"Mighty Mouse…" he said, again.

"Man, Mighty Mouse is like a hundred years old," Money said.

"I know…When my mama left me alone, I watched old videos of him…," Hustle said. "It was all that we had since we didn't have cable or anything."

"Isn't he a rat?" Money asked.

"Yep…"

*How appropriate…*I thought to myself.

We were silent for a second when Money looked at me and said, "Your turn."

I shook my head. "I don't get caught-up in the imaginary…make-believe shit…I spent too much of my life believing in shit that wasn't real."

We were silent again, when Money said, "I used to wrap a pillow case around my neck, put on a pair of my sister's tights…"

Hustle and I started laughing, but I quickly regained my composure.

"Don't act like y'all never put on a pair of lady's tights…"

"Naw Bruh…ain't nobody doing that shit…" Hustle said.

"Bruh, you got issues…" I said, still trying to keep it cool.

Money continued. "Anyway…I used to turn off the lights, stand on my bed, turn on a flashlight, point it towards the wall, and wait."

Curiously, I asked, "Wait for what?"

"To save the day…" he said, smiling and gazing out into the distance. "To save the day…"

"Boy…you really got some issues…"

"Fuck you," he said. "I didn't always want to be a villain…that's all I'm saying."

Remembering what brought us out here, I said, "Before we start giving each other blowjobs, can we get back to why we are here?"

Money snapped out of his daze and said, "Sure Boss."

I turned and looked at Hustle. "You know what this is about."

"I hope that this ain't about that girl."

"No, this is about time."

"Time? What about time?" he asked.

I looked out into the field. "As a child we were taught that there is a time for everything… 'a time to be born and a time to die, a time to plant and a time to uproot, a time to kill and a time to heal, a time to tear down and a time to build, a time to weep and a time to laugh, a time to mourn and a time to dance, a time to scatter stones and a time to gather them, a time to embrace and a time to refrain from embracing, a time to search and a time to give up, a time to keep and a time to throw away, a time to tear and a time to mend, a time to be silent and a time to speak, a time to love and a time to hate, a time for war and a time for peace…'"

"And you said all of that to say what?"

"That you've run out of time…"

Money watched everything without saying a word.

I shook my head and then continued, "Somehow, somewhere, things got fucked-up between us…"

"It was that girl…"

"Do you hear yourself? You are sounding like a girl…"

"What?"

"You sound like a bitch-ass nigga…you and I are not fucking…"

"What?"

"You got some 'closet' shit going on that I need to know about? Only a bitch would do the shit that you do…and I don't need no bitches working for me…"

"You're my boy…I just don't want to see you get messed-over by no hoe…"

"The only hoe messing over me is you…"

"But you're my boy…" he repeated.

"This ain't about you being my 'boy'…this is about business…"

"And I take care of business…"

"Yes, you do, but here's the problem…your bullshit is starting to fuck with my business…it's enough that I have to deal with the motherfuckers on the street, but now, I have to watch you too? I can't do that…"

"But I've known you since we were kids…"

"But we are not kids anymore…"

"I thought that she was ours like everything else," he said.

"Man, you can't be that fucking stupid," I said. "Cause I break bread with you don't mean you can take a bite out of my sandwich…"

"But I thought that we were tighter than that…"

"Well, that's what 'thinking' will get you…" I looked at Money who then turned and pointed the gun at him.

With his hands in the air, he said, "Money…you too?"

Money didn't say anything.

"There's a line that we should never cross…and you've crossed it."

"I love you, man…you are my brother," he said.

"That's why you gotta love some motherfuckers from a distance…"

"So…it's over?" he asked.

Mocking him, I said, "So…it's over?" I shook my head. "More bitch shit…you're fired."

"Don't do this man," he pled.

"Get the fuck out of here before I kill you!!!"

"Wait…think about this, Trey."

"I've thought about it."

He looked around. "Where the hell am I going to go?" he asked.

I looked at Money and nodded my head. Money pointed the gun at his foot and pulled the trigger. Purposely, missing his foot, he then pointed the gun at Hustle's head.

Jumping out of the way, he said, "Damn…okay, okay…I'm out of here." He looked around before walking away.

Money turned and looked at me. "You should have let me kill him."

"Naw, I think it'll be fine now. It's Hustle…what do I have to worry about?"

Money laughed. "Be careful who you trust, Bruh…remember that the Devil was once an angel too."

I thought about what he said as we jumped in the car and pulled off. I looked in my rearview mirror and watched him disappear into a cloud of dust.

Chapter 42

The next day, I got up really early because I had to make a run and pick-up some product. I'd been driving around all day and was looking forward to getting back to the house, but later that afternoon, my mother called me and asked me to take her to the store. I thought that this was odd, because they had a car, but when my mama calls, I don't ask any questions. I just move.

When I pulled up she was nowhere to be seen. I got out of my car that now had a kilo of drugs and $25,000 in its trunk. As I approached the door, I noticed that it was slightly opened. I pushed the door.

Slowly, I walked in. "Mama," I called out. "Mama," I called, again, but there was no answer. I pulled my gun from my waist and slowly moved throughout the house. "Mama," I called, again, but still there was no answer. I checked every room, but found no one.

When I arrived back into the living room, I called her on her cellphone, but there was no answer. Then, I called my father and again, there was no answer. I ran out of the house and jumped back into my car.

I drove frantically to the church to see if they were there, but I didn't see their car in the parking lot. I got out and ran inside. The pastor greeted me at the door. "Hey son…it's been a long time…where have you been?"

"Have you seen my mom and dad?" I asked, nervously.

"No son…they might stop by later…"

"Okay…well, could you tell them that I stopped by?"

"Sure…sure…" he placed his hand on my shoulder. "That's a nice car you got out there in the parking lot…when you gon' bring me…I mean, us…I mean, when you gon' bring the church some of that money?"

Biting my bottom lip, I said, "Now is not the time, preacher."

"Okay…okay…but I'll be waiting for you…I mean, I'll be praying for you…"

"I don't need the devil praying for me…" I turned and walked out of the church.

I kept calling their cellphones but no one answered. I drove to all of the places that I knew that they would visit, but no one had seen them.

Something was wrong. I decided to stop by the house to drop off the stuff that I had in my trunk before I went back out to look for them. When I returned to the house, I noticed that the house was dark. I parked and looked around before getting out of my car. The streets were unusually quiet. When I walked in, I pulled my gun out and carefully checked out every room. When I entered the last room, I flipped on the light to find Sarah tied-up and beaten, lying - in the middle of the floor. There were several kilos of drugs on the floor and money thrown everywhere. Before I could untie her, I heard someone kick-in the front door. Suddenly, I heard footsteps coming down the hall. Before, I could respond, they were on top of me.

"Get on the floor!!!" he yelled.

"What? What is happening?" I asked, but I knew what was going on. This was the end.

"Get your hands behind your back!!!" he yelled.

I complied as I looked at the white girl who was badly beaten, tied-up, and sitting across from me. I looked at the drugs and the money that was all over the floor. Then, he removed the gun from my waistband. Many times, I've heard people, who thought that they were dying, say that they saw their lives flash before their eyes, but I wasn't dying and I saw it all - my grandmother, my mom and dad, my brothers and sisters - all of the money, cars, and homes – all of it gone. As they pulled me to my feet, I said goodbye to it all. "Goodbye Sarah."

The police officer looked at Sarah's bruised face and then he looked at me.

He snatched my arm – almost pulling it out of its socket. He began, "You have the right to remain silent…"

I grimaced from the pain and mumbled. "Kiss my ass."

"Kiss these damn handcuffs," he said, overhearing me.

They dragged me out of the house and into the street. Now, the streets were buzzing. There were people everywhere watching to see the local pimp and drug dealer get locked up. As they walked me over to the police car, I saw them roll Sarah out on a stretcher. I looked at her as she reached out her hand to me. They threw me in the backseat of the police car.

As I sat there watching them pull all of the evidence out of the house, I noticed two cars that were sitting across the street. In the first car was my mom and dad. My mother was crying, as my father stared and shook his head. Slowly, the window of the second car rolled down to reveal the asshole sitting in it. It was Hustle, sitting behind the steering wheel, and smiling.

Chapter 43

During my arraignment, the only people there, were Sarah and Money. When they dragged me out from the back in shackles, she broke-down into tears. As I looked at those steel chains on my hands and feet, I wanted to cry too. I thought about everything that led up to this moment in my life. I'd fucked-up. I kept forgiving the unforgivable. I kept letting his ass slide, until it slid me right behind bars.

When they called my name, Miller, Trey Miller, the shit became real for me. Until then, I thought that I was trapped in a bad dream, just waiting for someone to wake me up, until finally, someone did.

"Miller, Trey Miller?" the bailiff said, again.

I stood and walked over to a table where the attorney hired to defend me was standing. It all felt so surreal. Everyone was talking and moving around me. I was the only one who couldn't do that. I stood there and listened until the Judge asked, "How do you plea?"

As I stood there, thinking about my answer, I couldn't help but think about the fact that I was about to add another lie to an already long list of lies. "Not guilty…" I said.

The Judge looked at me and said, "Bail is set at $300,000…cash or bond…" Then his gavel went down, loudly, scaring the shit out of me.

As I was walking out of the room, I looked at Sarah and Money. Sarah mouthed, "I'm going to get you out of here." While Money just looked at me.

He looked good. To stay under the radar, Money chose to cut his hair and put on a suit and tie for this event. If I didn't know who he was, I would have thought that he was an "honest" human being. Sarah looked beautiful. I knew that this was tearing her apart, but she looked like she was holding it together.

That afternoon, when I spoke with my attorney, she asked me if I had the money to post bond. Of course, I did, but here's the problem. A Black man with no job can't post $30,000 and then tell the court that he's not guilty. The first thing the prosecution would do is follow the "paper-trail", and I wasn't going to provide the breadcrumbs that would lead them to the truth. Nope, I was going to sit and wait this out.

But that was easier said than done. While I was waiting for trial, they threw my butt in jail. The "county" jail is where dreams go to die. Once you hear those steel bars close behind you, it's over. From the moment that you walk in, they strip you of everything that reminds you of the "outside", or reminds you of your freedom, and they do it quick; like ripping off a bandage – fast and very painful.

They don't give you a grace-period or a time to adjust. From the moment you're in, they let you know that they own your ass. I was their hoe now. There was nothing worse than having my movements controlled by another man or by another human being. I moved when they told me to move. I ate when they told me to eat. I slept when they told me to sleep. I felt like a child who had moved back into his parent's house except, I couldn't go out and play.

When they asked me to "strip and spread 'em" and another man kneeled down to look up my ass-crack, I felt a part of myself die. That was the most demeaning shit that I'd ever experienced in my life. I felt violated. No man should be forced to take off his clothes in front of another man, and no man should be asked to spread his ass-cheeks, and voluntarily let another man search their manhood. Now, don't misunderstand me. I get why they do it and I guess, if I didn't want it to happen, I should have chosen a different path in life, but it seems like they go out of their way to let you know that you are their bitch now.

And I was their bitch and they reminded me of it every day. The way that they treated me and the way that they talked to me would have gotten either one of them killed on the street, but in here, all I could do was comply. The funny thing is, one of the biggest fears that most people have, is being raped in prison and becoming somebody's bitch. Now, don't get me wrong, people are afraid of being "shanked" too, but being murdered is final. You can pray that it's quick, but at least in the end, it's final. But being raped, by another man or group of men would be a slow and agonizing death. After your body heals, you will be forced to relive that moment every day for the rest of your life. You can only pray that you will end-up only reliving it in your mind, because often times, when they take it the first time, they usually come back for more –

taking "it", until the person you once were no longer exists. That's kinda how I felt about my current situation. And this is not to diminish what a real rape victim goes through, because I've never experienced it and pray that I don't have to, but I felt like the system was forcing me into the same position. Every day, seeing me as nothing but a body, binding me, restricting me, and forcing themselves inside of me, inside of my mind, until the man that I once was, no longer exists.

Chapter 44

During my trial, I found out that Hustle had only beaten Sarah. My biggest fear was that he'd raped her, but he didn't. It didn't make it any better that he'd beaten her, but I can live with that. However, he'd committed another offense - he snitched, and in the "hood", that offense is punishable by death. You just don't do that, and I knew that he was behind it. Even without proof, I knew that he was the one that betrayed me, and if I didn't have those cuffs on my arms, I would have handled his ass right then and there.

Even though he'd betrayed me, Sarah respected my feelings for him. She didn't want to hurt me by turning him in, so she decided to keep her mouth shut. This was a smart move, because the streets hate snitches, and I couldn't protect her from in here. We both needed to play it cool, until an opportunity to fix things, presented itself.

The streets were buzzing with the knowledge that he turned on me, and a hit was put out on him by Money. I squashed it, because I knew that one way or another the trail would lead right back to me. When I get out of jail, I'm going to tighten-up all of my loose ends – him being one of them.

$$\approx$$

They gave me ten years for the drugs, but I was required to do eight. They weren't able to tie the pimping and any of the other crimes to me; which is good. I was lucky. There were no witnesses to my other crimes, other than the girls. I was

434

told that when everything went down, Bottom and the girls dispersed like women at a shoe sale. If they were able to tie me to any other crimes, I would have had to watch the Second Coming of Jesus from behind bars.

You see, if you get charged with pimping, you are looking at thirty years. Why? Because on the "books" pimping is considered White Slavery, and if you participate in it, your ass is going to serve as much time as a murderer. Doesn't matter if the woman is Black, Asian, Latino, whatever, or even if they give consent to have sex, you will be charged with participating in White Slavery. So you know what that means for a brotha. If you're a Black man, who's a pimp, you might as well tell your family to buy some shovels, because they're going to throw your ass under a jail, and that's where your family is going to have to visit you.

≈

She was my "ride or die." The entire time, I was locked up, she was there for me. She kept money on my books for snacks and calls. She visited me three times a week and she always wrote me. I found out that, the money that I gave her to invest turned out to be a good idea. She made a killing in the stock market and now, she was able to take care of me. Not to mention the money that I'd set aside for moments just like this. All she wanted was for me to get out, so that we could get back to what we started.

≈

Shortly after going in, she came to visit me. I noticed that she was putting on some weight. I know how sensitive women are about that thing, so I didn't bring it up. We were just talking when she said, "So how do you feel about becoming a daddy?"

"What?" I asked.

"Yeah…you're going to be a daddy," she said, rubbing her stomach.

I was in shock. I couldn't believe that – me, a daddy. If I hadn't had sex with her, I would have thought that she was lying.

When the visit was over, I went back to my cell the happiest man in the world, but then I quickly remembered that I was behind bars. What kind of father can I be as a prisoner? In that moment, the realization hit me that I wouldn't be there to see him come into the world, to hear his first cry, to change his diapers, to feed him, to burp him, to see him take his first step, or to hear him say "Daddy" for the first time. My joy slowly turned into sadness, as I looked at the wall that sat next to my cell-mate's bunk – his baby's life chronicled in pictures on a wall. It was then, that I realized that I needed to do everything that I could to get out of here.

And she did her best to try to make me a part of the experience. She brought me pictures of the sonograms. I saw the baby change from something that looked like an alien, into a tiny human being. Later, I learned that she was carrying a baby girl. When I first found out, I laughed. I felt that either God had a cruel sense of humor, or that Karma felt that he owed me something. Either way, I was a pimp who was becoming the father of a little girl.

She told me all about her cravings, and how the baby kept her up at night – kicking and moving around in her stomach. Then, during one of our visits, she kicked for me. When I placed my hand on her stomach, my baby girl kicked my hand. It was like she was giving me a "high-five". It was the most incredible feeling in the world.

And she visited for as long as she could, until she was too far along in the pregnancy to travel, but she continued to send me pictures of the baby growing inside of her. It made me feel good that something that I made, something that had my DNA was floating around in her belly, and was going to one day call me daddy.

Chapter 45

Doing time was easy. Once they gave me my sentence, they moved me from jail to prison, where I served the rest of my time. They don't send drug dealers to regular prison. They separate us from the murderers and rapists. It's weird, because they don't consider it a violent crime, even though it destroys the lives of so many people. We get to serve our time in Federal prison, which is like a college dorm full of men who fucked-up badly, and got caught. There were no bars. We have regular doors like the ones on your bedroom at home. We have cable, a workout room, and we eat good.

Life was good – about as good as it was going to get. All I had to do was avoid getting into more trouble, and I was out of here. The strange thing is, there was more illegal shit going on behind bars than there was in the streets. If I wanted to, I could get a hold of cellphones, cigarettes, drugs, and even pussy, if I knew the right guard. Some of the guards were dirtier than I was, but I was the one doing time.

One night, it was late when I was awakened by the sound of loud music. In a daze, I climbed out of my bed and dragged myself over to the door. Through the small glass window, I saw what I thought were women dancing in the hall, and I say that because, in here, it's not too much of a stretch to find a man prancing around in women's clothing. So I rubbed my eyes, and looked again. I saw three women, wearing nothing, but a G-string while dancing in the middle of the floor. I turned the knob to the door and walked out to find several guards, and a few prisoners cheering the women on. I stopped for a moment, when I realized that I wasn't dreaming, or that I hadn't died and gon' to Heaven.

The women were dancing seductively as the men took turns touching them. I was still standing by my doorway, when one of them slowly moved towards me. Over her shoulder, the guard yelled, "You better get in on this."

I couldn't believe my eyes or my ears.

The guard continued, "Take her in the room…we got condoms."

I was starting to think that someone had spiked my mashed potatoes, because I was clearly hallucinating. Suddenly, she leaned-in, and began to gently kiss my neck. I closed my eyes as the warmth of her mouth made my dick hard. She took her hand and slowly began to rub me between my legs. I opened my eyes to find that the other two women had walked into a room – followed by the guards and the prisoners. The one who was kissing me, stopped, and said, "Let's go have some fun." She grabbed my hand and led me to the room where everyone had removed their clothing, and were beginning to take turns having sex with them. The woman that led me to the room, turned, and dropped to her knees. "Let's see what you're working with." She lowered my pants to find that I wasn't no average motherfucker. Her eyes-widened as she licked her lips. She opened her mouth, and began to move toward me, when I saw it – Sarah's face. Immediately, my dick went from a foot-long to a six inch. She quickly went from smiling to frowning. I pulled my pants up, and went back to my room. I laid in my bed as the sounds of moaning filled the air. I grabbed my dick, and held it until I fell fast asleep.

The next morning, they all walked around like the shit didn't happen. I had convinced myself that it didn't, until one of the guards walked up to me and said, "Last night, didn't happen...okay?" I looked at him. I didn't like the position that he was putting me in, but I wasn't in here to clean-up the system. I was here to do my time and get the fuck up out of here, so I said, "Sure...whatever." He seemed happy with my response because he smiled, and walked away.

This went on for several months, until finally somebody snitched. At first, they thought that it was me, because I wouldn't participate in the "games," but after a "shakedown", they found the snitch in the infirmary being treated for the "clap." He was pissed that one of the girls set his dick on fire, so he told the warden. After that, the warden cleaned house, but not before finding the snitch – hanging from a bedsheet, in his room.

Chapter 46

While I was locked up, I decided to take some classes. As a child, my mother used to tell me that 'An idle mind is the Devil's playground." As a child, I didn't understand what that meant, but while in prison, I began to understand it. Counting your days is hard, but if you keep yourself busy, doing something positive, time seems to fly by. So I took some classes, got some training, and even started going back to church. Being conditioned as a child, it was easy to fall back into it. It was also something to do, and better than sitting in my "box" on a Sunday morning.

After a while, I threw myself back into the Bible. On the nights when I was at my loneliest, it actually gave me peace. Plus, I read it because it was the only book in the building that still had all of its pages in it, and didn't have sticky shit all over it. I wanted to read the magazines, but I couldn't, because these assholes would jag-off on any picture that had a human being in it. Even some of the pages with animals in them had stuff on them.

≈

When they told me that I had a visitor, I was at a loss. I knew that it wasn't Sarah, because she was preparing for the arrival of the baby. I knew that it wasn't Bottom, because she got the hell out of "dodge." I knew that it couldn't be my mama, because she told me that it would be a cold day in Hell before she ever visited a prison. So unless it snowed last night and no one told me, I wasn't expecting her.

"How are you doing, mama?" I asked, her.

"I'm fine son."

"So how's dad...I see that he doesn't come to visit."

"He's having a hard time with all of this, but he'll come around...one day...I promise."

I sighed. "I won't hold my breath."

"Son, this is not the life that we wanted for you..."

"Mama please...can't we just visit?"

"Okay, son...let's just visit...but just know that he does love you."

I ignored this comment. "How's everyone?"

"Well, everyone is about as good as they can be...you know?"

"I know, mama."

She took a deep breath, pulled out her Bible and said, "Let me read you something."

I really didn't want to hear it, but I didn't want to discourage her from coming to see me, so I said, "Sure mama."

She flipped through a few pages and said, "1 John 1:9 says, 'If we confess our sins, he is faithful and just and will forgive us our sins and purify us from all unrighteousness.'"

"Thanks mama…so what do you want me to do with that little gem?"

"I want you to ask God for his forgiveness…it's not too late, son."

"Ummmmm mama? Are you aware that I'm in prison…I think it's too late."

"It's never too late…God is just waiting…"

"So He got time to sit around and wait, when He could have intervened when those police were slapping the cuffs on me…intervened before I got into all of this mess?"

"Did you expect Him to intervene? We all have choices…"

"Well…if He didn't do it for Adam and Eve, why should He do it for me, huh?"

"Son…sometimes…we have to learn the hard way."

"You would think that Somebody who sees everything that we do, would prevent us from doing it in the first place."

"And then…how would you appreciate what He has in store for you?"

"I could appreciate it if He made an appearance every once in a while… instead of showing-up in a grilled cheese sandwich…or on a wall…"

"Maybe this is God's will…"

"God's will?"

"Yes…to get you to change…"

"Was it God's will to murder my brother…your son?"

"He picks and chooses…"

"So you're okay with that? A God who stood by while your son was being murdered?"

"If it's His will…what can I do?"

"Wow…" I shook my head. "So He decided to save a wretch like me…"

"That's how He do…"

Sighing, I said, "Mama….do you hear yourself?"

She looked at me for a second and said, "I'm going to pray for you…"

"Prayer doesn't work…this world is a prime example of that…"

She shook her head. "Son, what happened to your faith?"

"Look around you, mama…" I took a deep breath and continued, "Kinda hard to be faithful when everything is so messed-up."

"You have to believe…"

"I have to believe? In what? Lies?"

She looked at me for a second and then said, "Let's see what God has to say about that…"

"Even when the truth is right in your face you still have to look in that 'book', or ask someone else for the answers?"

"God is the truth and the light…"

"While His people remain in darkness…"

"Son…"

"There is nothing in that 'book' that has come to fruition…other than the stuff that would have happened anyway…or the stuff that man orchestrates to keep us bound and in fear…but all of the big stuff? Still waiting on it…it's all lies, mama."

"Don't say that…"

"An imperfect human being wrote the Bible...there is not one ounce of proof that God ordained that stuff...other than a man's word...that's man's agenda...and it's mankind who pushes it. Man has been the same since the beginning..."

"The pastor says..."

I interrupted her. "You worship these false prophets...put your soul in the hands of liars and thieves...and y'all call me the fool. At least, I'm going to walk out of this prison one day...you're going to die in yours."

"And then I'm going to Heaven...My Father is a Good God...a merciful God...as long as I got Jesus, I'm just fine."

"Your Father is a deadbeat dad...who doesn't provide for or protect all of His children...He ignores their cries... their suffering..."

"Don't say that...God provides for us all."

"Really? And sits idly by and does nothing... "Look around you, mama...I know that the truth scares you..."

She interrupted me with a scripture. "'So Jesus said to the Jews who had believed in him, 'If you abide in my word, you are truly my disciples, and you will know the truth, and the truth will set you free.'"

Frustrated, I said, "Did I miss something? We're Jews now? When did that happen?"

"That scripture is for all of us..."

"Or maybe it was for the Jews that He was talking to..."

"His word is for all of us..."

Rubbing my forehead, I said, "Gotta love the Christian-Psychic...He said one thing, but meant something else...not because He told you that he meant something else, but because you need it to mean something else...or maybe the person who wrote the Bible left 'us' out on purpose...or expects us to convert...or maybe, we need to take a hint, and realize that if we're going to believe in God, then we need to find our own way to Him…"

"We're running around in circles and getting nowhere…" She paused for a second and said, "There is only one way and that's His way…"

"Whose way, mama?"

She shook her head. "Not this again…"

"Exactly…" I sighed. "I get it mama…we all want hope, but there's no hope in lies…"

"We will all have to stand before Him and atone for the things that we all say and do." She pulled out her Bible to find another scripture. "I got one more for you…"

Suddenly, the C.O. walked up and said, "Visiting time is over, Miller."

Thank God. I stood to walk away. "I gotta go, mama. Thanks for coming to see me."

"Okay, son…"

Chapter 47

My time was going by really fast. Toward the end, every week, my mama came to see me. It wasn't until two years before my time was up that I found out the real reason why. When she first started seeing me, she looked good…healthy, but towards the end, she started to look ill. Something was eating her up. She'd lost all of her hair. When I asked her what was going on, she said, "I'm going natural…had to cut all of the perm out of my head…" That response would have made sense if she hadn't been the woman who spent so much money being "processed", that they erected a statue of her at the "no-lye" factory. Then, when she made the transition to wigs, and she began to lose more weight, I knew something was up.

Then one day, the visits stopped. When I saw Sarah again, she had pictures of my baby girl. She named her April after my mother. I was really happy that she did that, but the happiness was short-lived. She then handed me a piece of paper. I looked down to find a picture of my mother. It had her name, the date that she took her first breath, and the date that she took her last. I realized that I was holding my mother's obituary. I was devastated.

"My mama?"

"Yes, Love…she made her transition…no one told you?"

"Hell no, no one told me…" I said, crying and shaking.

"I'm sorry…I thought you knew."

"How would I know? I'm locked-up in here."

"Again…I'm so sorry…"

"What happened to her?"

"It was Cancer…"

"Cancer? How? Why? When?"

"She didn't talk to you about this?"

"My mama only talks about one thing…"

"I'm sorry…"

"It's not your fault." I paused and continued. "That bastard didn't even come here to tell me that my mama was gone…"

"Who?"

"My fucking daddy…", I balled my hands into fists and slammed them against the table. "That son-of-a-bitch." The C.O. looked at me. I tried to regain my composure, so that they wouldn't end my visitation. "I can't believe this shit." I put my face in my hands and cried.

The C.O. walked up. "Is there something wrong?"

Sarah answered, "His mother died."

The C.O. walked away without responding.

Sarah rubbed my hand. "Here…before she died, she told me to give you this."

With tears in my eyes, I looked at the long white envelope that had my name written across it.

"What is this?" I asked.

"I don't know…she just told me to give it to you."

"Thanks..." I said, staring at it.

"Not a problem…she had a beautiful service. "

"I should have been there…"

She looked at me for a moment before saying, "I know that you wish you could have been there, but by the end of her journey, she didn't look the same…you would want to remember her the way that she was."

I took the envelope, folded it, and placed it into my pocket. We spent the rest of our visit in silence.

≈

And just like that, she was gone. When I went back to my room, all I could do was think about her. I laid in my bunk staring at the envelope – wondering what was inside of it, but I couldn't open it. I knew that all it had in it was a bunch of scriptures, and I didn't want her preaching to me from the grave. I felt bad enough. I didn't need her adding religious "salt" to my wounds.

Even though, we had our problems, she was still my mother. She was the only other woman who'd loved me unconditionally. I knew that I'd let her down. I tried to make it up to her by showering her with material things - when what she really wanted was for her son to grow-up, and become a decent human being. But I couldn't do that, and for that, I will forever feel like I owe her something.

When you're a kid, you think that you know everything, and then you grow-up, and realize that you don't know shit. They do everything that they can to protect you from dumbshit, but we're drawn to it like a "moth to a flame." And sure this was a chance for me to turn my life around, but it was hard. It ain't as easy as people would like you to think it is. It isn't like I'm a caterpillar, being cocooned in a cell, waiting to become a butterfly. No, I was a leopard and a 'leopard never changes its spots.'

As I thought about my future, I looked at the envelope one last time. After placing it inside of the pages of the Bible that sat on the table near my bed, I fell fast asleep.

Chapter 48

I was in a bad place – still trying to process my mother's death, and still trying to figure out what I was going to do with myself, once I was released. It was during church one Sunday that I'd decided what I was going to do. An ex-con who was visiting, told us about his life, and how he had turned it over to God. Now, he was living the life that he'd always dreamed of, due to God's grace and mercy.

I listened to him talk, standing there in that bright-colored suit, alligator shoes, and diamond rings, and I was captivated. He was confident and arrogant. No one questioned or contradicted him. As I listened to him, I realized that he reminded me of someone, and that someone was me. I looked at him, and understood that I could do the same thing he's doing without changing anything, but the venue.

Later, I was in my room when I saw an ad on the back of a comic book. It was an advertisement that said, "Do you want to become an Ordained Preacher?" I thought that the shit was a joke, but decided to fill out the application anyway. It only cost me one dollar. What did I have to lose?

I actually had forgotten that I'd mailed it, until a few weeks later a large envelope came in the mail. I opened it, and inside was a large certificate and scrolled across the middle were the words, "Reverend Trey Miller." I nearly pissed my pants. They didn't do a background check. They didn't even ask me if I owned a Bible. They just sent me a certificate. I used to think that it was a joke when people said that they got their degree from the back of a cereal box. Now, I know that the shit is real. They gave this criminal a certificate to preach. That shit was so crazy. I looked at that certificate for about a month, waiting for someone to send me a letter, indicating that they had made a mistake, but it didn't happen.

So then it began, I was a Hustler hiding behind the "Word" of God. I spent the next two years studying my ass off. I learned the "word", and was so good at it that I started teaching Sunday school classes. The prisoners hung on to my every word. Things went so well that they allowed me to preach Sunday mornings. Those prisoners was sucking that shit up – the promise of a life after death. They were engaged, engrossed, and entrapped. This was better than trying to sell swampland in Florida. It felt good – standing in front of them and convincing them that I was a changed man – that God had "washed me and made me new." Even if I accept all of this religious stuff and changed my life, it wouldn't matter, because under all of that "change" was still a criminal waiting to do criminal shit.

Chapter 49

The day of my release, I was both excited and afraid – excited because I was getting the hell up out of here, but afraid because I didn't know the world that I was being released to. Time seems to stop when you're in prison. Once you're in, you are forced to relive the exact same day, over and over again, until the day that you're free again. I've eaten my meals at the exact same time, every day, for the past eight years, showered every week at the exact same time for the past eight years, and went to bed and woke-up, every day, at the exact same time, for the past eight years. No longer was I Inmate 421830, I was leaving these walls to become Trey Miller, again, a man who can now take a shit without another man watching him.

I was hours away from being able to hold her again. It's weird that I equated my freedom with having the ability to touch her without having someone tell me that I couldn't. I was thinking about all of the positions I was going to put her in, when my thoughts were interrupted by a knock on the door.

"You ready to leave, Miller," he asked.

"Ready since the first day y'all put me in here," I said. I grabbed the rest of my things and was headed towards the door. I stopped, turned back, looked at the table, and saw the envelope still sticking out of the Bible. I grabbed the Bible and was headed back towards the door when the C.O. said, "If you take that Bible, I'm going to have to charge you with theft."

I took the envelope out of it and said, "I don't want that...believe me, I don't."

≈

As I exited the building, I saw her in the parking lot waiting for me. With her arms wide open, I ran towards her and scooped her up into my arms.

"I missed you so much," she said.

"I missed you too."

I looked over her shoulder to find a little girl sitting in the backseat of the car. "Who is that?"

"That's your baby," she said, grabbing my arm and leading me to the door.

I looked at her. She looked at me. Sarah said, "April…this is your father."

April smiled and said, "Hi, ummmm…daddy?"

I've never experienced love at first sight until that moment. As I looked at her, I saw all of the daughters who once worked for me. My heart became full. For a moment, I regretted every bad thing that I'd ever done in my life.

April got out of the car and then walked up to me. She threw her arms open to hug me. I hesitated at first. She looked so fragile. Sarah looked at me and then nodded her head. I kneeled down on my knees, so that I was on her level. She threw her arms around my neck. I placed my head on her chest to hear her heartbeat. She smelled just like a baby. She held me tighter. "I love you, daddy," she said.

I stopped holding her and looked at her. "Don't say that you love me. You don't know your daddy. Let me work to become your daddy. Let me earn your love. Don't just give your love to me. Don't just give your love to anyone. Do you hear me?"

"Yes, daddy, I hear you," she said, throwing her arms around me.

I whispered in her ear. "Your daddy will earn your love...I promise you."

"Okay, daddy," she said.

Chapter 50

My first night, on the outside, was weird. I walked in my new home and dropped my bag. The first thing that I noticed, was the carpet on the floor. I removed my shoes and socks and placed my feet on the floor. It felt so good not feeling a cold hard floor underneath my feet. April grabbed my hand and said, "Come on, daddy…I want to show you my room."

I held her hand as she took me on a tour of my new home. We went from room to room, and when we landed into her room, I noticed that there was a photo of me on her nightstand – wearing my prison gear.

I looked at it. "We need to get you a new picture."

"Why, I like that one," she said.

"But look at daddy's clothes," I said.

She looked at me and said, "It doesn't matter what you got on...it's the man underneath the clothes."

I smiled and said, "Who taught you that?"

She said, "Well, I learned in Bible School that Jesus walked around like a regular brotha...he didn't wear no fancy clothes, no flashy jewelry...no gold teeth..."

I laughed. "No, gold teeth, April?"

"Nope...He was regular and guess what?"

"What, baby girl?"

"He is our savior...he wasn't frontin', 'cause he didn't need to."

I laughed. "Wow, and you learned that in Bible School?"

"I learned the basics…mama taught me the rest. She also told me the story about the wolf."

"The wolf?" I asked, curious.

"Daddy, you don't remember the story of 'Little Red Riding Hood'?"

"Vaguely…"

"Well, you see…there was this little girl who was running around the woods…going to see her grandmother, but what she didn't know was…the wolf had eaten her grandmother…so the wolf dressed-up in her grandmother's clothing, and waited for her to come over, so that he could eat her too. Here's the thing, he thought that by putting on her grandmother's clothing, she wouldn't notice his snout, his claws, and his big teeth. He was a killer…dressed like a lady."

"And what does this have to do with your daddy…or with Jesus?"

"Clothes are a distraction...if you focus on the person wearing them, then you can see the wolf hiding underneath."

"I like that..."

"No matter what you put on, you can't cover-up the truth," she said.

"And the truth about me is?"

She looked at me. "Well, I don't see a snout or claws, but I guess time will tell..."

I laughed.

≈

That night, I knocked on her door. "Hey, baby girl...what cha' doing?"

"Nothing, daddy...you need to talk?"

I laughed and I looked at the little girl curling up with a teddy bear. "No, but I was wondering if I could read you a story?"

April started laughing. "Ummmm, I'm a little too old for that."

"But not too old for teddy bears?"

"Teddy bears protect you from the monsters…"

"Well, daddy's home…you don't have to worry about that."

"Daddy…you always have to worry about monsters…always."

I sat down next to her. "Why don't you tell me something about you?"

She smiled and said, "My name is April and….my mama's name is Sarah and my daddy's name is Trey…"

I smiled. I hung on to her every word, until she fell fast asleep.

≈

After taking a long hot shower, I climbed into the bed next to Sarah. As my body

473

sunk into the mattress, I found myself waiting for someone to say, "Lights out!" but it didn't happen. Sarah began to kiss me, slowly as she removed her nightgown. I looked at the silhouette of her body as the moonlight touched her skin. Moving from my neck, to my chest, she slid her hand between my thighs and began to stroke me. She began to kiss my stomach, sliding her tongue over my navel. As her head moved toward my crotch, I realized that "he" wasn't responding to her touch.

"What's wrong?" she asked.

"It's been a long day…I'm sorry," I said, embarrassed that I couldn't give her what she needed. "He misses you…he's just a little tired."

She looked at me and said, "It's okay…we have all of the time in the world."

"Thank you, baby," I said, as she climbed into my arms.

"I'm glad that you're home," she said, snuggling up next to me.

"Me too."

≈

The next morning, I awakened to find her gone. I listened carefully – hearing the sound of water running in the bathroom. I got up and walked towards the door. When I walked in, I pulled the shower curtain back. She wasn't aware that I'd entered the room. I watched as the soap dripped off of her skin. I began to touch myself as I watched the water run down her spine, and down the crack of her butt. I removed my clothing and climbed in behind her. Startled, she said, "Hey you…good morning."

I smiled and grabbed her hand and placed it on the "hard" spot between my legs. She looked down and said, "Damn…good morning."

I smiled as she got down on her knees. I grabbed her hair and by the back of her head, as she kissed me, gently.

Chapter 51

I thought about him every day. I didn't want to know why he snitched on me. The "why" didn't matter – the fact that he did it was what I needed to deal with. I thought about what I would do to him once I saw him again. Yes, I could have just let by-gones be by-gones, but he started it, and I couldn't move on until I finished it. At first, I thought that it would be satisfying to open his ass up like a fish and gut him, but that would be messy. Then, I thought about shooting him and filling his ass with so many bullets that his ass looked like Swiss cheese, but then I remembered a story that my mother read to me about a woman who was stoned to death. That didn't seem like a "hood" way of handling a snitch, but it sounded painful, and I wanted pain for his ass.

I went looking for him even though it was against the rules of my probation. The hood was the same, but I was no dummy. Although, I had a lot of friends, I had my share of enemies too, so I decided to pick up some "heat" just in case. You can't go back to a neighborhood that you used to run, after eight years, and expect things to be the same – for people to be the same. So I had to travel like a man walking across a minefield – watching every step.

First, I looked for Money, but no one had seen him. My sources said that he'd just disappeared, but I made sure that he knew that I was looking for him. Then, I set-out to find Hustle. When I found him, he was back on the 'block.' He looked horrible. He was on that shit, and it had really messed him up.

"Let's talk," I said., walking up on him.

"Oh my God...BRUH...look at you...man, did I miss you..." he said, wrapping his arms around me.

I grimaced and pushed him off of me. "Let's talk."

"Sure," he said, wiping powder from his nose. "Man, I'm so glad that you're back home. The game hasn't been the same since you left it."

I looked down and said, "Yeah, about that...so I found out that you were behind the set up..."

He interrupted, "Naw man...who told you that? That hoe?"

"Man, I know that you set me up and don't call her that."

"Man, I would never do that to you," he said, nervously.

"You did," I insisted and before he could lie to me again, I said, "Let's take this around back. I don't want folks in my business." I proceeded to walk around to the back of the house. He followed me without even asking why. He still trusted me, or maybe the drugs were making him delusional. Once we were back there, I looked around to make sure that we were alone.

Sniffing, he said, "Man, I'm ready...we should get back into the game."

I frowned. "That's done."

"Naw, it can't be done...I've been waiting for you to get out. You my boy...we can do this."

"I'm your boy, but you never bothered to visit me. You never wrote me a letter...sent me a fucking card. You never put any money...any of the fucking money that I gave to you...on my books...," I said, still looking around.

"I'm sorry man, but shit got hot after you left. I had to protect myself," he said.

"Shit got hot because you set the damn fire...you ratted me out."

He walked up to me. "It was that girl..."

Confused, I said, "What girl? Are you talking about Sarah?"

"Man, I just couldn't believe that you let her come between us."

"Are you serious? You set me up over my relationship with Sarah?"

"I didn't set you up...did you ever think that it could have been that bitch?"

"Don't call her no bitch, man."

"See...that's what I'm talking about. Every other girl you knew was a bitch...you pimped them...you didn't give a shit about them...you never loved them either..."

"You're right...but Sarah is special..."

He laughed. "Man, do you hear yourself talking? That hype was about to blow you for some drugs, and you thought that she was special...that is the funniest shit that I've ever heard."

The more that I talked to him the more I regretted not killing him when I had a chance.

"People change," I said.

"They all would have changed if you would have given them the same opportunity that you gave that 'chicken head', but you fed off of their weakness and their willingness to please you. You don't think that any of them would have got off of their knees for a chance to start over?"

I didn't respond.

"That skank was going to do for you what all of the others did...and because you poured some soap on her ass, didn't wash the stink of an addict off of her. Wave some of that shit in her face, and she'd jump like a fucking gymnast to get to it. An addict is always an addict..."

"That's some interesting shit coming from a fucking addict. The first rule of the game...never use your own shit. You are a walking contradiction…Dealer turned addict…" I said.

"Man, this is just a temporary set-back."

"Get out of here with that bullshit…"

"I'm telling ya' man…I'm going to get off of this shit and you and I can start all over…" He looked around before saying, "I even tried to keep things going after you left…"

"So, wait a minute, I got locked up and you tried to take over my business?" I became numb. Suddenly, I couldn't hear anything – the birds chirping, the horns blowing, the children playing – nothing. The only sound I heard, was the sound of my heart beating against my chest. I was so angry, I couldn't even think. I couldn't believe this shit – the levels of betrayal. I didn't care that I was on probation. Traitors need to be dealt with. I pulled my gun from its hiding place, and then pointed it at his head.

"Get on your knees," I instructed.

Kneeling, he said, "Bruh, not this shit again."

"This is something that I should have done a long time ago."

"Man, I know that I really messed up and I apologize for hurting your girl. She just made me so mad trying to tell me what I couldn't do…"

"It's too late."

"But I'm sorry," he said.

"Me too," I said, before pulling the trigger, over and over, until the gun was empty. He looked at me and reached out his hand. His body made a loud thumping sound as it hit the ground. I was walking away when I felt something tugging at my leg. I looked down. "Why Bruh?" he asked. I shook my leg loose, put the gun in my pants, under my shirt, and got out of there.

≈

On the news, that night, there was a report of a "John Doe" that was found behind a known crack-house. I looked at the TV and smiled. I was happy that now that part of my life was over.

Chapter 52

I decided to marry her. It's weird, because as much as I love her, I couldn't see myself married to her, or anybody else for that matter. I used to think about my parents' marriage, and I felt like getting married was like going from one prison sentence to another. But she was there for me when others turned their backs on me. She used to tell me how lucky she was to have me, but in truth, I was the lucky one.

In the beginning, we lived like "normal" people. We cut our grass, went to PTA meetings, and we went to church. For a while, I even tried getting a regular job, but it didn't happen. People aren't interested in hiring ex-felons. I needed to find something to do with my life, because now, I had a family to take care of. It was when we went to church on Sunday morning, and they were passing the collection plate around, that God sent me another sign.

I started off slowly. First, I became a member of the congregation. After a few months, I introduced myself as a pastor, showed them my "comic-book" credentials, and then I was in. At first, I was preaching only when someone was absent, or teaching Sunday school classes every now and then. At that time, I was considered, a visiting preacher, so they paid me a portion of the collection for that day, but before long, I was preaching almost every Sunday.

I will never forget my first day in front of them. I stayed-up all night the night before looking for a scripture that would be a good ice-breaker, but that is what all preachers do, so I decided that I would do something different, and begin with a joke to sorta get things going. It was an oldie, but a goodie. I thought that they would like it. I wanted them to see that I was "progressive", and not like the old shit that they'd become accustomed to.

So that morning, as I rose from my seat, I could feel every eye in the building watching me. I walked up to the mic and did a few "Hellos" and a few "Giving honors to", and then I went right into the joke. I adjusted my tie and said, "Four nuns were in a church one day. On this particular day, it was extremely hot, so they decided to take off all of their clothing. They threw everything on the pews and proceeded to walk around the church, naked, in an attempt to cool off. Suddenly, the doorbell rang. One of the naked nuns walked up to the door and asked, 'Who is it?' 'The Blind man,' the voice answered. The nuns decided that it was safe to open the door because the man was blind. He walked in, looked at them and said, 'Nice tits.' Where do you want me to install these blinds?"

I was waiting for applause, but instead, they all stared at me. You could hear crickets chirping it'd become so quiet. I tapped the mic and asked, "Hello? Hello? Is this thing on?" But no one answered. Suddenly, I began to sweat. I thought that a man dressed in a clown suit was going to tap dance across the pulpit, and drag my ass off of it with a big hook, but then suddenly, I heard a little "snicker" on both the left and right side of me. Then, the snickers turned into laughter and then, I heard someone say, "You never know when He's coming."

I smiled and referred to the Bible by saying, "'Be dressed in readiness, and keep your lamps lit. 'Be like men who are waiting for their master when he returns from the wedding feast, so that they may immediately open the door to him when he comes and knocks.'"

Someone hollered, "Amen" and another hollered, "Preach Pastor" and then it was 'on' from there. I had them standing on their feet. "You can't be getting ready...

you have to always be READY!!!" They rose to their feet. They loved it. One woman stood and started doing a dance that looked like she was killing roaches. The organist began to bang loudly on the piano's keys and the drummer joined in.

"ARE YOU READY????" I asked.

"YES!!!!!" they responded.

"I SAID, 'ARE YOU READY???"

"YES!!!!!!"

Then I began to chant…

"FEELS LIKE FIRE…!!!!"

"FIRE!!!" they responded.

"SHUT UP IN MY BONES!!! JUST LIKE FIRE!!!"

"FIRE!!!" they responded.

"SHUT UP IN MY BONES!!! I SAID, 'FIRE!!!"

"FIRE!!!" they responded, again.

"SHUT UP IN MY BONES!!!"

Then I took a handkerchief, wiped my mouth and forehead, and then threw it in the air to signify that I was almost done. "Amen?"

"Amen..."

I walked back and forth, mumbled, and made up some shit about my life, quoted scripture after scripture, and when I took off my coat and threw it on the floor, a woman stood and fell out. They were having a good time. If you ask me what I was talking about, I can't tell you, but by the end of my presentation, folks were running up and down the aisles like the building was on fire and they were trying to find an exit.

I ended my sermon in prayer. The only thing missing was someone "beat-boxing" in the background. "Bow your heads...Lord, I thank you for the blessing and the opportunity to speak to your people, today...Only you, Lord, know the way...thank you for giving me the right words to say...to keep evil at bay...because the Devil does not play...in his attempts to lead us astray…touch us, Lord. Do not delay…It is your will that we will obey…in this here, USA…in Jesus' name we pray…Amen…"

"Amen…" they responded.

$$\approx$$

The congregation liked me so much that they had a meeting and voted me in as the new "Pastor" of the church. The previous Pastor was asked to sit-down due to some alleged "sins" that he'd committed. It is my understanding that they asked him to give-up his seat due to drug use, infidelity, and his affinity for little boys and strippers. I can only assume that this is true, because those who worked closely with him was forced to sign a Confidentiality Agreement. They cloaked him in secrecy. No one talked about what he did. He was still receiving a salary and he sat second chair. I found it interesting that they protected him knowing his crimes, but there was not a day that I stood at that pulpit, looking down at all of those little boys and not wanting to cut his dick off and shove it up his ass.

Becoming "Pastor", has its perks too. I receive a housing allowance, expense reimbursements, health insurance, Health Savings Account, Group Term Life Insurance, Cafeteria Plans, 401(k) Retirement Plan, a car, an amour-bearer, a driver, and a clothing allowance, and that's on top of a salary, and when and if I decided to stop preaching, I would receive a very nice severance package upon departure. They couldn't fire me. I mean, they could, but it wouldn't be easy. My contract specifically outlines under what conditions they could ask for my removal, but anything short of me fucking one of the ushers in the ass during Communion, I was pretty much untouchable. As long as I didn't track my "dirt" inside, I was good.

I was able to provide a good life for my family. We lived in a very nice home –

probably better than most of the members in the church. While they were praying and praising, my pockets were being filled with all of their hopes and dreams. It was the fastest "come-up" that I'd ever seen. I couldn't have asked for more. If I'd known that it was this easy, I would have never become pimp or drug dealer, even though what I was doing was kinda the same thing. I didn't have anything to worry about, so I thought.

Every Sunday, I stood before them, reading shit that they'd heard a million times before, and they loved it – they needed it. I was amazed at how the "system" worked. It was like being in a club every Sunday morning. They all showed-up to hear the music and to watch the entertainment. Then, after everything was "said" and done, they left intoxicated by the "word." I was like the stripper in the club that they threw money at. The more that I took off...the more that I showed them....the more they gave. By the time it all wore off, they were standing at the church's door, the next Sunday, looking for their next 'fix.' I was in my element – like a drug dealer or a pussy supplier.

I gave it to them. I yelled, I screamed, I cried, I made that "hacking" sound that the preacher at my church made, I got on my knees, I did whatever it took to keep the collection plates full, and they were. Saving souls was big business and business was good.

≈

And the ladies loved me. They wanted to take care of me. I never had to ask for anything. They wanted me to be happy. I was their man. Their husbands and their boyfriends just didn't know it yet. And I could have had any one of them, if I wanted them.

Who didn't want to fuck the preacher? They say that they wouldn't, but a woman would leave her man for the "Man of

God" faster than a choir member could get their hands on a tambourine. I was their ticket to the "Pearly Gates." It didn't matter that I was married, they would have done anything that I asked – anytime I asked for it. And as tempting as it was, I didn't indulge, because I didn't have time for it. There was too much going on in my life, but it was nice to know that it was there if I needed it.

Chapter 53

The problem that I have with churches is that there are no bouncers at the door. Now, I see why some preachers have security guards, and why some preachers carry guns, because no matter how much you "believe", no one can stop evil or the truth from getting through the doors.

On Sunday, I was calling people to the altar when he stood up and proceeded toward the front of the church. I froze as I watched him get closer and closer. I recognized him. He was thinner, cleaner, and he was alive. It was Hustle – alive and in the flesh. I saw his ass and couldn't help but think about the story of Lazarus who rose from his grave. When he approached the altar, he smiled and kneeled down to pray with everyone else who had come up. I was so stunned, one of the deacons had walked up, and touched me on the shoulder to remind me why I was standing up there. "It's time to pray, Pastor."

I looked down at Hustle and stuttered, "Yes...right...prayer."

When we were done, Hustle decided to give an impromptu confession. He turned to the congregation and said, "Giving honor to God, the Pastor, deacons, members, and friends...I stand in front of you, today, a changed man. You see friends, I was once a drug dealer. Then, I turned around and committed the worst kind of sin. I stabbed my friend in the back. My friend was sent to prison, but he cared enough about me that he didn't snitch on me. I was free, but I felt so bad about it, that I ended-up doing drugs – trying to numb the pain and the guilt that I felt." He paused and then looked up at me before continuing, "And then my friend found me and he shot me six times."

The congregation gasped. My heart fell between my legs and sat squished between my dick and my balls.

He continued, "But I don't blame him...I know that this might sound weird, but it's because of him that I am alive today. After he shot me, I was rushed to the hospital. They told me that I wasn't going to make it. I told the Lord that if He saved me, I would turn my life around and He did it...He saved me. So I stand here today a changed man...a saved man. 'I was blind, but now I see.'" The church erupted in applause. Then, he turned and looked at me. "Pastor...please baptize me...I want to be saved."

The whole congregation looked in my direction. I nodded and smiled uncomfortably. He smiled again and walked back to his seat. I spent the rest of the service sweating like I was lying on the beach in the summertime. My thoughts were racing all over the place.

Another hour had passed before service was complete, but before I could dismiss everyone, he stood and walked out of the church.

≈

That night, after April went to bed, I found myself staring at the walls. Sarah could tell that something was wrong.

"Baby, are you okay?" she asked.

I looked at her. "Baby, do you believe in ghosts?" I asked.

She laughed before saying, "I believe in the Holy Ghost."

"No…not that," I said. "Do you believe in folks dying and then coming back to life?"

"Are you talking about reincarnation?"

"No...he wasn't reincarnated...he is still the bastard who got shot," I said, still staring at the walls.

"Trey, what are you talking about?" she asked.

I looked at her and said. "Nothing...I'm going to bed."

"Ummmm, okay...I hope that the big bad ghost don't get you."

"Me too," I mumbled. "Me too."

504

Chapter 54

The following Sunday, I baptized him. As he walked into the baptistry wearing a white robe, I couldn't help but remember how many bullets that I'd put into his body. There we were, staring each other in the eye as I read scripture and prayed for him. Even as I held his body to dip him in the pool, I could feel the bullet holes, in his chest, through his clothing. He watched me at I touched him, feeling my handy work. He didn't say anything. He just smiled. When I dipped him in the water, I saw him looking up at me. I was taken back to the day that I'd shot him; the way that he looked at me as he was dying. Then, he reached out to me for me to pull

505

him out of the water and again, I was reminded of that day. I was starting to panic. If there weren't so many people watching me, I would have held him there – under the water, but I didn't. When he came up, he smiled and then said, "Thank you."

For the first time in my life, I was afraid. I was sure that he felt that he owed me something, because I'd shot him and left him for dead. He was a problem that could potentially put me back in that "box" for the rest of my life. I couldn't let that happen, but if he suddenly disappeared, I knew that it would find its way back to me.

But after months of watching him and interacting with him, I realized that he was sincere. It was strange. He'd actually turned his life around. He became a valuable member of the congregation. He paid his tithes, faithfully. He joined the choir and he even volunteered for events.

He was truly a changed man. Not like me. I changed my clothes. I changed my shoes. I changed my drawers, but he was truly changed. I actually forgave him for the fucked-up shit that he'd done to me.

Months went by and we were cool again. I even invited him over for dinner. Sarah still hated him, but April loved him. She started to call him, Uncle Hustle. We hung-out with each other, almost every day. We watched basketball games together, and I even let him stay over a couple of times. I allowed him to play video games with April.

I began to feel really bad about what I'd done to him, so one day, after service, I pulled him to the side to talk to him. The congregation was leaving the church when he walked up to me.

"Great service, Miller," he said.

I smiled and said, "That's Reverend Miller." It felt weird to hear myself say that. Especially, saying it to a person who knew me – who knew the real me.

"He smiled and said, "Yeah, Reverend, got it."

We were talking about the service when I interrupted him by saying, "So, ummm, about that....ummmmm thing...so you know that was only business, right?"

Suddenly, his eyes turned cold. "Business?"

"Yeah...you know that it was just business, right?"

He looked at me for a second and then said, "You weren't in the game anymore...you looked for me...hunted me down...to get pay-back for some shit..." He stopped, grabbed his mouth, remembered where he was, and then said, "Oops...sorry about that, but...you took me behind that house to kill me. If it wasn't for that dope-fiend, who'd found me..."

I interrupted him. "Another dope fiend...remember you were on that shit too." I stopped, looked at the ceiling, and said, "Sorry..." like I expected God to respond and say, "Don't worry, Nigga...we good."

Hustle continued. "Yeah, I was on that shit…" He didn't stop to apologize this time, because he didn't care. "You could have walked away, Trey…but you looked for me…to kill me."

"Naw, man…it wasn't like that. I mean, I wanted to kill you…then you started on that stuff about Sarah, and you admitted that you tried to fill my shoes…like…they were yours to fill…like I was stepping down because I wanted to…it was because of you that I had to leave the game."

Hustle looked at me for a long time before he responded. For a moment, I thought that he'd fallen asleep with his eyes open…while standing up…but then he said, "But all of that's over now…we good now."

The abrupt change in his tone bothered me, but I really wanted to end the conversation, because we were still in the Lord's House. "We good?" I asked.

"We're good, REVEREND Miller." Then he smiled and hugged me.

This time, I hugged him back. It felt weird, but for some odd reason, it felt good. From that moment on, things were good until things began to take a turn for the worse.

Chapter 55

That weekend, he came over to watch a game with me. Suddenly, we both became tired, so I told him that he could stay overnight and leave in the morning. It was around 2 a.m. when I was awakened by a sudden urge to use the bathroom. It's weird, because I couldn't help but think about how incredibly quiet things were. Hustle is a snorer. You could hear him snoring from another block, so I thought that it was odd when I didn't hear him. As I slipped my feet into my slippers, I thought about how great things were going between us. Slowly, I walked across my bedroom to use the washroom.

When I was done, I decided to walk downstairs to get a glass of water, when I noticed that Hustle wasn't on the couch. I thought this was weird, but thought that maybe he decided to go home anyway. I was walking down the hall, when I noticed that the door to April's room was slightly open. When I approached the room, I noticed that it was dark. Her bedroom was never kept dark because she was afraid of the dark. When we moved in here, we'd bought her a nightlight that she kept burning every night until the sun came up.

I walked into her room and turned on the light to make sure that she was okay. She was sleeping peacefully – still holding her favorite teddy bear. I walked over to reconnect her nightlight. I was turning to leave the room when I noticed something moving in the corner of my eye.

I adjusted my eyes to make sure that I wasn't seeing things, but I wasn't. In the corner of her room was Hustle, naked from the waist down, and masturbating.

He was staring at me with his mouth hanging wide-open. He was moaning and breathing hard. Just as he started to cum, I snapped and ran towards him. Before I knew it, I was on top of him. I started beating him over and over again. Blood was flying everywhere. The sound of his screams woke up April. "Daddy, what are you doing?!!!!! Why are you hurting, Uncle Hustle and why is he naked?"

I looked at April and yelled, "Get out of here!!!" I continued to whoop Hustle's naked ass. Before I knew it, I had my hands around his neck trying to choke the life out of him. Then over my shoulders I heard, "Baby Stop!!!!"

"Daddy Stop!!!!"

I looked down at him. He was gasping for air.

"Daddy, please…!!!!"

I released him, but before getting up, I hit his ass again. "Get your ass up and get out!!!!" I yelled.

"But…but…" he said, pulling up his pants.

"GET THE FUCK OUT!!!!!" I yelled.

Hustle stumbled out of the room and out of the house.

$$\approx$$

"Call the police," she said.

I tried ignoring her, but she said it again. "Call the damn police, Trey."

I stopped pacing long enough to say, "I can't."

"What do you mean you can't?" she asked.

"I can't," I said, again, after resuming my pacing.

"What do you mean? That doesn't make any sense."

I took a deep breath and said, "I killed him."

Confused, she said, "What?"

"Sarah, I killed him."

"Who?"

"Him…" I confirmed.

"Him, who?"

"HUSTLE DAMN-IT!"

"That motherfucker didn't look dead to me. That wasn't no ghost in my baby's room beating his 'meat', Trey," she said.

"Sarah…" I paused, took a deep breath and continued, "When I got out…I looked for him and when I found him, I emptied my gun in his ass and left him for dead."

"Well, Trey, unless they changed the definition of dead to mean 'alive and jagging-off in a little girl's room,' you fucked up…because that motherfucker ain't dead," she said.

"Something must have happened…"

"Yeah…you missed…"

"No, Sarah…he was dead…"

"Well…like I said…unless dead means something else…"

"And I can't call the police because my ass will end-up back behind bars forever…do you want that?"

She took a deep breath and said, "No, but I don't ever want to see him again…do you understand?"

I didn't like the way that she was talking to me, but I understood where she was coming from. I allowed that piece of shit back into my life, and he fucked with the one thing that I love more than my life – my baby girl.

Chapter 56

The next day, we were sitting at the breakfast table. The only sound was that of the forks hitting the plate. Finally, I broke the silence. "Baby girl, I'm sorry about last night."

April looked up. "It's okay, daddy...he didn't touch me or anything...he was touching himself."

Hearing her say this made me sick to my stomach.

She continued. "Mama, already talked to me."

Then I asked, afraid of her answer, but I had to know, "Is this the first time that he did that?"

She swallowed a mouthful of orange juice before saying, "I don't know…maybe…"

Sarah and I stopped and looked at her.

"What do you mean, maybe?" I asked.

"Well…One night, I did see him leaving my room, but I didn't think about it, because I thought he had just came in the wrong room…you know? He got lost looking for the bathroom."

My mind went blank. I stood from the table and began to walk out of the room.

The vision of him playing with himself in my baby's bedroom while she slept made me want to find him and kill him again.

Sarah ran behind me. "Baby please, he's not worth it."

I kept walking. "Sarah, go back in the kitchen."

She pulled my arm, trying to stop me. I stopped and looked her up and down. "Sarah, you want to let me go."

Crying, she said, "I won't. You can do whatever you want to do to me but I'm not going to lose you again. I need you. Your daughter needs you. Those people at that church need you."

Her tears softened my anger. She was right, but I wanted that man's body dismembered, and his head hanging on my wall over my fireplace.

"Breathe baby, you know that I'm right. He didn't touch her and you know that if he did, she would tell you. Now, he's done a lot of bad shit to you…to us, but he's not worth a life sentence. Please, I'm begging you. Let it go."

I took a deep breath, collected my thoughts, and then pulled her into my arms. "You're right?"

"Maybe he'll leave us alone now," she said. "I'll pray."

As she quietly recited the Lord's Prayer, I thought about Hustle and all of the horrible things that I was going to do to him when I found him, again.

≈

I tried to let go of it, but for days, weeks, and even months after that, all I could do was see him sitting in the corner of her room, in the darkness, touching himself, while she slept only a few feet away. I hated him and I know that it is wrong to hate someone, but I hated him and no amount of prayer was going to change that.

For weeks, I went through the motions. I got up, got dressed, and went to the church. I did what I needed to do and then I went home. I didn't sleep at night because I spent every night watching over her – protecting her.

≈

I was in the church's study taking care of business when I received a troubling phone call. Sarah was frantic. "What's wrong?"

Between breaths, she said, "I can't find April."

Trying to calm her down, I said, "What do you mean, 'you can't find April?'"

"I CAN'T FIND APRIL!!!!"

"Did you look in the gym…in the music room…the library? Did you ask her friends where she was?"

"Yes, of course," she said. "No one has seen her."

"Did you two have a fight or something?"

"Of course not," she confirmed.

"Look, let me try her and then call you back." I called her cellphone, but the call went straight to voicemail. I waited a few minutes, but she didn't call back. I called Sarah back. "Look, I'm on my way home."

"Okay baby, hurry."

All the way home, my thoughts raced. I couldn't imagine where she could be. She was a good girl, and never went off by herself. Moments later, I was driving down my street. I could see Sarah's car still sitting in the driveway, and behind it were two police cars. I parked behind them and ran into the house. As I walked in, Sarah stopped me and said, "I filed a missing person's report."

One of the police officers turned towards me and said, "We're going to put out an Amber Alert. Most of the time, we're able to find a child, safe, within the first 24 hours…sometimes they stray off to visit one of their friends, or they are still at school…we never know, but again, we will get the alert out. If you hear anything, please contact us, and we will contact you if we receive any updates."

I reached out my hand to shake his, and said, "Thanks officer."

"We will find her," he said, as he and his partner left the house.

When they were gone, Sarah walked up to me and said, "We have to find my baby."

"I know…I know…let's drive around the neighborhood," I said.

She grabbed her purse and said, "Let's go."

We drove around for several hours, but wasn't able to find her. We returned home and began to call all of her friends, again, hoping that someone had heard from her, but no one had.

That night, Sarah cried until she couldn't cry anymore. She was a mess. I carried her upstairs to lie down. As I placed her onto the bed, she asked, "She's okay, right?"

I looked at her. I didn't know what to say to her. I kissed her hand and said, "Try to go to sleep."

She closed her eyes and I walked out of the room. I went downstairs and called the police department to see if there were any updates, but no one had heard anything. I walked over to the front door and turned on the front porch light just in case she found her way home. Then, I walked over and sat on the couch and waited for her.

Hours later, I woke-up to complete darkness. When I turned toward the front window, I noticed that it was dark outside. Someone had turned out the porch light. I stood to walk over to the door. "Sarah!" I yelled. "Did you turn out the porch light?"

"No!!!!" she yelled, downstairs.

I could hear her stirring upstairs. Then, I heard her walking out into the hallway.

I looked toward the stairs. "You didn't have to get up. I'll check it."

Now, at the top of the stairs, she said, "Have you heard anything?"

Walking towards the door, I said, "No…the police haven't heard anything."

I flicked the light switch a few times, but the light didn't come on. Looking at her, I said, "Could you grab a bulb? I left the light on for April. It must have blown out."

"Okay," she said, walking into the kitchen.

I opened the door. I reached up to unscrew the light bulb, but couldn't reach it. I stepped down on the porch, but noticed something soft under my feet. I stepped over it, and walked around it to get to the light. Sarah came to the door. "Here," she said.

I took out the old bulb, and then screwed in the new one. Suddenly, Sarah let out a scream that pierced my eardrum.

"NOOOOOOO!!! OH MY GOD, NOOOOOOOO!!!! NOT MY BABY!!!! NO GOD! NOT MY BABY!!!" Sarah dropped to her knees and scooped April into her arms. "Not my baby…not my baby…not my baby…" she repeated over and over again. As I looked at them, I couldn't move. I couldn't speak. I couldn't breathe. I saw her, limp in her mother's arms, with her eyes still open – looking up at me. The same eyes that looked at me as she told me that she loved me. The same eyes that looked like mine. As Sarah held her rocking her back and forth, I could hear April say my name, calling me, "Daddy."

≈

I can't remember dialing 911, but moments later, they were there. As the police and medical personnel surrounded my home, I stared at my socks which were soaked in my baby's blood. I was numb – unable to think – unable to feel, unable to do, anything.

"Noooooooooo!! Nooooooooooo!!!!! Noooooooooo!" I fell to my knees.

"No Lord…please, Lord, nooooooooo!" Sarah cried.

The police officer tried to ask me questions, but I was too upset to answer.

Still holding her teddy bear, they placed her body on a gurney and then covered it with a sheet. They began to take her to the ambulance. I could hear Sarah scream, again. "Noooooooo!!! Not my Baby!!!!!!"

As they swarmed around the front yard looking for evidence, I watched them as if I was watching a movie. Suddenly, an officer said, "You want to grab some things…I think it'll be a good idea for you to stay with friends or go to a hotel…"

Blankly, I looked at him. Snapping out of my daze, I said, "Okay."

As I dragged myself upstairs and walked down the hall, I noticed that April's nightlight was on. I walked in, and written all over her walls were the words, "What's yours is mine. What's yours is mine."

Chapter 57

The next few days are a blur. We decided to have the funeral at my church. There were so many people at the service that they began to line up along the walls. I remember sitting there looking at the beautiful white casket – no bigger than a trunk surrounded by white and yellow lilies. Sarah thought that it would be a good idea to wear white. April hated the color black because it reminded her of the darkness, while white reminded her of the light.

She was having such a horrible time accepting that our little girl was gone. Today, at breakfast Sarah made April a bowl of cereal. When April didn't come down to eat it, Sarah broke-down in tears. She still spoke of her in the present-tense. She sat in the living room hoping that it was all a bad dream, and that one day, April would return to us, but I knew better. As I looked at the casket, I knew that she wasn't coming back, and I knew why.

That afternoon, as they placed her body in the ground, Sarah and I remained there holding each other; assuring April that she was not alone, and that we would never leave her. As I watched her casket which was now surrounded by dirt, I remembered what the medical examiner said, "She was strangled and stabbed to death." I couldn't believe that he would do that. It took a "special" kind of evil to do that to an innocent child. He was stupid. He was crazy, but this? I didn't want to believe it. I tried to convince myself that someone else from my past had done this, but when I saw those words on her wall, "What's yours is mine," I knew who was behind this.

≈

I wanted to die. I couldn't find another reason to go on. I thought about her smile, her hugs, and the way that she said the word, "Daddy." She was my baby girl – my seed…my blood, and now, she was gone. I tried to live, but there was no life without her. I tried everything to get through this – to numb the pain, but there was nothing. I tried praying, but that bullshit didn't work. I wasn't happy with God and I'm sure that he didn't like my ass either. I couldn't understand how He stood by while that piece of shit choked and stabbed the life out of my baby girl. What kind of God sits back and doesn't intervene when innocent people suffer…when innocent people die? I always believed that He was a figment of people's imagination, but it was solidified the day that He turned his back on my little girl. There was no purpose. I no longer had hope. My hope died the day that my baby died.

≈

And out of the blue, my father showed-up on my doorstep. He'd heard about my baby's death and decided to come to her funeral. We didn't speak at the church, because he knew better. But then, he rang my doorbell. Now, he was trying to make up for lost time, but I had no respect for a man who turned his back on his son. Sure, he had a million fucking reasons for why he couldn't come, but there was one good reason why he should have. He was my father, but the truth is, he was ashamed of me. Even though he'd lived the same life, he felt that because his ass never got caught, that he was better than me. So now, he's here smiling in my face like being a sperm-donor affords him some special kind of pass. If only he knew that the day that my mother died, his ass died too.

"Son, you have to snap out of this. There are too many people depending on you," he said.

I looked at him through swollen eyes. I'd cried so much that my eyes burned. "Look who's talking about dependence. Your kids depended on you."

"Son, I'm sorry, but I was so busy…"

"Busy doing what?" I asked. "Cause you wasn't busy being a father…you didn't even bother to tell me that mama died. Who does that? You hated me that much that you couldn't tell me that mama was sick?"

"Listen to yourself…did it ever cross your mind that it was hard for me…knowing that I was going to wake-up, alone, without the woman that I spent most of my life loving? My wife? My best friend?"

"MY MAMA?"

He couldn't answer my question.

"Sarah, hand me my checkbook so that I can get rid of this motherfucker."

"Son, I don't want your money," he said.

"Don't call me son."

"What would you like for me to call you? Pimp, Drug Dealer, Prisoner, or the new scam that you're running...Pastor?" he asked.

"You bring your ass into my life after all of these years...when I'm at my lowest...and you insult me? If you were a better father, I probably wouldn't have become a pimp or a drug dealer."

"You wanna blame those fucked-up ass decisions on me?" he asked. "Decisions that you made?"

"Why shouldn't I?" I asked.

"So you wanna blame me because your ass grew-up to be the stereotype...all of the shit that you could have done with your life and you decided to follow my dumbass..."

"You were my example...my role-model...my father..."

"And clearly you didn't hear a word that I said to you...you didn't have to succumb to stupid shit...once you know better...do better...it's simple..." He shook his head and continued. "You know why ignorance is bliss?"

I didn't respond.

"Because simple motherfuckers like doing simple shit...they like being ignorant...they like being told what to think and what to do...but that ain't you..."

"But I needed you..."

"I didn't want to see anything that I helped bring into this world, locked behind bars..."

"So you chose not to see me at all..."

"To see you behind bars…in chains…behind a glass wall…like an animal? I can go to the zoo for that shit."

I didn't respond.

"Think what you want, but I do love you…"

I stood to leave the room. "I liked it better when you were dead."

"Dead? What do you mean dead?" he asked, as I left the room.

Chapter 58

It was too hard to go back in there. Her room was the only room that wasn't cleaned after the murder – it remained protected by police tape. We just closed her bedroom door, and kept it that way. I would walk pass, place my face up against the door to listen for any sense of life – music, her TV, her laughter, or her talking on her cellphone, anything, but there was nothing.

After a while, Sarah and I barely spoke to each other. We were more like room-mates than husband and wife. We stopped touching each other. We just existed.

We were eating dinner when she broke down and cried. "I can't do this anymore. I can't just pretend that nothing happened. My baby is dead." She stood up and grabbed her head. Then, she grabbed her plate of food and threw it across the room. She pointed at me. "You know who did this shit...now, you must fix it. Do you hear me? You and your damn boys....Find that motherfucker and kill him!"

I looked at her. "You're willing to lose me?"

"Look at us, Trey...I've already lost you. We are dead without her."

"Sarah..."

She continued. "This is what happens, Trey, when you don't handle your business..."

"Sarah..." I paused, but couldn't continue.

She walked up to me and said, "He's a fucking weed...A FUCKING WEED!!!

And you know what you do to weeds? You pluck them and that's what you should have done a long time ago…PLUCKED HIS ASS!!!" She walked around the room for a few minutes before she grabbed her purse and keys. "I need some air…"

"Where are you going?" I asked.

She walked towards the door, but then turned and walked upstairs. Suddenly, she returned and stomped passed me. I stopped her. What are you doing, Sarah?"

"I'm going to get some weed killer."

≈

The next day, Sarah was acting funny. It should be expected, we had lost our daughter, but this was something different. She was tense, jumpy, and always looking over her shoulder. When asked, "What was wrong?" she would shrug me off and ask me, "Don't you have some shit to do?" This wasn't like her. She never talked to me that way, but I let it go because I knew that she was dealing with a lot.

≈

For almost a year, we hadn't seen or heard from him, but then out of nowhere, Hustle started messing with us. One day, he drove passed my house, slowly, like he was getting ready to do a drive by. He started coming back to church. He used to sit in the back and stare at us – always making his presence known. Also, there were times, I would come home to find him standing outside of my house – watching us. I wanted to approach him and finally put an end to it all, but I couldn't and he knew it.

≈

After months of him stalking me, I decided that enough was enough. After a long day at church, I loaded up my gun and I went looking for him. I drove through the alleys, looking in the crack houses, sitting outside of his mother's house – just waiting, but he never turned up. Finally, after several hours of nothing, I decided to go home, but I'd promised myself that this time, I wouldn't make the same mistake. I was going to put an end to this.

Chapter 59

The house held too many bad memories for us. After two years, Sarah and I decided to sell the house and move on with our lives. It was the most difficult decision we had to make. When we packed-up April's room, we had to decide to donate her things or hold on to them. Sarah didn't want to let her things go, but I convinced her that holding on to those things wouldn't bring her back. She had to let it go.

There was a point, after we moved into the new home, when Sarah stopped eating, and had to be rushed to the hospital. Watching her suffer, put me in a bad place. She'd been through so much. I wanted it all to stop.

≈

Another two years had passed, when I finally got a call from the police indicating that they found the man who'd killed April. They needed us to come down to the station to see if we recognized him. As I held the phone, I thought that my heart was going to explode in my chest. I'd been waiting for this moment for such a long time. I was so happy that they'd found him. Even though I wished that he was dead, a life behind bars was just as good, because in there, prisoners hated people who committed crimes against children. If we couldn't get street justice, we would settle for jail-house justice.

≈

When we arrived at the police station, they took us into a room. An officer came in the room and said, "I'm going to show you six photos. We need you to identify anyone that looks familiar." Slowly, he turned over the photos. We both looked at them. When we spotted him, Sarah grabbed my hand and then looked at me. She had a look on her face that told me that she didn't want this. She gently squeezed my hand. The officer asked, "Do you see anyone that looks familiar?" Sarah squeezed my hand again. We looked at each other, again, and then we both said, "No, we don't see anyone."

The officer asked, "Are you sure?"

We looked at each other again, and then said, "No….we don't see anyone."

"Okay, thank you so much for coming down," he said.

"What's going to happen now?" Sarah asked.

The officer said, "Well, we think that we have someone who was involved in the murder of your daughter. We will continue to investigate and keep you updated."

"He's here?" Sarah asked.

The officer said, "We're still investigating…we'll keep you updated."

I shook the officer's hand and said, "Thank you so much. We appreciate it."

Forty-eight hours later, they set him free. They said that they didn't have enough evidence to hold him, but they were going to keep doing everything they could to put him behind bars. We were sitting outside of the police station when we saw him exit the building. When Sarah saw him, she said, "He doesn't deserve to live."

As her husband and April's father, I felt that it was the least that I could do. If it wasn't for me April would still be alive. She died for my sins.

"I want to be there this time…to make sure," she said.

I grabbed her hand and kissed it. "Okay…let's do this."

We followed him all day. As we drove around, she asked, "Are you scared?"

"Scared of what? Killing him?"

"No, dying."

I thought about it for a moment and said, "No…I'm not afraid."

"Why not?"

I frowned. "Because evil people never die, Sarah. They never fucking die."

We watched him go to the liquor store, go and visit his mother, and we watched him go into the old house – the one that we all once shared together. We sat outside, watching, and waiting until nightfall. How fitting that all of this would end where it all began.

≈

I looked at her and said, "You ready?"

She nodded. "Let's do this."

"Grab the flashlight."

"Of course…who the hell looks for the Boogey-man in the dark?"

When we entered it, we noticed that it was well-maintained. After all these years, a lot of the old furniture was still there. Things looked the same except that it was now covered in dust and spider webs.

Slowly, we entered each room until we found him sitting on the toilet with a strap tied around his arm, and a needle dangling from a vein. He was sitting back, eyes rolled in the back of his head and his mouth was hanging wide open. I walked up to him and slapped his face to wake him. He looked up to find us standing across from him.

"Well, lookie here…it's my brother from another mother. What's up 'fam'?"

I didn't say anything.

"Hey Bruh, why you looking at me like that?" he asked, and then looked at Sarah. "How have you been?"

"You sick son-of-a-bitch…" she said.

I heard the steps creak behind us, but I ignored the sound. I wanted this to be over so, I pulled out my gun and pointed it at him. I looked over to see Sarah, who was staring at him and balling-up her fists.

"You here about baby girl ain't you? Well, about that…it was just business…" He laughed. "Sounds familiar?"

I was still looking at him, pointing the gun at him, when I heard a loud *BAM!!!!!* The sound left my ears ringing. I closed my eyes, and when I opened them, I found Hustle sitting back against the toilet with his head plastered against the wall behind him. I then looked over at Sarah who was holding a gun with one hand, and her ear with the other. We looked at each other.

"Did you?" I asked.

She shook her head. "No, did you?"

I shook my head, "No."

We both turned and looked over our shoulders.

He smiled. "You turned on the light," Money said, as he turned to leave the room.

$$\approx$$

We didn't say a word all the way home. Every once in a while, I would look at Sarah to see if she was okay, but for some odd reason, she looked fine. She didn't look like she was struggling at all with what happened. For the first time, in a long time, she seemed at peace.

Finally, it was done. When we walked into the house, Sarah went straight upstairs. I was tired, so I decided to follow her. By the time I got up there, she was already removing her clothing. I grabbed the remote and climbed onto the bed. She was walking into the bathroom, but turned around and said, "I forgot something." She walked over to her purse, reached in, and then pulled out her gun. "Here…put this up with yours."

"Okay," I said, removing mine from my waistband. I walked over to the closet and pulled a steel box off of the shelf. When I pulled the box out, an envelope fell onto the floor. After putting the guns in the box, I picked up the envelope. It had my name on it. I stared at it. I'd almost forgotten that I had it. I decided that enough time had passed since she made her transition. I turned on the light and then opened the envelope. I looked at the piece of paper, slowly. When I was done, I looked at it again. My eyes filled with tears. I was staring at the paper when Sarah walked into the room.

"What is that?" she asked.

Still trying to process the contents of the envelope, I said, "It's the letter that my mama gave me."

Drying her hair, she said, "You're just now reading that thing?"

I sucked my teeth and said, "Yeah."

She sat on the end of the bed. "Well, what does it say?"

I handed her the piece of paper. She looked at it and read it aloud. "Psalm 37:27-29 - 'Turn from evil and do good; then you will dwell in the land forever. For the Lord loves the just and will not forsake his faithful ones. Wrongdoers will be completely destroyed; the offspring of the wicked will perish. The righteous will inherit the land and dwell in it forever.'" She frowned and continued, "What the hell?"

I didn't respond. Instead, I rested my back against the bed, and stared at the ceiling.

Coming Soon...

Six Degrees of Separation

Spring 2017 in paperback

A preview of my next novel…

"Six Degrees of Separation (also referred to as the "Human Web") refers to the idea that, if a person is one step away from each person they know and two steps away from each person who is known by one of the people they know, then everyone is no more than six "steps" away from each person on Earth." -- Frigyes Karinthy

So now we must ask ourselves, "Where the hell did he come from?"

Prologue

Excuse me sir, do you have any change?" she asked, with the most beautiful blue eyes I've ever seen. I looked into my pocket and retrieved some small bills and handed them to her. It was cold out. Her teeth 'clicked' together as she thanked me. I had to admit that I felt sorry for her.

"Look, let me buy you a hot meal," I said.

"Oh, thank you, that would be nice," she responded.

We walked down to the corner diner. From the moment we entered, all eyes were on us. I ordered us some coffee to get us started. While we waited, the woman went on and on about the road that led her to this place — this moment in her life.

"He was a football player," she said, as if I gave a shit. "Yeah, he even went pro," she continued.

I looked around the room for the waitress who was taking so long to bring us our coffee that I was beginning to think that her ass took a trip to Columbia to hand pick the beans herself. The woman sitting across from me was still rambling.

"I really loved his ass too…for real…no kidding. Everybody thought that I was only with him for his money, but I ain't no gold-digger.

No matter what they say," she spat through the gap in her front teeth.

The people in the diner watched and whispered as she took me down memory lane. She noticed it. I couldn't tell if she was embarrassed or not because her face was hidden under several layers of dirt. When the waitress finally arrived with the coffee, the woman excused herself, went to the bathroom, and when she returned it looked like she tried to clean herself up. She had pulled her matted hair back and she tried to wash her face. It was evident that she scrubbed really hard because now her pale skin was even redder than before.

As I ordered, I could tell that the waitress was staring at me.

I didn't acknowledge her because I wasn't interested. When she realized that I wasn't going to give her the attention that she was seeking, she took the menus, placed them under her arm, rolled her eyes at the woman sitting across from me, huffed and then walked away.

Still talking, the woman said, "That motherfucker even had the nerve to be on the down-low. Man, I heard she cut the shit out of his ass."

Now, she had my attention. "She who?" I asked.

"The bitch he dumped to marry my fine ass." She smiled. "Then he dumped me to get back with her. That's why I'm glad that he's dead…with his triflin' ass," she said, like a person who was trying to make Ebonics a first language.

Curious, I asked, "So, she killed him?"

"Naw," she began. The waitress walked over with our plates. She paused and threw some fries into her mouth. "Like I was saying…naw, that motherfucker got him some 'jail-house justice.' They raped his ass to death. He was a loser in life. Now, he's a loser in

Hell." She went on like this for another hour.

I watched her thinking about what she may have looked like when she was younger. She was probably really pretty 'back-in-the-day.'

Now, she was just an empty shell — one of life's walking dead.

When she finished, I paid the tab and then we left the diner. I was about to walk away when she said, "I really appreciate what you did for me. Nobody has been that nice to me in a long time. Let me do something nice for you." She looked down at my crotch.

Frowning, I said, "There's nothing that you could do for me. Just take care of yourself."

"Please let me do something…it's the least I could do," she pleaded. She began to lick her lips seductively.

What a waste. I thought to myself. "Look, I'm good."

"Well, I promise that I'm going to do something really nice for myself. I might even use the money you gave me to go to the clinic and get myself cleaned up. Wouldn't that be nice? Change my life…become respectable," she said.

I looked at her. "Take care of yourself." I turned and walked away.

Later that evening, I was walking back in the direction where I left the woman. I walked passed an alley where I could hear someone both crying and laughing. I walked toward the sound. In the dark, it was hard to tell who it was. As I got closer, there she sat with a rope wrapped around her arm and a needle sticking out of her vein.

"Hey, I told you I was going to do something nice for myself," she said, recognizing me.

I looked at her; disappointed and angry. It was disgusting looking at her lying in the alley like trash that someone had thrown out. I leaned over her and then removed the needle from her arm. Lying on the ground next to her was a spoon, a lighter, and a couple of rocks that looked like heroine. I placed a 'rock' on the spoon and began to heat it. She laughed to herself. When the rock melted and became a liquid, I filled the syringe with it. As she mumbled and laughed to herself, I asked her for her name.

"My name is Sandy," she said, enjoying her buzz. I hit the syringe with my finger, found her vein, and then plunged the needle deep inside of it. Initially, she smiled and closed her eyes. Suddenly, she looked at me as if becoming lucid just long enough to realize what was happening to her. I smiled at her. Before ramming the needle deeper into her arm, I said, "My name is Izrael. It was nice meeting you."

Other Titles

- *Never What it Seems*
- *Autumn Leaves*
- *Fallen Angel*
- *Never What it Seems II – A Mother's Love*
- *Kiss My A@@ - This is Not Your Typical Self-Help Book*
- *Somebody Else's Baby*
- *Somebody Else's Baby (Stage-play)*
- *Peaches – Always Kiss Your Baby Goodnight*
- *Officer Friendly*

Website:
http://dianemartin.weebly.com